DEAD MAN'S LEGACY

PETER BONO

 FriesenPress

One Printers Way
Altona, MB R0G 0B0
Canada

www.friesenpress.com

Copyright © 2024 by Peter Bono
First Edition — 2024

All rights reserved.

ISBN
978-1-03-919267-6 (Hardcover)
978-1-03-919266-9 (Paperback)
978-1-03-919268-3 (eBook)

1. FICTION, CRIME

Distributed to the trade by The Ingram Book Company

For my awesome grandchildren, Luke and Ivy…

…and great appreciation to Anthony Curto for his tireless encouragement (badgering), which proved instrumental in completing this novel.

CHAPTER 1

"Morning Lieutenant, what we got today?" Sgt. Richard Falco asked.

His partner, Brian O'Reardon, replied, "Just that liquor store thing over on Elliot Avenue. That's what I like about winter, keeps the culprits indoors. *Don't say it*—I know, Rich, you hate when it's quiet."

"Never said that. Not looking for Harlem craziness out here, but a bit of Bed-Stuy will do, though."

O'Reardon, after twenty-nine years on the job, was just looking to ease through his last few weeks before retirement without any major cases tying him down.

"Finish your coffee and we'll head over. The owner is meeting us there at 8:30."

"Mr. D'arpa?"

"Yes. You must be Detective O'Riley?"

"Detective Lieutenant *O'Reardon*, and this is Sergeant Falco. We're from Robbery/Homicide. I realize you're busy so we'll make this brief. I take it you weren't harmed in any way?"

"Other than having a gun shoved in my face, no."

"The report says he was a Spanish guy, and we saw the description you gave. He took a hundred and seventy dollars, that correct?" O'Reardon said.

"Yep, and he also grabbed two bottles of cheap vodka on the way out, which were sitting right next to an expensive Russian brand. Didn't even know the difference, the *bassa vita*."

O'Reardon looked at Falco. "Uh, *lowlife*."

"Did you ever see him before?" O'Reardon asked.

"Nope, he was a strung-out junkie, I know that. His nose was running, he was shaking, face was gaunt. I can't understand why these guys allow themselves to become fuckin' zombies. For what?"

O'Reardon snapped closed his notebook, then looked around. "It doesn't start out that way, I can assure you. If by chance you see him around the neighborhood, Sgt. Falco will leave you a card. Don't hesitate to call. By the way, do you keep a firearm here?"

"Nope, haven't picked up a gun since the war!"

"I get it, but it won't be a bad idea, nonetheless. This is a different ballgame! We're in the *sixties* now, Mr. D'arpa." Falco nodded in agreement as he dropped his card on the glass counter.

Falco steered the beat-up Plymouth toward the neighborhood hangouts looking for someone fitting the description of their perp.

"Ya know, Brian, what's insane is, some of these junkies have to come up with twenty, thirty bucks a day to keep going," Falco said.

"Yeah, what's even crazier is that's just to get straight, they really don't even get high anymore," O'Reardon answered.

Since drug addicts normally have their "wake-up" shot next to their beds, the detectives didn't expect to see much activity this time in the morning, so after a few laps around the neighborhood they headed back to the precinct.

"Thought I was done with these losers when I left narcotics," Falco groaned.

* * *

The usually bustling neighborhood of Maspeth, Queens, was quiet this frigid Saturday, the first weekend in 1964. All seemed well with the Marchetti family of six. There was little Paulie, the ten-year-old oops kid, and the big guy, Mike, college grad, married, and at twenty-four, making quite a name for himself with a brokerage firm in the city. Mike was the vast Marchetti clan's very first college graduate. Sal had barely managed Mike's Hofstra College tuition and shuddered at the thought of more tuition down the road. The only girl was vibrant fifteen-year-old Angela, who constantly struggled to stay fashionable on their meager budget.

Salvatore Anthony Marchetti had been working at the Morgan Trust bank since 1932, starting as a teller trainee and working his way to assistant manager of their Maspeth branch. Thirty-two years with one company, one neighborhood, one local bank. Sal was turning fifty-five next month, and his hairline and waistline were moving in opposite directions, not to mention his energy level was that of a seventy-year-old! Sal was a heavy smoker and border-line obese.

To the dismay of the Marchetti family, money was a constant concern. Their tight budget was reflected in their well-travelled 1952 Pontiac, affectionately referred to as "Dreamboat" by Sal. Their six-room apartment, though large by Queens standards, was situated above an old bakery on busy Flushing Avenue.

Seventeen-year-old Tuddy, whose actual name was Salvatore Marchetti Jr, was super close to his parents, but like his brother Michael, plans on moving far away from his neighborhood after high school.

"We're going over to Mike and Pat's for dinner; they have an announcement to make," Laura said, sarcastically stressing the word *announcement.*

"Ma, we already know she's pregnant!" Paulie snickered in his worldly knowledge of such things. Not worldly enough, however, to know what having a small, pouched belly meant when a bride had only returned from her honeymoon a month ago.

"Hi Mom, Dad, how are you?" Dramatically exclaimed their daughter-in-law, Patricia. "Hurry in, it's freezing out there."

Laura, not entirely comfortable with her new title, hugged her. Then Angela and Paulie took their turn.

"Where's Tuddy?"

"Oh, he's not feeling well, stayed home," Laura replied as they trailed up the four steps leading to the spacious, though mostly empty, living room. Michael Vincent Marchetti, thanks to an excellent first year selling long-term bonds at Lehman Bros Brokerage firm, had managed to put a down payment on a split-level house in a new development in East Meadow, Long Island. This was the family's first real visit there, not counting the actual helping of the move.

"Where's my son?" Sal asked, looking around. "Did he skip town already?"

Angie laughed as her mother nudged her in disapproval.

"Not yet, Pop," an amused Mike replied as he emerged from the garage entrance. "Unable to, until I fix the timing chain on that piece of shit MG. Hi, Ma."

"You kiss your mother with that mouth," his mom hissed.

"Nice dress, baby sis, new?" Mike remarked while looking around. "Where's the king cobra?"

"They lost their game, Mike, they got eliminated" Paulie hastened to say.

"Tuddy was still in bed when we left this morning," Angie added.

No way! They lost to Ossining? How?" Mike asked.

"Those boys were very good," Laura replied.

"Did Tuddy get in?" Mike asked, slumping into the armchair.

"GET IN? HE STARTED, scored twenty points too," Sal exaggerated.

"Eighteen, Dad," Paulie remarked, quickly correcting the old banker's math.

"Did he really! Patti, hear that?" Mike yelled toward the kitchen. "My kid brother scored twenty points in the quarterfinals."

"Anybody hungry?" came her reply as she carried a tray of broccoli lasagna into the dining room.

"So, how are you kids liking suburban life?" Laura asked as they collected their seats in the virgin dining room.

"What's not to like, quiet streets, clean air, no gang fights outside your window. I love it," Mike bragged.

"The house is just lovely, isn't it, Sal?" Laura hastened, trying to distract her husband's attention away from the meat-free lasagna he was leering at.

"Oh, yeah, very nice, a little too quiet out here for my taste but that's me. Very nice though, uh, do they have butcher shops out here?"

"Of course, Dad, why?" an unsuspecting Patti replied.

"Just wondering."

Laura wanted to kill him. Angie giggled.

Mike came to the rescue. "So, Dad, how's the bank doing?"

Mike expected his father's answer to be brief.

He shrugged, "Same. Got a new girl there, though. Marie Werner left."

Laura looked surprised. "Oh, you didn't tell me." Laura managed an expressionless face. She despised her. Marie Werner was a stunning woman who had worked there for nearly twenty years and was a bit of a flirt. Laura had a less kind description. They'd nearly had it out at the Christmas party eighteen years ago. Laura was pregnant for Tuddy, was how she remembered the year. They'd never buried the hatchet throughout the many years. The rare times Laura entered the bank Marie would look down as if counting money or otherwise busy.

Finally, Laura said, "Is her husband still the security guard there?"

"Yeah, Chubby's still there. We had to get him a chair because he can't stand up too long. So, now we have the only bank guard who is seated at the entrance half asleep."

They all laughed. It was the most Sal had ever spoken about his workplace. The *Bank*. Dad's bank. When Mike was a kid, he was proud his father wore a jacket and tie to work. Usually rumpled but still smarter looking than the other kids' dads, who wore overalls. He had his own desk behind the tellers. Mike remembered when the Dodgers finally beat the hated Yankees in the '55 series, how he'd rushed into the bank after school and hugged him. Good old Morgan Trust. Mike also knew his father grew to resent the place. Thirty-two years and rose no higher than assistant manager of a local branch. His twenty-four-year-old son, barely out of school, was making nearly three times his salary, owned his own home, and drove a new '63 Impala. To make matters worse, Sal's boss, the branch manager, was fifteen years younger than him, *and Puerto Rican*. Sal Marchetti, a proud, honest man blamed his mediocre career on the bank's inept upper management, not his *own* complacent, lackluster work ethics.

After dinner, Laura noticed her son reaching in the refrigerator and coming out with a bottle of champagne. Here it comes, she thought. Handily extracting the cork, Mike looked up at the waiting faces.

"Patti and I have an announcement . . . *We're having a baby.*"

He avoided giving the date. Their guests sprang to their feet in mock surprise and took turns hugging the proud parents-to-be. All the while Laura was eyeing Paulie, hoping he wouldn't spoil the moment.

"If it's a boy we're going to name him John Fitzgerald."

"After Kennedy?" a surprised Laura asked, reminded of the awful assassination, which occurred the day before Mike's wedding. It nearly caused a postponement and certainly put a dark cloud on the occasion.

"The very," Mike answered. Their dad, unable to mask his disappointment, preferring of course Salvatore III, remarked, "Great idea, Mikey, and you can name the next one *Lyndon Baines* after they shoot that Texan stinking up the White House now."

Angela broke the stunned silence, turning toward Patti. "And if it's a girl?"

"Laurie."

"*After Mom*, how cool," Angie replied, feeling her mother's glow beside her.

Their dad forced a smile through his champagne glass.

CHAPTER 2

"Good morning, Mr. Marchetti."

Everyone looked up. Even Sal was surprised, not unpleasantly, by the new girl's formal referral to her superior. Two other tellers, in unison, sang, "Good morning, Mr. Marchetti." Sal was in no mood this today for their humor. Ignoring the duet, he responded, "Good morning, Dana."

Dana Jankowski was a local girl, slightly overweight but very pretty, with short blonde hair and flawless skin. That probably had a lot to do with Manny's hiring her. She was a welcome sight next to the other two. Sal settled in behind his desk, quickly remembering he was running the show this week when he didn't see his early-bird boss in his office directly behind him. Manny Figueroa, a forty-year-old divorced father of two, had been hired two years ago after the Hamburg Bank, where he was their financial officer, was taken over by Greenpoint Savings. Figueroa had a bachelor's degree in finance acquired from night courses at Adelphi. He was taking his first vacation since coming to Morgan, choosing Acapulco, Mexico, as the place he was going to wed his new girlfriend. Chubby Werner emerged suddenly from the men's room folding a newspaper under his arm.

"Hey Sal! How was your weekend? Did you go out to the Island?" he asked in his German accent.

"Yeah Chub, Mikey's got quite a place."

Sal looked on as the punctual bank guard checked the clock above the front door and wasn't satisfied that it was the correct second to open the bank's massive door. He had no guilty feelings for the shivering gray-haired woman glaring at him from outside as he settled onto his folding chair under the clock. Old man Werner had come to America from Germany in 1922 after a stint in the kaiser's army during the First War. He had learned English while a prisoner of the British in Alsace, France. After a few odd jobs, he became a member of the New York City police force and served thirty years, mostly in Brooklyn, without once firing his service revolver. After a few restless years of retirement, he returned to work with his beloved Marie at *her* bank. Unbeknownst to most, his real first name was Adolph, and he'd quickly adopted his nickname when World War II emerged. With Aryan precision, Chubby opened the door at the very stroke of nine. The frosted, annoyed woman waiting outside brushed past him, entered. Thus, another week at Morgan Trust began. This one, however, was to prove very different from any other.

* * *

"I'm telling you, Hector. This old Jew's gonna recognize us . . ."

"Listen, Junior, then just wait out here. I'll do it myself."

These two drug addicts, along with Whitey Aparicio, called themselves the three *amigos*, having grown up together on the same block. Their gang-fighting lifestyle had been swiftly interrupted by the trickle, then flooding, of narcotics into the neighborhood.

Hector Maldonado strolled into the large grocery store and beelined toward the meat section in the rear. Looking nothing like a morning shopper, he got busy, nonetheless. The porterhouse steaks were the first to get stuffed inside his overcoat pockets. Then the rib steaks went into his loosened pants. Hector no sooner looked up than Junior was right alongside him loading up.

Hector smiled. "*My man*, we doin' some rustlin' now!"

Cattle rustling was street slang for shoplifting packaged meat, usually steaks. It was then sold in the neighborhood at half the marked price. The urban cowpokes had their regular customers who would eagerly await the bargains. No questions asked, of course.

"Com'on this way." Hector motioned, as the two suddenly obese junkies waddled toward the exit.

"This shit's dripping down my fuckin' leg," Junior cried out, laughing.

"Shuddup, he'll hear you."

Which he did. **"Hey, you!"** the grocer yelled as he rushed around his counter. **"Stop!"**

The two began running out the door, laughing as their bounty bounced around inside their clothing. "Com'on Junior, hurry up." As they headed toward the train station, a winded Junior finally called ahead, "Wait up Hector, that old fuck ain't coming. He can hardly walk!" They took the train two stops, got off, and walked to Wilfredo "Whitey" Aparicio's three-room apartment on Rust Street in the Greenpoint section of Brooklyn, near the Queens border and just a half mile or so from Maspeth. To their delight, he had just returned from their heroin connection and was in the living room holding a Zippo lighter under a discolored spoon.

Whitey's girlfriend, Sandy, was feeding their six-month-old son at the kitchen table, ignoring, and long resigned to the lifestyle of her drug-addicted boyfriend. He'd gotten his nickname from his grandmother because of his pale complexion. He and his friends had been together from grade school through high school, where two of them dropped out at sixteen, allowing a more focused Whitey to graduate and then serve four honorable years in the Navy.

In '62 he was aboard a heavy cruiser, in formation during the Cuban missile blockade. As soon as he was discharged, he returned to his friends, who were by then deeply submerged in the neighborhood's drug culture. Before long, Whitey, much to Sandy's dismay, fell right into Greenpoint's heroin pit. The three friends became inseparable again. All of them were twenty-two years old but Whitey was always the alpha. Hector and Junior were glad to have their old crime partner back in civilian clothes.

Whitey had plans for a serious heist he was about to spring upon the guys. After dumping their cattle booty onto Sandy's kitchen table, they hurried in toward Whitey to get their shot before he entered oblivion.

* * *

Laura Marchetti's week also began at around nine when she was seated on the BMT subway train headed toward lower Manhattan's Canal Street. There was not one discount store in this enclave of bargains that she was unfamiliar with. With the flags from the municipal buildings still hanging at half-mast mourning the slain young president, she wound her way through the scurrying New Yorkers.

Laura, the daughter of a prominent Sicilian "plumbing supply and waste disposal" entrepreneur, had had a very comfortable childhood on Staten Island. She was a somewhat timid woman and a devout Catholic. Laura was the type that walked around the house as if on eggshells so not to disturb anyone. She'd met Sal on the Staten Island ferry during the war and married him a year later. With all the local guys her age away at war, thirty-year-old Sal was a catch. Her father gave them a generous wedding gift, but Sal refused all the subsequent offers of help from her income-suspect family. She moved with Sal from small apartments to larger apartments all in the same neighborhood. They were a far cry from the beautiful house she'd lived in during her earlier years. She wanted so much to provide her children with a similar lifestyle.

It was still early in the day, so the shops weren't crowded. She bargained and bartered, speaking English and Italian, all the way down Canal and into Little Italy. By the time she arrived home she had two shopping bags of discount clothing, mostly for Angela, and a pair of sneakers for Paulie. Laura was tired from the journey and feeling a bit melancholy. She slumped into an armchair and flipped on the radio, daydreaming, like many middle-aged people, about the *what ifs* of life. What if she had not, much to her father's dismay, broken up with Augie Pantina two months before she met Sal. What if she had not spurned the repeated attempts for a date by that landscaper/medical student whom her father had hired that summer of '39 to tend to their garden. There was also her father's driver, Mario. Laura, like most mothers when the doubts creep in, would look at her children's pictures located everywhere in the apartment and dismiss the thoughts, reasoning, *I wouldn't have my children.* Okay then, what if her husband had listened to her and taken those accounting courses back in '46. Laura always realized that it wasn't Sal, himself, that she had second thoughts about; it was the lifestyle he provided. The damn payday-to-payday existence is what she wanted no more of. True, Sal's lackluster professional drive was surpassed only by his more lackluster sex drive, but Laura long ago had come to terms with that and with her turning fifty in a few years, it was not even an issue any longer.

Unmistakably, being at her son Mike's new house and seeing the manicured homes throughout his neighborhood was the topper. What's more, she knew her husband felt the same way. She probably could convince that old Italian hardhead to allow her to work—*hell, this was 1964, not '54. But what about Paulie? A ten-year-old couldn't look after himself. Tuddy and Angela had their own lives. It wouldn't be fair to ask them to stay with their baby brother after school. Besides, how much of a difference would her salary make anyway?* She turned up the radio and forced herself out of the chair and out of the dream.

"Ma, didn't you hear the bell? What's with the loud music?" Angie yelled, turning it down and, of course, changing the station. "I hate coming in through the bakery. Mrs. Girardi gives me the creeps."

Lina Girardi gave most people the creeps, but especially Angela, who'd had to spend the last three summers down there working alongside her. The old lady had been in this country more than half her life and still struggled to put together a full sentence using only English words. When Angie refused to work on busy Sundays, Mrs. Girardi and her mom weren't happy with her.

Sal too, for that matter, was very intimidated by the old woman. Lina was only in her sixties but with that ever-present black dress draped over her bent frame combined with the white-grey hair of hers in a permanent bun, the whole neighborhood had always only known her as "the old woman." Her husband, Joe, who had opened the bakery with her forty years before, had been adored by everyone, especially Laura and Sal.

Joe had died ten years ago on Christmas Eve, in Laura's arms, of all people. Laura broke down every time she told the story of the day a bakery customer frantically rang her bell yelling that the guy behind the counter was having a heart attack. She had kneeled to pull him away from the hot oven when he suddenly gasped and rolled his eyes back in a way she'd never forget. To make matters worse, Laura had to be the one to break the news to frantic Lina, who was pushing her way past the gathering onlookers. Lina, who had rarely left him alone since his first heart attack, had to choose that hour to pick up his Christmas gift. Somehow, her flailing arms never let go of the package that contained the hand-carved pipe Joe would have loved. What an awful day. Lina had remained dressed in black from that day forward. She also remained unbridled from then on. Without her polite husband around to see to it that she kept her nose out of everyone's business, especially their tenants, she became unbearable. So much so, that the apartment on the third floor had had a different tenant nearly every year. Lina would know what time they were leaving in the morning, who was coming over for dinner, and often what they were having for dinner. The old lady's senses, much to Laura's dismay, hadn't aged as prematurely as the rest of her. She would occasionally have periods of generosity though. She had a soft spot for Little Paulie and would often call him in and give him a bag of cookies to bring upstairs. Laura avoided her as much as possible, more so when the rent was overdue. Often it meant approaching the house from the other direction so she wouldn't have to walk past the bakery window. They all did have one thing in common though, they *still* missed Joe.

Laura could tell by the sounds in the hallway who was coming home. This time the two-steps-at-a-time pounding meant Paulie was rushing through the two obstacles between him and the refrigerator—the stairs and the front door.

"Anyone call?" he asked the slice of Swiss cheese.

"Who'd call you?" his sister remarked.

"Yes Tud, Eddie said to call him," Laura answered. Laura looked at her son. Even bent over in the refrigerator he looked so tall. He had passed his father last year and now was taller than his older brother and still growing. Even though he was only seventeen, Laura still worried about the military draft. He was not likely to go to college as his brother did, so the draft board would be snatching him in a few short years. *He's just a boy,* she thought, and let out that sigh that mothers save for moments when issues concerning their children are beyond their control. Vietnam War, another sigh, followed by the sound of Paulie storming in. Jacket and books flying, he went straight for *Soupy Sales* on Channel 11.

"How was school, Paulie?"

"Good."

She noticed the brand-new Captain Marvel comic book drop out of Paulie's loose-leaf. "Where'd that come from?"

Now she had his attention.

"I, uh, bought it, Mom.""

"With your lunch money?"

"….. Yeah."

"Tell her the truth, Paulie," his sister said as she approached with her hands on her hips.

"Tell me what?"

"He stole it from Feldman's." Angie added, "He always does, and I told him to stop."

Laura was beside herself with anger. **"Always does? Tuddy come in here!** You knew about this too?"

Tuddy confessed. "Yeah, Ma, he has a whole collection downstairs in the bin."

The *bin* was a small private storage area each tenant was allowed, in the cellar. Tud hid his cigarettes there, and Mike still had his *Playboy* magazines moldering away in there. The place was so cluttered you could probably stash a Volkswagen in there and no one would see it. Not unexpectedly, a livid Laura led Paulie out the door, turning back to tell the other two that she wasn't done with *them.* Down the hallway steps and then down the creaking cellar steps, her hand grasping his collar, they went. She unlocked the door and saw about thirty comic books and *Mad* magazines. "Pick them up, *all of them,*" she commanded.

A flustered Paulie gathered up his collection and feared his immediate future. Out the front door they stormed, past a puzzled Lina, who of course had heard them down there. Paulie's fears were realized when they headed down Flushing Avenue toward Feldman's. Paulie prayed the candy store was empty.

"Mr. Feldman, my son here has something to tell you."

Ivy and Anita, Paulie's classmates, looked up from their seats at the soda counter.

Mr. Feldman, eyeing the books, sensed what was unfolding and came around from behind the counter. He looked sternly at the child. Laura yanked on his collar to help him get the words out. Paulie wished he was dead.

"I'm sorry, Mr. Feldman."

"For what?" Another yank.

"For taking your comic books," Paulie whispered, glancing at the girls, who snapped their noses back into their chocolate egg creams.

Laura felt so sorry for her son, but this was necessary. Kindly Mr. Feldman, losing track of the years, leaned down and said, "I'm surprised at you, Tuddy."

"This is Paulie, Tuddy's brother, Mr. Feldman, and he's going to be sweeping your sidewalk and he'll clean the inside of your store as well, if you trust him enough to let him in." Laura finished the sentence with her face inches away from her trembling son.

"I guess I won't call the police then," winked the old gentleman. Laura led the boy away. Two blocks up the avenue she weakened and put her arm around his shoulder.

CHAPTER 3

It was a mild Thursday by January standards. Sal's fourth day at the helm, and past the halfway point of Matty's vacation. Sal was settling in as the acting manager. He had done this often in the past, when Matt was out sick or just off for the day. But Matt had always seen to it that he was there, personally, for large payroll deliveries such as this one, even if he had to leave his sickbed. Today was the exception.

The Morgan Trust Flushing branch held the payroll account for the nearby Schaefer Beer brewery. Shaeffer had an arrangement where their employees could cash their checks there every other Friday. This particular Friday also fell on the third of the month so many Social Security recipients would be in. Accordingly, that afternoon was the Wells Fargo delivery to cover Friday's withdrawals. Sal again read through Matt's notes. The amount of the Wells Fargo delivery should be just short of two hundred and fifty thousand. Nearly double the normal payroll delivery. The scrawling on the hidden loose-leaf paper also carefully laid out the new sequence of numbers and key turns necessary to open the recently upgraded main vault. Matt and Sal had had a dry run last Friday, so Sal sort of felt confident with it.

Right at 2:30 the truck rolled up and double-parked outside the bank. Out bounded two Wells Fargo guards, each with a large satchel in one hand and a .38 revolver pointed at the ground in the other. As is customary, a third guard, usually the driver, stayed inside the vehicle. Chubby heartily greeted the older guard, who had once been his desk sergeant at the 83rd Precinct. Sal got up from his desk and unlocked the steel-barred door that led to the main vault and safe-deposit box room. The four of them entered. Along the way, Chubby was laughing at his friend's whispered remarks.

Sal approached the vault and read the note he was holding . . . Insert key, turn dial twice around to the left to 14, then once around to the right to 36, then back left once around to 6, then to 31, remove key, spin handle . . . *nothing.* The younger guard was observing while the other two continued their reminiscing. Sal tried again: Insert key, turn dial left to 14, right to 36, 6, 31, remove key, try handle, again . . . still nothing. He let out a groan in disgust and all three were watching him now. He tried a *third* time . . . approached closer the vault and slowly followed the note he was holding. Insert key, turn dial twice around to the left to 14, then once around to the right to 36, then back left once around to 6, then to 31, remove key, spin handle and . . . *still locked.* Sal tried a fourth time, nothing.

What the hell am I doing wrong? He stubbornly tried *still* again with no luck. About now their driver entered. They saw him standing inside the door of the bank pointing to his watch. The three tellers never looked up from their work, which involved balancing the busy day's receipts. Sal apologized and told the guards to leave the bags right there on the ground and he signed their ledger and thankfully off they went. He then shrugged at Chubby as if to say, "What now?" He attempted the combo one last time without luck, then lifted the bags off the floor and went out to Manny's office. He unlocked the door and entered with Chubby. Sal muttered to his sympathetic friend, "Why does this shit only happen to me?"

"Just be glad tomorrow's Friday and by Monday Mr. Wonderful will be back and you can return to your normal *shit.*"

"My normal shit! Now there's an enticing thought I always look forward to," Sal remarked as he unlocked a large metal file cabinet and stuffed the loot inside. He turned toward an amused Chubby and declared, "It'll be okay in here for now. Tomorrow morning, I'll call the main office and find out what I'm doing wrong." Chubby took his seat and noticed he had ten minutes until 3 pm lockup time.

Sal rested his head in his hands while he stared down at the numbers. "Damn."

After dinner that evening, Sal and Tuddy, on the spur of the moment, decided to take a ride out to East Meadow to watch the Knicks game at Mikey's. It was rare that Sal ventured out on weekdays, Laura thought, let alone a long drive out to Long Island.

He just wanted to spend some time with his older boys and unwind. He liked long drives and was looking forward to stretching out in his son's home far away from the noisy city life he *still* claimed he preferred. Mike and Patti, not really knowing anyone out there, welcomed their visitors. The boys watched the Knicks beat the Celtics and woke their father after the game. On the ride home he talked basketball with Tuddy while he sped along the newly built Long Island Expressway. The trials and tribulations of the day, which as usual he kept to himself, were forgotten.

The day ahead of him, however, he wouldn't soon forget, nor would many New Yorkers.

* * *

Hector lifted his head when he felt his cigarette burning his fingers. He'd been pretty much out cold for the last two hours, opening his eyes just long enough to light another cigarette.

"Where the fuck Junior go?"

"He's picking up something for me in the city," Whitey replied.

"Picking up what?" Hector asked, more awake now.

"Listen Bro, I was going to wait until he got back to tell you . . . We got a job tomorrow."

"Huh?"

"Junior is buying a couple of pieces for us up in El Barrio."

Hector was stunned. "Pieces, as in guns? For *tomorrow*?"

"Yeah, I waited 'till now to tell you 'cause I know how retarded you get with shit like this."

"Shit like what?"

They both looked up when the bell rang, and Sandy let a nervous-looking Junior in. He looked at the empty glassine envelopes next to his friends and quickly asked, "You didn't do mine, did ya?"

"No, shithead, did you see him? What happened?"

Junior smiled, reached into his bulging overcoat, and pulled out a taped-up bag. "Got two .22s and a fuckin' cannon .45."

Whitey jumped up and slapped him five. "How much?"

"Not cheap. Two-fifty, but they're clean, no numbers."

"Fuck, that's a lot. I don't give a shit about serial numbers, after the job they're disappearing anyways."

As Junior was searching for what was left of his veins, Whitey looked at Hector. "You okay? You look like you're shittin' yourself, bro."

Hector changed his expression and forced a smile. "You gonna tell me what the fuck's goin' on?"

Junior was shaking as he fumbled with the needle. "I don't believe you didn't tell him yet, Whitey," he mumbled through the leather strap in his teeth.

Whitey shot a look at Junior. "What's the difference, I'm telling him now, ain't I?"

"Hector, open your eyes and look at me. We're hitting a bank over on Flushing Avenue tomorrow."

"A bank, tomorrow? Aren't you supposed to plan shit like that?" Hector looked in the kitchen at Sandy then back at her boyfriend.

"Don't worry, she's cool. That's our driver."

Hector's hesitation reflected the fact that this was way out of the league of these three neighborhood junkies. They'd done robberies before, but mainly only street muggings and using knives not guns. Junior had held up Gito's candy store once while Hector was overseas, but this was way different.

"Everything's been planned, and it's happening tomorrow. They do payroll and shit on Friday, so it should be a bitchin' score. I was there Monday, they got this old fuckin' guard, a couple of women tellers, and another old dude in the back. Easy as it gets, my man. No more cattle rustling bullshit, mi amigo."

Junior finished with his shot and his shaking and stood up to put his belt back on. The heroin helped the reluctant Hector gain courage.

"Fuckin A, dudes, it's about time we did a real score."

They spent the rest of their coherent evening going over the plan. Afterwards, a disgusted Sandy came in to pry the smoldering cigarettes from their motionless hands.

* * *

Sal woke up Thursday and, unlike other mornings, Laura wasn't next to him. He found her on the living room couch listening to the stereo. Not a good sign, he thought.

"You okay, dear?"

She was startled by his voice. "Hi, I'm fine, couldn't fall back asleep."

Sal knew she always played Sinatra records when something was bothering her. He went into the kitchen and made a pot of coffee. "Tea, honey?"

She didn't hear him.

He went back in and sat beside her. "Would you like some tea?"

"No, I already had—what are we gonna do about Angie's braces, Sal?"

Sal gave her a sideways glance. "Is *that* why you're up?"

"Well yeah, that and all the rest."

"Such as?"

She became annoyed. "Such as the car transmission, such as Paulie probably going to P.S. 147 instead of St Bridget's next year, such as—"

"Okay, okay, spare me the sermon. What can I tell you, Laura? We'll get through it, don't we always? We got no choice."

"But we do . . ."

"No, forget it."

"Sal, he won't mind."

"No, I'm not asking Mikey for *anything*. Laura, it's not gonna happen."

"What about Dad, then?"

Ignoring her, he got up and stormed into the shower. She reached over and slammed shut the hi-fi, scratching the record.

* * *

"Good morning, Sal."

He looked over. "Mornin' Dana, mornin' Rose. Paula not here yet?"

Chubby broke in, "She's across the street getting cigarettes."

Sal winced. "It's probably those damn things that got me breathing like an old man. If only I knew better."

Chubby walked over to Sal's desk and asked in a low voice, "Figure it out yet?"

"What's that, Chub?"

"The combination," he replied, motioning his head toward the vault.

"Oh, actually I think so. I was racking my brain last night. I think I gotta leave the key *in* throughout the process. I was removing it. I *hope* that's it."

It was 8:55. Chubby sat in the chair alongside Sal's desk.

"How are the kids?"

"They're good, Chubb. Michael's settling in out there. The rest of 'em are doing their thing, and I'm waiting to be a grandfather."

"Ahh, there's nothing better, Sal. Little Susie starts school in September." As expected, Chubby went into a dialogue about her. This time her reading ability. Sal interrupted him between breaths.

"What's Marie been doin' with all her time these days?"

"Well, it's been a couple of weeks now," Chubby replied, referring to her retirement. "She seems to be settling into a healthy regimen of shopping."

They laughed. Sal kind of missed her.

"Tell her to call Laura for some pointers," Sal joked, knowing that Laura would prefer having her fingernails pulled out. Chubby looked up through the cigarette smoke billowing from behind the teller's counter, toward the old clock.

"Bout that time, folks." He got up from Sal's desk and started toward the door. He noticed a black Rambler sitting off to the side with four people inside. It was beginning to snow. He unlocked the door and sank in his chair with a groan. Not a minute later, three Puerto Rican men entered. In unison they transformed their caps into ski masks and were reaching into their coat pockets.

Whitey put the .45 to Chubby's temple and said in a calm voice, "Do what I say, Pop, and no one will get hurt. Get up and lock the door." Hector was rushing toward the women, waving his gun and screaming, **"Back up! Get Away from those fuckin' buttons and come around here!"** Junior went straight toward Sal, who was still seated behind his desk.

"Get up motherfucker."

Hector was still screaming at the terrified women. **"Over here, get on the floor, face down!"** As planned, he herded them away from the windows.

Everyone obeyed.

Rose started to sob. Whitey calmly disarmed Chubby, slid his revolver across the floor, then led him off to the side where the women were lying.

"Down, Pop, on your stomach." The three pulled out large shopping bags from inside their jackets. Whitey and Junior shoved Sal toward the vault entrance while a ranting Hector went behind the tellers' counter and began to empty the drawers, all the while screaming threats at the trembling people on the ground.

"Open it," Whitey commanded, rattling the bars with the barrel of his .45. Sal produced the keys, realizing suddenly his life depended on his opening the vault inside. They went into the vault area and Sal pulled the piece of paper from his top pocket.

Junior held his .22 against the back of the trembling man's head. **"Hurry up or your fuckin' dead!"**

Whitey looked out toward the front door and was relieved that no one was waiting to get in. Sal's weak heart was beating furiously.

"Okay, okay, listen, I'm not the regular guy here so I need time to open this thing."

"Don't fuck with us, just do it!" Junior pushed the gun hard into Sal's head, causing a cut.

Sal started. Insert key, twice around to the left to 14 and once to the right, to 36, then left once around to 6, right to 31, *don't remove key*. He gasped as the wheel spun in his hand and released the lock.

"On the floor!" Whitey pointed. The two of them proceeded to fill the bags and glanced confidently at each other. They were under control. The hostages were under control. It was looking like they'd soon be heading out the door with everyone intact. The bags were half full, and Whitey was already glancing outside for his ride. Suddenly...... **POP!** A loud shot and screaming from inside the teller area. Whitey whirled, then looked at Junior.

"Keep going, I'll be right back."

He pointed his revolver at the now shaking assistant manager, "You stay down, mister," and quickly headed out front. The group of hostages were lying still, except for the bank guard, who was writhing on the floor with a low gurgling sound coming from his throat.

Blood was streaming onto the tiled floor. Hector was frantic. Whitey yelled for the first time, **"What'd you dooo, man?"**

"He went for the alarm Whitey. I think he hit it. Let's get the fuck outta here!" Whitey ran to the back and into the vault where Junior was still stuffing the bags. Junior saw that their leader had finally lost his cool.

"He shot the guard! Let's go!"

Junior was already about done in there. "What about the boxes?" He said, referring to the safe-deposit boxes they were planning on emptying.

Whitey was breathing heavily. "No time, com'on!"

They stepped over Sal and hurried to the front, where Chubby now lay face down in a large pool of blood. The quivering women never looked up. Rose was passed out.

"The keys, the keys!" Junior was rattling the locked door. **"They're under him!"**

Hector motioned toward Chubby. Whitey reached under the motionless guard and pulled out a set of bloody keys. His second try opened the door. Luckily, the sidewalk was clear. Outside, he waved to Sandy to bring the car up. The other two hurriedly walked out while pulling up their ski-masks and hopped into the back seat of the car. Sandy sped away from the curb and headed west. She knew from their faces something had gone wrong. Whitey and Junior were talking at the same time. Junior was the louder, **"Why did you shoot him?"**

Hector seemed in a trance while staring out the side window.

"What happened out there, Hector?" Whitey asked, looking back at his friend.

"When I turned to look in at you guys, he started crawling over to the alarm button under the counter. Dumb motherfucker. **Dumb** motherfucker."

Sandy slumped in her seat and exhaled dramatically. Whitey looked up ahead. "I guess he hit it." Two 104th Precinct radio cars screamed past them, and they heard more coming down the parallel street. They continued along Bushwick Avenue. The traffic was light, probably due to the snow forecast.

Whitey caught his breath and leaned back. He replayed the whole event in his mind. A few silent minutes later he spun around. "Hector, did you call me by my *name* in there?"

"Wha?" He turned and looked straight at Whitey. "No!"

"Think! Did you say my name at any time?"

"Nooo, Whitey, *no*, when?"

Junior, looking to calm things down, hastened. "I didn't hear him say your name, Whitey."

Whitey took a deep breath and thought out loud, "I fuckin' hope not."

Sandy, shaking her head slightly, turned into a side street where they abandoned the stolen Rambler and jumped into their '59 DeSoto.

Whitey settled in the front seat, removed his gloves, and again looked back, repeating, "I *really* hope not, Hector,".

* * *

"Don't touch anything till Homicide gets here."

An NYPD sergeant repeated this to each late-arriving pair of uniformed officers that rushed in. Sal, Dana, Rose, and Paula were seated in the rear lunchroom, out of sight of their covered, lifeless old friend. Two of the women had overcoats draped over them to try to ease the shaking. One of the cops helped Rose light her cigarette. She was still crying. Young Dana remained brave, trying to comfort the other two. Sal was hyperventilating, hoping this was all just a bad dream and Laura would wake him.

"You okay, mister?" the same cop asked.

Sal looked up. "Uh, yeah, I'll be all right," he lied, wondering now about the tightness in his chest.

Two burly men in tan overcoats pushed their way through the large crowd outside the bank.

"Through there, Lieutenant," the sergeant motioned.

"We don't need all these people here, Sergeant," Lieutenant O'Reardon replied, referring to the sea of blue uniforms gathered in the bank. The two detectives went over to the covered bank guard and the older one, noticing his right hand sticking out and seeing his ring, asked, "Anyone notify his wife?"

"A car is on the way to his address now," a uniformed officer replied. He knelt and lifted the blanket. "I hear he's a retiree from the job; that true?"

"Looks like one entry, through the back of his neck and out his throat, small caliber." The younger detective was busy writing the information in his notepad.

The sergeant, hearing the question, moved closer to the detective. "Yes, his boss in there said he's been retired from the force for about ten years now. His name is Adolph Werner, known as Chubby here, though."

The duo moved into the lunchroom toward Sal. "I'm Detective Lieutenant O'Reardon and this is Detective Falco. I understand you're the assistant manager here."

"Yes, I am," Sal replied.

"Is the manager around?"

"No, he's away on vacation."

"Okay, would you please come in here, sir?"

They led Sal out of the back room and sat him down at his desk. Sal noticed the camera flashes coming from the side of the counter where Chubby was lying. Detective Falco re-opened his notebook and spoke for the first time,

"Mr. Marchetti, what happened in here?"

Sal explained the event to them. All the while Richie Falco was scribbling on his pad, repeatedly asking him to speak slower. When he got to the part of hearing the gunshot, O'Reardon interrupted and asked, "Did you see him fire the shot?"

"No, I didn't, I was lying down inside there," pointing to the vault.

"Okay, continue."

Sal finished his detailed statement and noticed what apparently was the coroner approaching them. Motioning toward Chubby, he asked O'Reardon, "You guys done over there?"

"Yeah, you can have him," the lieutenant replied.

"Ok, Mr. Marchetti, that's all for now, thank you. Could you please return to your lunchroom?"

They led him in and escorted Rose out to Sal's desk. They got her statement, with even more pertinent details because she had been out there with Chubby.

"One of them was named Whitey—the short one."

"You heard his name mentioned? Was he the one who fired the shot at the guard?"

"No, that was the other one. The tall skinny one."

"You heard someone say the name Whitey, ma'am?" Falco asked.

"Yes. Clearly."

There was suddenly a commotion at the bank's entrance. It was Chubby's wife, Marie, being restrained by two policemen. She had not been home when the police went to inform her and found out at the grocery store that there had been a holdup at the bank. What's more, that the bank guard had been shot. Everyone watched as she was led away and taken to the morgue for identification. Other family members started showing up and were herded into a separate area inside the bank. Sal wondered where Laura was.

When the detectives were done with the preliminary questioning, they asked Sal to escort them into the still-open vault. He noticed that another team was there taking fingerprints. "You had mentioned they were wearing gloves, sir. Did you notice if any of them removed them at any point?" O'Reardon asked.

"Not that I saw." Sal noticed Laura had arrived and was behind the other cops, straining to look inside the vault. Sal waved at her and asked if he could go out there.

"Sure."

She wrapped her arms around his neck and was bawling.

"I'm fine, I'm fine." She wouldn't relax her grip. "They shot Chubby, Laura, he's gone."

"I know, it's on the radio," she murmured.

"Do the kids know?" he asked.

"Angela and Tuddy do. Paulie doesn't and I haven't spoken to Michael yet."

"Go on home to them," Sal said. "They shouldn't be alone. I'll be there in a bit." She finally let go, then grabbed him again and kissed him on the cheek and turned and left. Sal rejoined the detectives, who were busy thumbing through items that remained in the vault. "Mr. Marchetti, how much money would you estimate was in the bank when you opened this morning?"

"I'd say over three hundred thousand, probably three ten."

They both turned and looked at him.

"Tomorrow is the brewery's payday *and* Social Security day."

The detectives looked at each other with a *this was a big one* look.

"You said you thought they were Puerto Rican?" Falco asked. "Did they speak Spanish?"

"No, but they were. They had that Spanish accent kinda. They also sounded like junkies."

"*Sounded* like junkies?" Falco looked puzzled.

"Yeah, you know, that voice they have, kinda raspy like."

O'Reardon knew the voice. They led him out of the vault area. He noticed the women were already gone.

"This, I take it, is the manager's office?"

"Yes, Manual Figueroa."

"Is it always locked?"

"Yes, it is, I have the key though."

"You stated they rushed out after the shooting and didn't go into the safe-deposit box room," O'Reardon said.

"Correct."

"I take it they didn't go in here either." He was referring to the locked office.

"That's also correct."

"Mind opening it?"

Sal went into his desk and came back with the key. O'Reardon and Falco stepped in and looked around while Sal watched them from the doorway. They looked in Manny's desk and glanced in a few file cabinets. "What's he keep in here?" O'Reardon asked, trying the large, locked metal cabinet.

Before Sal could answer, he asked, "Do you have the key?"

"Mostly loan records and such. No, I don't. He probably has it with him." Sal waited a few seconds then hastened nervously, "I could look around for a spare."

The lieutenant hesitated, looked at his watch, and said, "No, that won't be necessary, we're done for now, but what I *would* like you to do is, like I told your tellers, this evening, slowly go over everything that occurred in here today and try to remember something, anything, that you didn't already tell us. The slightest detail may be more helpful than you think."

Sal walked them to the door. It was nearly one o'clock. There were still the fingerprint guys and a cleanup crew from the coroner's office inside with him. He noticed the patrol car posted outside. Two executives and a security team from the head office in Manhattan were on their way. They were scheduled to meet the insurance company people there at two o'clock. Sal had some time alone for the first time. He sat behind his desk and buried his head in his hands. He was struggling with his conscience.

What on earth made me do that? he thought, referring to the incident in Manny's office. *Am I crazy? That's a quarter-million dollars sitting in that cabinet.*

What puzzled him the most was there was no particular time during this whole day that he'd decided he wanted that money. It had just happened, as if another being within him had acted independently. What's really crazy, he thought, was if someone had asked him earlier if there was cash left behind, he would have said, "Yes, in the manager's office."

Whatever the reason and whatever the outcome, the reality is, *too late now. The money cannot just turn up.* He knew he had to find a way to get those bags out of there. When? Before the bosses got there would be the logical solution, but the police were outside the door. He couldn't just waltz those large bags past them to his car. He decided his only choice was to leave them there for now. The executives, like the police, had no reason to look in that locker. If for some reason they wanted to, he would tell them, like he told the police, that the key was probably in Manny's possession.

His palms were sweating. He lifted his head off them and looked over at the guys in white coveralls heading to the door with their cleaning gear. He hopped up and let them out. He noticed the crowd outside was gone. It was eerie how the neighborhood just carried on as if nothing had happened. Sal strolled around the inside of the bank then walked into Manny's office and sat down. He was tempted to peer into the locker but dared not since there were cops still around. He then started dwelling on the positive aspects of that amount of money. *That's twenty years' salary in there. My family's new home is in there. Laura's happiness is in there.* His desire to see his wife happy was what this was all about. Her not worrying about braces and tuitions was what this was all about. Most importantly, moving her out of that apartment. This was all for his wife. He was now content with his decision. Then a visit from reality entered his mind. *What if I get caught? What will happen to my family if I get arrested and go to prison? They'd wind up wards of Mayor Wagner's home relief program.*

His chest felt tight again, and his breathing hastened. He wondered why he'd stopped taking his blood pressure medicine.

CHAPTER 4

Whitey, Junior, and Hector had been in the apartment for several hours now. The white powder on the coffee table was now a half-ounce mound instead of the usual ten-dollar pinch. Whitey was the only one awake. He was smoking a cigarette and staring at the ceiling. He wished the heroin would soothe him as it did his friends. Well, actually, it *did* soothe him, what he needed was for the drug to make him *forget*. The shooting this morning weighed heavily on his head.

He spoke to his half-asleep cohorts. "Shit, if only I'd laid the old man down on the other side." He closed his eyes tight. *Fuckin' murder, in the process of a bank robbery. Mandatory chair in New York State*, he thought. All for what! Whitey was also brooding over the amount of money they got. He had been told there would be much more there. With three heroin addicts and a girlfriend already planning her shopping spree, how long was fifty thousand dollars going to last them? He was sorry he ever did this. He was also scared. Several minutes later his worries were gone as was his coherence.

* * *

Sal heard voices inside the bank. The honchos from the head office had arrived. Roger Bilkey, the executive vice-president, apparently had his own key. The four men walked over to Sal with a look of condolence. They each shook his hand. Mr. Bilkey put his palm on his shoulder and said, "Salvatore, I'm so relieved you're not hurt. As you know, we at Morgan Trust view our employees' well-being during these incidents, as the primary concern."

His associate was all the while nodding in agreement. Sal was certain Bilkey made that little speech before.

"Well, sir, I appreciate you finding the time to come all the way out here." He lied. He wanted these people there like he wanted polio. Sal noticed the fingerprint duo were finally done and went over and thanked them as he let them out.

He was about to relock the door when he noticed two guys in suits walking across the street toward the bank's entrance. No doubt, the insurance adjusters. He held the door for them while they introduced themselves. Sal, in turn, introduced them to the waiting foursome. They all filed into the only spot that could seat them, the lunchroom.

It was now 2:30. Two cops were still outside keeping customers away. Sal wanted to call home but decided instead to follow them in. He took a seat, not even sure if they wanted him in there. Turns out they did. He was asked for the ledgers and records and receipts. Sal was glad he was a tidy record keeper and was able to quickly produce everything they requested. He was surprised to see that Bilkey already had a copy of the preliminary police report. Papers were spread out all over the table and everyone was filling out forms. Sal started to daydream about being wealthy again when he was interrupted by Bilkey who was seated beside him.

The vice-president leaned over and spoke to him almost in a personal whisper, "We have been in touch with Mr. Figueroa. We reached him at his hotel in Mexico. He offered to cut his vacation short and come right up but we felt it wasn't necessary, so he'll be back here Monday. Nothing can be done over the weekend anyhow and tomorrow is only a half-day."

Sal could barely hear him over the racket the adding machines were making.

He continued. "Let's give the tellers the day off, but I would like to post a representative outside to assure our customers that this was an isolated incident, and we'll return to business as usual on Monday. It would also be useful to direct them to our Greenpoint branch if they need a transaction before then. John and I will be stopping there when we're done here to get them situated."

Sal offered, sensing an opportunity. "I can be here tomorrow, to do whatever's necessary."

"Good, I would also like you to take care of a few things for me while we finish our work here. I need you first to show Jeff and Mark from our security department whatever they require. Then, I want you to box up all your active customers' records, so we can bring them with us to Greenpoint. They'll return them before opening Monday."

The trio exited the lunchroom and went behind the tellers' counter. Jeff and Mark began going through the drawers, looking under mats, taking notes, photos, occasionally asking Sal about items they were unfamiliar with.

"I get it. Much of this stuff hasn't been upgraded since this branch opened in the twenties," Sal said.

After a short while they moved into the vault area. They asked to go into the safe-deposit box area first so Sal unlocked the door. They entered and started looking around. Sal was concerned because the detectives, when informed that the gunmen had never entered the room, were uninterested themselves in going in. He wondered how thorough these guys were going to be when they headed into Manny's office. They asked a few questions about the branch's procedure with customers who used the safe-deposit boxes. In all, they went through the area pretty quickly.

Next stop was Manny's office. Jeff was looking through Manny's desk drawers, while Mark read Manny's framed diplomas and awards that adorned the wall behind his desk. He also seemed interested in the pictures of the kids on the desk. Suddenly, one of the insurance adjusters walked in and asked Sal to come back to the lunchroom. Sal sat down alongside Roger Bilkey and answered a variety of accounting questions, all the while concerned about what was going on next door.

"Will that be all?" Sal hastened.

"Yes, I think so."

Just as he was about scurry out, another guy would ask another question. Sal was growing frantic. Finally, he didn't ask, he just got up and went right toward Manny's office. He drew a deep breath as he walked through the door not knowing what these two had gotten into. He saw the metal cabinet was still locked and he exhaled.

"Mr. Marchetti, what does he keep in this drawer here?" Jeff asked, referring to the locked top desk drawer.

"I have no idea; I suppose pens and pencils." *Dumb question,* Sal thought.

"What about the cabinet there?"

Sal strained to remain composed. "He keeps the loan records in there mostly, blank forms as well."

"Do you have a key?"

"No, I don't. If you guys don't mind, I have to put together those records for Mr. Bilkey before he leaves."

As soon as he heard *"for Mr. Bilkey,"* the security chief didn't hesitate. "Sure, go right ahead."

Sal saw this as a chance to get them out of there. He waited at Manny's door, looking at them, and it worked. Mark placed the picture of Manny's girlfriend back on the desk and they filed out.

"Nice, huh," Sal said as he closed the office door.

"Yeah, I'd say," Mark replied.

He was getting better at this. Within another half-hour they were wrapping the whole thing up. It was nearly four o'clock. Sal led them all to the door and Bilkey suggested before leaving that he not linger too long and get home to his family.

"I'm just going to set the alarm and I'll be out of here."

Bilkey made a rare attempt at humor. "Alarm? What for, money's already gone." He then grinned and patted him on the shoulder and Sal responded with an exaggerated laugh.

Sal quickly set the alarm, put on his coat, took a last look at what was left of his once-tidy bank, including the now bleached area, shut the lights, locked the door, and stepped out into the snowy evening. He saw the patrol car still was out there. *They better be gone tomorrow.* He took his first breath of fresh air as he walked briskly to his car.

Lina was the first to encounter Sal when he arrived at the front of his house. Noticing his strained expression, she emerged from the bakery. "Madonna—Sal, are you okay?"

"I'm fine, Lina, thank you." He started up the hallway stairs before she had the chance to give him the third degree.

She yelled up at him, "I hope they shoot up thosa bastards."

"Me too, Lina."

Tuddy was waiting at the top of the stairs and Laura was in the apartment doorway motioning them in, knowing their nosy landlord was in the hall. Inside, they all took turns hugging him. Mike was also there. They were all talking at once.

Finally, Mike spoke the loudest, "Dad, tell us what happened."

They sat down at the kitchen table. Sal noticed there was a pot of sauce cooking. He wondered why he hadn't smelled it first. He told them the story from beginning to end. There was a brief silence.

"The pasta's boiling over," he said finally to his entranced wife.

"Angie, lower the flame," Laura relayed.

"Dad, how much did they get?" Tuddy asked excitedly.

Sal took a breath. "A lot, over three hundred thousand dollars."

Angie and Tuddy instantly looked at each other.

"WOW," she said.

"Imagine, Ang," Tuddy added, "what we could do with all that money!" Their eyes widened while they exchanged fantasies. Little Paulie even pitched in his wish list.

"Ok, you three," Laura reeled them in. "Angie, set the table please."

Sal hadn't eaten all day and wasn't a bit hungry.

"This phone hasn't stopped ringing today," Laura complained as she got up and grabbed the receiver.

"Oh! Hello, Monsignor." Laura looked surprised and motioned for everyone to quiet down. "He's fine, Father, thank you." She was listening intently to his phone sermon. "Yes, Monsignor, he *was* watching over him. Okay I'll tell him, Monsignor, thank you. Okay, goodbye." Laura looked at her husband.

"I didn't know Monsignor Tucci *knew* how to use a telephone!"

The kids giggled.

Mike remarked, "I didn't know you understood Latin, Mom."

Everyone laughed now. The monsignor was eighty years old but still an active patriarch of St. Bridget's. He had married Sal and Laura. His phoning the house was truly an event.

"What'd he say?" Sal asked.

"He quoted a passage from *Matthew*, then said he was praying for you."

"Good," Sal replied, then thought, *I'll need it.*

The conversation turned to Chubby, and the atmosphere grew serious again. Sal told a few stories about him and fondly mimicked his accent. His wife's name wasn't mentioned.

Michael changed the subject. "What happens now, Pop?"

"Well, I expect a big investigation by the police, for one. Morgan will no doubt come up with unnecessary new security procedures. Other than that, not much will change."

"You won't be fired then, Daddy?"

"No, Paulie," Sal mused, "I won't be fired. Any more questions before we close this matter and have dinner?"

No one answered and Laura started filling the plates.

CHAPTER 5

"Want half?" Detective Falco held up his meatball hero to the lieutenant. O'Reardon looked up and made a face.

"No, Rich, I had *dinner* at Smitty's," he joked, referring to the beef jerky he had with his gin and tonics.

These two handled quite a few robbery/homicides together at the 104th; however, when the robbery was a bank and the homicide was an ex-cop guard at that bank, it took on an even larger priority. Next to actual on-duty police murders, this was the most serious. No one was going home tonight. O'Reardon had just finished briefing the team of detectives he headed.

They knew they were looking for amateurs. They had a name. Whitey. They had a description of him: short, Puerto Rican, maybe five foot five. They knew the murder weapon was a .22. They had the getaway car. It was found in Greenpoint, a '62 Rambler that was reported stolen last week. It was now outside the precinct under a flood light and the same two lab guys were removing the fingerprints from it. That's all they had. The detectives and some uniformed teams headed out to start rounding up the known junkies and stoolies from the surrounding precinct. O'Reardon wanted the word out to them. If they wanted a peaceful winter, they'd better come up with this Whitey guy quickly. O'Reardon looked at Falco. "The thing I don't get, Rich is, these guys were too clumsy for this to be an inside job, yet it's just too much of a coincidence that they hit it with that much loot in there."

"Well, let's figure; if it's inside, there's only what, five or six people who work there? Then there's still the Brinks people and for that matter the *entire* Schaefer Brewery knows when and where payday is. Coulda been anyone."

"True, not to mention Social Security Day . . . Still, I don't know . . ." His voice trailed off as they hopped into their black Plymouth and headed west, to Brooklyn.

It was cold and pitch-dark now. The snow had stopped after an inch or two, settling mostly on the cars. Even though it was only seven o'clock the streets were desolate. These detectives had both served in Narcotics at different times in the past, but they had long since lost touch with their connections in New York's drug subculture, Falco more recently. They headed to his old precinct, the 83rd: Up DeKalb Avenue toward Knickerbocker Park. A junkie haven, no matter what the weather.

At the entrance to the park, at first sight of their car pulling up, the rumpled group huddled in there started loosening their grip on their cellophane packets, allowing them to float onto the dark concrete path. They walked calmly in separate directions as if a local PTA meeting had just concluded. Falco, a step ahead of the lieutenant, zeroed in on the short one in the leather jacket. They flanked him.

"Joey Prez, my old pal, when did you get out?" Falco said as he felt around inside his leather jacket pockets. Prez had gotten his nickname when president of his local gangbusting group, *before* the drug epidemic. He was twitching and his nose was running. They knew he was sick. He looked at Falco.

"I been home almost a year now and I'm doin' good. I'm clean now." He rolled up his sleeve and showed his arm, knowing the cops couldn't see his tracks in the dark. "*I swear on my mother,* I just smoke pot now . . . I got a job and a kid and a real good old lady."

Falco was still going through he pockets. "Joe, we're looking for Whitey. You know where he is?"

"Whitey who?" The junkie looked puzzled.

"Whitey, a short Puerto Rican."

"Wrong place, dude. There ain't no spicks up here."

The park was three or four street blocks east of the ethnic line. O'Reardon spoke for the first time, "Listen, dope fiend, the next time you go down into *their* turf I want you listening for the name Whitey!"

"*I* know. This is about that guard that was shot this morning, ain't it."

"We WILL be back here to see you in a few days," O'Reardon said, "Do **not** disappoint me."

The two got back in their car and drove off.

"See, Lieutenant, the narco is still in you."

"Like riding a bicycle," he replied while eyeing two of the stragglers from the park.

* * *

Saturday morning was abnormally warm. Salvatore started his car and sat for a while. He just needed a moment to gather his thoughts and get his head straight. His mind had been racing all night allowing him only a few hours' sleep. His thoughts ran the gamut from agony to ecstasy, depending on what scenario his imagination led him to. One minute, he would feel the happiness and contentment that comes with wealth. Next minute, his pessimistic side would take control and he envisioned disgrace, scandal, and prison. He realized this roller coaster ride was to be expected given the circumstances, but wondered why the lows were so much lower than the highs were high. He was frightened, plain and simple. He again felt his blood pressure soaring, even with the medication.

He put his car in drive and headed to work, not sure who or what awaited him there. He knew that he had to somehow get those bags out of there today. It was imperative that he find a parking space as close to the entrance as possible.

It was only 7:30 when he pulled up to the bank. He hadn't realized that he was a half-hour early. Surprisingly there were parking spaces all over. What a difference Saturday makes, he thought. He parked in an ideal spot on the side street maybe twenty yards from the entrance. No one was there. *Shit, why not right now?*

He unlocked the front door and rushed right into Manny's office, locking all the doors behind him. He took out the small key that he'd kept with him overnight and opened the cabinet. He drew a breath. "Wow." The bags were bigger than he remembered. He proceeded with his removal plan. He went outside the office and removed the large empty drawer that had contained the records that Bilkey had taken to the Greenpoint office. He brought it inside and stuffed one of the canvas bags in it. It *just* fit. He lifted it and carried it out. To a casual onlooker he would appear to be removing records.

He headed down the side street and finally reached his car. He laid the drawer on the back seat upside down and lifted the drawer up so the bag would fall onto the seat. Sal then covered it with his jacket. He shut the door without locking it and headed back with the empty drawer. He repeated the process with the second bag. Now the jacket wasn't big enough to cover them both. Sal calmly looked up and down the block. He decided then and there not to wait until later to bring the money home.

He returned the empty drawer back into its cabinet. He started hyperventilating again. He quickly went into Manny's office, relocked the cabinet door and beat it out of there.

Even jacketless in January, he felt the sweat as he pulled away from the curb and turned onto Flushing Avenue. He checked his rear-view mirror the entire way. Saturday shopping traffic was starting to build. He detoured through side streets just to make sure no one was behind him. He noticed his beaded face in the same mirror and smiled. One more obstacle, he thought: Lina. Two, actually: his own guys. He approached the house from the opposite side of the bakery. Shutting down, he reached under the seat pulling out Laura's laundry bag. Leaning over to the back seat he stuffed the two bags snugly into it. He then got out, threw the bag over his shoulder, and strutted toward his house. He suddenly felt the laundry bag was a dumb idea. All that was missing was a big dollar sign on it. It was just paranoia he reasoned.

He made it into his hallway and headed straight toward the cellar door, flicked on the light, and went down. He unlocked the bin door, and pulled the canvas bags out and placed them under a sheet that covered Paulie's old baby carriage. He carefully relocked the bin and headed up the cellar steps. When he turned to go out through the hall he nearly jumped out of his skin. Sure enough, the old lady was out there, right in front of him.

"Good morning, Sal. I thought I hearda somathing."

"Mornin', Lina, yes I had to put some clothes away, how are you?"

He was back outside before she could answer. He went straight for his car and noticed, as he drove past his house, Tuddy was walking out carrying a football. *Close call*, he thought.

When he arrived back at the bank it was a little after eight. Sal dashed across the street and picked up a newspaper. The Daily News headline read *BANK GUARD KILLED IN BROOKLYN. THIEVES ESCAPE WITH LOOT.* He sat down behind his desk and read the story. *Get away with $300,000 in unmarked bills, mostly twenties and fifties.* There was a picture of Marie being restrained outside the bank. He read the story three times. They spelled his name with one T, he noticed.

The morning proved uneventful. Surprisingly, only a handful of customers had to be redirected to the alternate branch. The brewery must have gotten word to their employees about the new arrangement. Throughout the day he pretty much ignored the ringing phones. He spent much of the day getting the bank straightened up. Just before noon the detectives showed up again. They had more questions, the main one being if he remembered any other details about the robbery. Sal did remember tight pants and pointed shoes on one of them. That was about it. Truth was, if Sal had a photo of them, he would have torn it up. He obviously didn't want them captured and disputing the amount of the haul. He asked Falco how the investigation was going.

"It only happened yesterday."

"Yes of course, I forgot you guys actually go home at night."

They asked about Chubby's wife. "Tell us about Marie Werner," O'Reardon said.

"She worked at this branch for nearly twenty years. She was a Miss NY State finalist, and she got her husband his job here. Marie is a woman of impeccable character is really all I can say. May I ask why?" Sal queried.

"She's going through a hard time is all, she looked pretty broken up yesterday." Falco answered. "Does she have family?"

"Her parents are still alive, live in Forest Hills, got a married daughter as well."

After several more mundane questions, the detectives left another card with the same instructions, "If you think of anything new call us."

He watched them leave and started to feel more confident. Next step, he thought, was when and, more importantly, *what*, to he tell his family about this money? Every idea he thought of seemed worse than the last one. There was plenty of time before he really had to act on that. He knew he wasn't going anywhere near that baby carriage any time soon. He still wondered why the police asked him about Marie. He should call her and find out how she was doing and what Chubby's funeral arrangements were. He did just that at his desk.

"Hello Sal, how are you?" He heard the grief in her voice already.

"I'm fine, Marie, how are you holding up?"

"I'll be okay, Sal, I suppose we all must deal with stuff like this and just learn how to carry on. You can't imagine how tough it is, though."

Sal got startled when she started crying. He managed to calm her down and they spoke for a while. She even started to reminisce and mentioned the afternoon when their casual flirting got out of hand the first time. Sal felt uncomfortable. He reasoned that although it was still morning she was drinking again and the vodka was talking because they never before spoke about that. Even though it happened eighteen years ago it was still vivid in his mind. More so was his wife's reaction when she noticed the lipstick on his white shirt that evening. They had one more encounter after that, but Sal ended it before it got out of hand. Luckily, as far as he knew, Chubby never had a clue. All the years since never soothed the animosity between the two women.

The day dragged by. It was nearly two o'clock and he finished a few last chores and went home for the weekend. Sal had never spent that much time alone in the bank and he relished the calm.

* * *

Sandy Cruz was beginning to worry about her boyfriend. Whitey was normally the sensible one of the trio, but he hadn't left the house now in two days and had been sleeping, shooting dope, smoking cigarettes, watching TV, and doing little else. Hector and Junior had been over several times to hang out and get high. Even they seemed to be functioning better than Whitey. She sat down beside him, holding the baby in one arm and shaking him with the other.

"WHAA?" he murmured before becoming semi-conscious. He looked at Sandy. "Hi, baby, what are you doing up?"

"I've been up for three hours, Whitey. It's eleven o'clock."

"In the morning?"

"Yes, Sunday morning. What's up with you, babe?"

"Meaning what?"

"Meaning you been sitting here stoned since Friday. I thought this money was supposed to get us out of this shithole instead of keeping us prisoners here."

"*Listen to this shit, Whitey,*" Hector said from across the room. "They're saying on the radio that three hundred thousand was stolen."

"No shit? These fucking bankers are bigger thieves than us. They say that bullshit to cheat the insurance company. I'll be a . . ."

Sandy interrupted, "Can't we go look at that apartment over on Powers Street I told you about?"

"Sure, baby, this afternoon, come here." He patted his legs and she got up and sat on his lap. "My babies," he said, hugging her and his son.

"Watch your damn cigarette before you burn up your babies."

"I'm sorry, Sandy."

"Don't be sorry, just put it in the ashtray."

"I'm not talking about the cigarette, I'm sorry about this whole thing. When all this shit blows over, we'll get back to the way things used to be, I swear."

"This *really* isn't you, Whitey, not getting high *this* much."

"I'm just a bit scared and stressed, that's all," he replied as the doorbell rang. Junior came in looking haggard. "What's the matter, bro?"

"Shit, Whitey, I just heard something."

"Yeah?" Sandy stared at him.

"Cops were at Willie's Pool Room last night. They got your name, man, they're looking for you."

Whitey slumped into the sofa and put his hands through his hair. He looked up at Junior. "My **whole** name?"

"No, just Whitey I think."

"Fucking Hector, I *knew* it." He got up and started pacing. Sandy was sitting there motionless. Whitey went to the window and looked out through the blinds.

"You see the news, Junior? They're saying we got three hundred thousand. Imagine that shit." He peeked outside several more times while walking around the apartment trying to digest it all. "We can't stay here," he said finally, while closing the blinds. "Too many people know where I live. Sandy, call that lady about the apartment."

He leaned over and took another scoop from the dwindling pile and carefully patted it into the spoon. He took his belt off again and settled down into his sofa. Sandy walked their baby into the kitchen and fought back her tears.

CHAPTER 6

"Salvatore Marchetti?"

"Just a second." Paulie called down from the top of the hallway stairs. He went inside. "Dad, there's a coupla guys downstairs to see you."

Sal rushed out and went down. He was relieved to see one of them was carrying a camera.

Okay, he thought, newspapermen. Before they could speak in the hallway, Sal brought them up into the privacy of his apartment.

"Bob Williamson, *Daily News*," the taller one said without introducing his photographer. Sal held out his hand. "Sal Marchetti, and this is my son, Paulie." He looked around for his wife, as she emerged from her sixty-second miracle makeup job.

"This is my wife, Laura."

"Pleased to meet you." She beamed. "Please sit down, can I get you gentlemen coffee?"

"That would be great, only if it's already made." They took their seats at the kitchen table. "I see you're a big fan of ours," Williamson joked, referring to the copy of the rival *Daily Mirror* sitting on the table.

"Oh, we read them *all*," an embarrassed Laura hastened to say as she placed coffee cups in front of them.

"If you don't mind, sir, I'd like to ask you a few questions regarding Thursday's events and perhaps take a few pictures."

Sal paused, "Okay, under one condition: you don't put my address in the paper."

"Wasn't gonna do that anyhow." He took out his pad while Laura poured the coffee.

"First sir, is your name spelled with two t's?"

"Yes."

"Why do you suppose they shot the guard?"

Quite a jump, Sal thought, in just two questions. "Well, I was in another part of the bank when the shot was fired, so I didn't see. My teller said that Mr. Werner, the guard, reached to set off the alarm."

"Can you tell me what kind of guy Mr. Werner was?"

"Sure, I'll tell you what kind of a guy he was; with a gun pointed at him, I heard him telling one of the robbers that their foul language wasn't necessary." After a pause Sal finally said, "Need I say more?"

The reporter was writing feverishly, loving that. "Was he from Germany?"

"Yes, he actually fought for the German Army in the first war and was captured by the British."

"His real first name was Adolph," Paulie added needlessly.

"Three hundred thousand was taken," Williamson said. "Do you always have that much money lying around such a small branch?"

"No, not always, but Friday was expected to be an especially busy day for us.

"So, since they hit you when you had all that money in the bank, would you say they were incredibly lucky, or do you think it was an inside job?"

Sal was caught off guard. "I'd say it was no secret what day Social Security checks are cashed, and large company payrolls fall on; therefore, any fool can figure that we were loaded that morning."

Laura smiled at Sal, showing her approval of his sidestep.

"Will Morgan Trust be changing any procedures to prevent a recurrence of this?"

"Short of keeping the bank door permanently locked I'm not sure there *is* anything else that can be done." Sal was growing tired of him. They asked several more questions and then requested a picture of him with Laura. "No, I'd prefer it if my wife wasn't photographed."

"Sure thing, Mr. Marchetti, please stand over there," the photographer said motioning toward the kitchen wall. The flashbulbs went off and Sal showed them to the door before they could sit back down.

"I'm not sure this interview was a good idea," he whispered to Laura afterward.

That evening, after the bakery closed, Sal couldn't resist going down to the cellar and checking on the stash. Upon entering their storage bin, he noticed a pack of Marlboros sitting near the baby carriage. No doubt Tuddy's. He wondered if it was about time he gave his son permission to smoke. Maybe next year, he decided. He reached under the sheet and pulled out one of the canvas bags and broke the seal for the first time. He noticed the control numbers on the seal and wondered if he should discard it or leave it attached. He reasoned that it wouldn't be found if it stayed on the bag, so he left it alone. He reached in and pulled out a pack of twenties. As expected, they weren't new and therefore not traceable. He played with the money for a while then placed it all back in the canvas bag and again covered it with the sheet. As he locked the bin door, he made a mental note to replace the lock so Tuddy couldn't get in there.

Back upstairs, he opened the newspaper and turned to the real estate section. Four bedroom, Tudor-style home in Forest Hills, his dream neighborhood, $29,900. He poured over the entire classified section, cars included, wondering how long he must wait before he could actually begin buying these things. Months? Years? It all depended on the circumstances the next few weeks, he reasoned.

Laura was watching the news in the living room when still another follow-up story came on. Hearing it, Sal walked in and saw his friend Chubby's picture on the screen. The commentator was discussing his accomplishment on the police force and spoke of his German heritage. The camera also panned the exterior of the bank. "Police are currently looking for a Spanish-speaking male said to be named Whitey." Sal winced, hoping the name the police had went nowhere.

"Chubby looked good in that photo," Sal offered. "I wonder if they got it from Marie."

Laura chose to ignore the reference to Marie.

In church on Sunday, many of the parishioners approached Laura and Sal and offered their condolences. During the oration part of the Mass the priest spoke of the event and asked that the families involved find "strength in Christ" during these trying times. Monsignor Tucci tracked down the two of them after the Mass. He asked them to join him in the rectory for a cup of coffee. They spent an hour with him. The three discussed the robbery briefly, prayed together a while, and just mostly spoke of day-to-day family events. Laura was very moved by the monsignor's attention as was her husband. Sal was curious why he felt no guilt or even shame for his crime while in the company of this man.

* * *

"Hey Sangenito, why aren't you in church?" Falco asked the desk sergeant as he entered the station house.

"I knew there was something I forgot to do this year, Richie."

Falco headed up the stairs and went through the old door marked robbery/homicide. "Hey Brian, what's up? You know I hate being here on Sunday. My kids forgot what I look like."

O'Reardon had been there all morning. "Your junkie friend called."

"Who, Joey Prez?"

"Yup, wants to meet us at noon. Grab a couple of bags from 217," O'Reardon said.

Room 217 was the loosely monitored evidence room. When necessary, they'd removed small glassine envelopes from the shelves. It came in very handy for investigators at times like this. It worked wonders *improving* their informant's memories. They knew that addicts would turn in their mothers for free dope. They headed back to Knickerbocker Park in Bushwick.

The block long park looked a lot more community-oriented than it had when they were here Friday night. The freezing weather didn't keep the old timers from their Sunday bocce ball game. The locals, mostly Italian-American working-class people, were strolling through carrying home their pastries and rolls. They *loathed* sharing the park with the haggard addicts. The detectives drove to the rear entrance of the park and Joey Prez emerged from a nearby hallway and hopped into the back of their car. Falco drove off. O'Reardon wasted no time.

"What have you got?" He saw that Joey was sick.

Joey was also to the point. "I found out who this Whitey guy is."

O'Reardon leaned he head back. "I'm listening."

"He's not from this neighborhood. He's from Greenpoint. Little guy. Lives on Humboldt Street, I don't know what number, but he drives a green Dodge, a '53 I think."

"That it?" O'Reardon said, purposely sounding disappointed.

"Wha? That's not gonna help you?"

They continued driving. Joey Prez was very uneasy riding around his neighborhood with these two. He couldn't have slumped farther in the seat without sliding off.

"Tell me, Joe," Falco said through the rear-view mirror, "how did you find this out?"

"Let's just say we have a mutual friend on Bushwick Avenue."

"Is that right? Here ya go, these'll save you a trip to your *mutual friend* today," O'Reardon sniped, as he tossed two glassine envelopes back onto the junkie's lap.

"Don't fucking OD on it, it's stronger than the garbage you're used to," Falco warned.

They came around the park again and dropped him off in front of the same building, watching him jog up the stoop and into the hallway, to reap his bounty.

"Whatdya think?" Falco asked.

"That way," was all O'Reardon said, pointing west toward Greenpoint.

They got to Humboldt Street, which was more than a few blocks long, and made a left onto it.

"Holy shit, right there, Rich," O'Reardon said. A dark green DeSoto was parked on the first block they went down.

"Don't slow down, keep going," O'Reardon muttered as he looked up at the windows, wondering which one of these tenements he was holed up in. They drove off knowing that the sight of their car on his street would have Whitey gone in a heartbeat.

Falco looked at his partner. "Looks like we'll be spending time back in the shitty smokeswagon again."

He was referring to the VW van with Triple R Tobacco Distributing painted on the sides. It had been confiscated from a guy in Williamsburg, who was distributing more than cigars from it. It was the 104th Precinct's unofficial/official surveillance vehicle. The fact that it's registration and insurance expired months ago bothered no one. The two detectives were feeling stoked as they headed back to the station house. They knew if they bagged one guy, chances were, they'd get all three.

* * *

When the Marchetti family returned home from church, Sal got busy trying to convince Laura to accompany him to Chubby's wake that afternoon. "Most of the people were there yesterday, I'm sure things have quieted down."

"Sal, I don't want to go. I'm sorry for Chubby but you know how I feel about *her*."

"Laura, do it for me, it won't look right if you're not there. We'll be in and out before you know it."

She exhaled and rolled her eyes.

They left Paulie with his sister, Angela, who had nothing better to do on this frigid Sunday afternoon. They headed down a deserted Grand Street. Sal liked driving on Sunday; all the stores were closed and the streets were quiet. It was a little after three when they arrived at Weitz Funeral Parlor. The parking lot was jammed. Laura gave him an annoyed look: *All of Brooklyn and Queens are in there!*

When they entered the lobby, the first people they ran into were Sal's boss, the well-tanned Manny, and his new wife. Manny threw his arms around the two of them. "Sal, Laura! How are you two doing? This is all a nightmare. Sal, you already know Claudia. Claudia, this is Laura Marchetti, Sal's wife."

Laura smiled and lifted Claudia's hand. "The ring is beautiful, congratulations."

Sal noticed how enormous the diamond was, especially compared to Laura's. "Congratulations you two," he managed.

There were a bunch of uniformed cops in the lobby milling around.

"Chubby must've been a popular policeman," Laura said. She was glad that they had company with them when they walked into the main room. She followed behind the other three as they entered. Laura heard buzzing and noticed some heads turning. She knew they were looking at her husband, knowing he'd been there when it happened. She couldn't help but feel there were a few surprised to see *her* there. The four of them walked up to Marie. Manny spoke first and he held her affectionately, exaggerating remorse. *What a phony*, Laura thought. Sal then approached and hugged Marie.

When it came time for Laura, she just held out her hand and managed, "I'm very sorry about your husband." Marie was equally formal and thanked her. The two couples noticed the unmistakable smell of alcohol on Marie's breath. They made their rounds and greeted some of Morgan Trust's main office people. Sal felt uneasy when he noticed Mr. Bilkey taking Manny aside and speaking with him.

Manny was wearing a sharkskin suit that fit him perfectly. He was a flashy person who somehow managed to always live above his means, right down to his new Mustang. Sal looked like a pair of brown shoes standing next to patent leather when he was with his younger boss. When he looked over at his wife talking to the stunning Claudia, he noticed there was even a larger disparity between those two.

The short time they stayed, Laura couldn't help looking over at Marie. She glanced down at her still-shapely legs. She wondered how long this flamboyant, attractive, forty-three-year-old would remain dressed in black. No more than a week she figured. Sal and Laura went out and sat in the lobby. Sal noticed his wife discreetly eyeing the other women, many of whom seemed well-to-do with their shimmering jewelry and fine clothing. He wished he could tell Laura that the Marchettis now had more cold cash than just about all of them. He wished he could tell all of *them*. With his money woes now history, his new wish was for better health. The shortness of breath and occasional chest pains really had him worried. His father had had a fatal heart attack at fifty-two. Sal even avoided making love with his wife for fear of having one himself.

"I think I'm going to go see Dr. Rossoff this week," he said matter-of-factly to a surprised Laura.

She leaned her head back in the chair. *"Finally."*

CHAPTER 7

Whitey was home minding his baby son, Victor, while Sandy was out getting groceries. Sandy never worried too much about leaving the baby with him despite his heroin habit. As reckless as he was, he knew he had to remain coherent, at least until she got home. Junior was with him as they were looking through the apartments-for-rent section in the *Daily News*. The place on Powers Street that Sandy had been so big on was already rented when they'd gone there yesterday. They had a few prospects circled and were planning on checking them out when Sandy got back.

The baby woke up in the bedroom and started crying. Whitey went in and picked him up. He adored his son more than anything and made sure he always had what he needed even when there was little money for anything else.

Junior winced. "Whoa, Pop, I think your boy left a little something for you in his diaper."

"Damn, what's she feeding you?" Whitey moaned as he started removing his diaper on the table. "Poppy, how you gonna get through college smelling like this?"

Little Victor was kicking his arms and legs while smiling up at him.

Sandy arrived home with arms full of groceries.

"Hope you bought diapers, there's only one left," was Whitey's greeting.

He and Junior were heading into the living room to get high before she had her coat off.

"Baby, me and Junior are gonna go look at two places now. One on Graham Avenue and one over in Williamsburg down by the Navy Yard."

"About time you're leaving the house, it's been what, five days?"

It was 11:15 Tuesday morning. Whitey shielded his eyes from the bright January sun when he entered the street. There was little wind, but the twenty-degree weather caught his attention. They headed across the street to his car.

"I hope this bitch starts!" Whitey said.

"Whatya talking about, didn't Sandy just get out of it?"

"If Sandy was driving it why the fuck would I be worried about it starting. She *walked* to the store. The woman walks everywhere."

Whitey cranked the DeSoto a second time and they drove off. They were in good spirits; the radio was blaring, and Junior was dancing in his seat to the beat of Tito Puente. Whitey noticed the van behind him had made the same three turns he did. He lowered the radio and said to Junior, "Don't turn around, I think that van is following us."

"Make a left here, Whitey." They headed down a long side street. Whitey had his eyes glued on the rear-view mirror. Sure enough, he saw the van turn with him. That was all he needed; he was just about to floor it when he saw two radio cars pull up and block the intersection ahead of them. Another radio car sped up behind the van. Lights were flashing everywhere. Whitey hit the brakes.

"LET'S GET THE FUCK OUT OF HERE." They flew open the doors and ran in separate directions. Whitey knew the best escape in the city was through backyards, so he ran into the nearest hallway while the cops poured out of their cars after them. The door that led out back was locked, so he ran up the hallway stairs to get to the roof. He heard the footsteps hurrying below him as he reached the third floor. Tenants' doors were opened then quickly shut as Whitey ran up each flight two steps at a time. He scampered up the ladder and out on the roof and started running over the adjoining rooftops.

The pursuing cops were screaming at him from thirty yards back. He could still hear the sirens of the responding police cars. Windows were opening everywhere. He saw over the roof's edge that Junior was on the ground spreadeagled. A herd of bluecoats were hovering over him. He heard a warning shot fired by a young plainclothesman that was coming up behind him. Whitey hopped onto a fire escape but right above his head was a snub-nosed .38 pointing down.

"I'll fucking waste you right here, Poncho."

"Okay, okay" He threw his hands up. **"I didn't do nothin', man!"**

"Slowly climb up here."

At least a half-dozen cops waited for him up on the roof. Another four were down in the street had he chosen that route. Whitey started up the ladder and as he reached the top, he was grabbed by two bluecoats by his hair and collar and thrown to the frozen rooftop. He felt nightsticks jabbing him and one wildly clubbing him in the knees. He was screaming in agony while trying to fend off the blows. People looking out of their upper-foor windows across the street had a clear view of the commotion on the shorter roof. They began to yell at the cops. "STOP HITTING HIM!"

More attention was drawn to the action by the residents. Soon they were screaming and cursing in both English and Spanish. Finally, the older sergeant, sensing the dangerous climate, stepped in and ended the beating. They half carried, half dragged, their bleeding prisoner down the hallway stairs past the wide-eyed tenants and into the street. When they got to the street all he saw were police cars gridlocked from one end of the block to the other.

Whitey started to struggle, screaming in Spanish, **"Help me, help me!"** He figured his last hope was to cause an all-out riot and somehow get loose. The cops were trying to get him in the back seat of the radio car, but Whitey's legs were flailing.

"They're going to kill me!"

"Leave him alone!" A woman was screaming in broken English as she ran up to the car. The uniformed police captain who arrived on the scene saw his younger officers yelling up at the windows in response to the curses hurled at them from the Puerto Rican inhabitants.

The captain, sensing a disaster, started shouting and waving his arms at his men. **"Get in the cars and get out of here!"**

They started to do so, but they couldn't leave until the cars on both ends of the block moved first. Just as the captain feared, the objects started to rain down. He noticed groups gathering on the rooftops and now larger items came crashing down. Whitey was picked up by four cops and thrown head-first into the backseat. One cop was pushing the frantic woman away. She lost her balance and fell to the ground. A large metal bar crashed through the windshield of one of the cars, injuring the driver. The captain's dilemma became a nightmare when two young cops, seeing where the bar came from, bolted out of their car and into the building. Others followed with their guns drawn. Things were now out of control. More sirens were heard. It was the tactical units.

The bloodied cop was removed from his car and stretched out.

"Get an ambulance!" someone called out.

Four of the cops instead carried him to the police car at the end of the street and rushed him to Wyckoff hospital. The residents from surrounding blocks were beginning to merge onto the scene. The tactical police were now running down the block. Whitey watched from his seat, straining to look at the rooftops. From the screaming coming from up there he knew there was another beating taking place. There was pushing and scuffling in more than one place on the street level. More arrests were being made.

The arriving captain now had a bullhorn. **"Go back inside or you'll be arrested!"** The locals either ignored or didn't understand him. He was also calling out for his cops to come down off the roofs. Suddenly there was a thud in an alleyway toward the end of the block. People down at that end were screaming. The captain ran toward it and saw the crumpled figure of a youngster lying motionless in a rapidly widening pool of blood. The kid, no more than fifteen years old, had fallen between the buildings while trying to run away from a rooftop beating. Now the commander *had* to get his men out of there. He ran back to the middle of the block and started screaming at the officers to get into their cars and leave. They started dispersing amid the projectiles from the now angrier and bolder residents. The captain's car was the last one out of there. He heard stuff hitting his cars and the sidewalk. He radioed the dispatcher a warning not to send an ambulance crew in there until things quieted down. One dead was enough. He didn't want two more.

* * *

From behind his desk at the bank Sal heard the flow of sirens heading west. "I wonder if they hit another bank," he called into Manny's office. Manny never looked up. He was preoccupied with the mountain of work that was waiting for him. Being a hands-on person, he delegated very little to Marchetti and the others. Sal had no problem with that.

The new bank guard, who was sent over from another branch, was looking at the torrent of radio cars going past his window.

"I thought you said this was a quiet neighborhood," he said to Sal without diverting his stare from the street.

Rose, who was listening to her portable radio in the lunchroom, emerged, shaking her head. *"They're rioting in Greenpoint."*

Manny called Sal into his office a half hour later. After thumbing through the papers in front of him he looked up, "Sal, we haven't had a chance to really talk yet. How have you been feeling?"

"I've felt better."

"What's your doctor saying?"

"Saw him just yesterday, says I need open heart surgery."

Manny got up out of his chair and walked over to Sal. "Surgery?"

"Yeah, my plumbing is pretty clogged," Sal said, tapping his chest.

Manny knew Sal wasn't well, but he didn't expect this. Standing alongside him, he placed his hand on Sal's shoulder, "Listen, if you're going to need any time off you just say so."

"Well actually, Manny, I've been speaking with Laura and we're thinking that it's about time I start taking it easy, ya know, start spending more time with the kids and all."

Manny looked surprised, sensing where Sal was going. Losing, what he considered, his *dead weight* assistant manager was a welcomed scenario. "I know what you mean, my father went through that. He waited too long though. Listen, if you want to put in for an early out, I'll start the paperwork for you when I'm done with all this shit."

"I think it's time, that holdup kinda did me in. I would appreciate your doing that."

They spoke for a while longer then Sal settled in behind his desk feeling relieved. He looked around and a sad smile came to him. *Thirty-two years looking at these walls. A half-dozen different managers. Countless tellers. All the changes, except me . . . until now, that is.*

He was finally leaving Morgan Trust. His next task now was to sit down with his son Michael and make some painful but necessary arrangements. He was dreading this meeting, not knowing what his son's reaction would be when told his father had embezzled a quarter-million dollars from the neighborhood bank. He'd pored over every possible scenario, and this was the unavoidable way to pull this off. Tomorrow night he'd take a drive out there and get it over with.

Sal's ringing phone snapped him out of this dilemma and into the next one.

"Mr. Marchetti, Detective Falco, just wanted to let you know we believe we have at least one of the guys in custody, probably two."

Sal dropped his head into his hand. This was a worst-case scenario, he thought.

"Hello, you there, sir?" came the voice.

"Yes, yes. I'm overwhelmed. That's great. Great work, Detective."

"Well, that remains to be seen. Meantime, I know their faces were covered but if you and the girls could stop down here after closing and hear their voices it might be helpful."

Sal was trying to sound detached. "*I'm* certainly willing. We'll speak with the tellers and call you back."

"That would be great, but we need to hear from you soon."

"Did you recover the money?"

"Not yet, we just got the search warrant a little while ago. We're headed over to his apartment now."

Sal was stunned. He went in and told Manny, who went over to talk to the women. Manny begged out of accompanying them which Sal thought odd. Sal walked into the bathroom and washed his face. Looking at himself in the mirror, he reasoned, *they'll never believe these drug addicts if they claim they only got fifty thousand. Why would they admit to anything?* He realized. *They're facing the death penalty.*

* * *

"Police! Open the door!"

Sandy started circling the apartment in a panic.

"Open this fuckin' door!" The hammering got louder.

She realized there was nothing she could do but comply. Guns drawn, three detectives hustled in, led by O'Reardon. Thrusting the search warrant on her table he shouted, "Does Wilfredo Aparicio live here?"

Sandy tried her best. "He used to; he moved out."

"You're right about the *used to* part, he's living with us now," O'Reardon barked.

Sandy put her hands on the kitchen table to steady herself. She couldn't hold the tears back. "*He was arrested?*"

Her question was ignored as they panned out and started their search. The young detective that accompanied them made the first find in a living room drawer. "Heroin," he said after touching his tongue with the tip of his finger. "With syringe. Looks to be about two grams, Lieutenant."

Sandy watched as her clothing was flying in different directions. They woke up the baby. Sandy, still crying, straightened up and went over and picked him up. Falco looked up.

"Is that Aparicio's kid?"

"Yes, it is." She smiled, sadly.

After about twenty minutes of searching, O'Reardon popped off the back of the hi-fi speaker and smiled. "What have we here?"

He walked into the kitchen with a stuffed paper bag. Onto the table he dumped a pile of twenties. "Your baby's college fund, is it?"

Sandy instinctively denied knowing the money was there. Falco thumbed quickly through it. "There's only about fifteen thousand here." They had found Whitey's cut of the loot, although it was well short of what they expected.

"Keep looking, tear out the damn walls if you have to." O'Reardon was pissed.

Falco looked at the trembling woman trying to soothe her baby and felt bad. He hated this part of his job. "Miss, is there someone you can call to come over and look after the kid? You're gonna have to come with us."

Sandy looked stunned. "Why? Are you arresting *me*?"

O'Reardon snapped at her, "Lady, you have a pile of heroin and stolen cash in your house, you *comprende* what that means?"

"But it's not mine. I don't use dope," she cried, holding out her free arm, veins up.

"Please call someone or we'll have to bring over an agency," Falco said, pointing to the phone.

They continued tearing up the apartment until the lieutenant was satisfied they'd found everything they were going to find. A cousin of Sandy's rushed over from up the block and took baby Victor with her while they led the sobbing woman outside and into their car.

Upon arrival at the 104th Robbery/Homicide Office, Falco sat her down and started the good-cop routine.

"Your friends call you Sandy?"

"Yes."

"Sandy, I really don't think your chances of seeing your son anytime soon are too good."

"I did *nothing* wrong." She was a streetwise woman and aware of police tactics in these situations.

"Can you tell me where you were at 9 am last Friday?"

"Yeah, where I am every morning at that time, home feeding my son and changing shitty diapers."

Falco leaned in closer. "Guess what? We have an eyewitness who saw a young woman with long hair just like yours driving the car the holdup men got into carrying three hundred thousand dollars."

"That may be, but it wasn't me. Shit, I wish it was. Three hundred thousand would solve *all* my problems." She felt herself feeling less frightened, the more she spoke. "Can I have a cigarette?"

Falco reached into his pocket and handed her a Pall Mall.

"This is a very simple offer I'm making," he said, lighting her cigarette. "You tell me where the rest of the money is, and you'll be back with your son by dinnertime."

"Officer, do you think for one minute if I had that much money I'd be anywhere near here?"

Falco tried a different angle. "We have a confession from Junior Saez."

She wasn't buying it. "I don't know no Junior Saez."

O'Reardon, who was listening from behind the one-way mirror, saw this was going nowhere. He'd have his turn later. After watching another twenty minutes of questioning he went over to the lone female cop in the precinct. Motioning to the interrogation room, he said, "Carmela, please take her downstairs for processing."

Seated out in the hallway watching the two women go by were Sal, Dana, and Rose. The third teller, Paula, had to pick her daughter up at school.

The trio were led into the same area facing the interrogation room. They watched and listened as first Whitey, then Junior, were questioned. The women winced at the sight of their swollen faces.

Afterward, O'Reardon entered. "Anything?"

Sal shook his head, as did Dana. Rose spoke up.

"The short one with the black shirt, that's the one called Whitey."

Sal spoke out of place. "Rose, you're just saying that because of his height."

O'Reardon gave Sal an annoyed look before turning back to Rose. "Was it his voice, features, mannerisms, why are you saying he was the one? That one *is* Whitey, by the way."

"I'm pretty sure that was him, but I can't swear to it because his face was covered." She turned toward the detective. "*What happened to their faces*, Lieutenant?"

"They resisted arrest." He answered with a tone suggesting she had no business asking that question. He was growing impatient. They were brought to Junior's cell and all they saw was a rolled up withdrawing addict.

"Saez!" He tried to get him to speak. Nothing. He knew this was a waste of time. "Thank you all for coming. We'll be in touch."

O'Reardon went back into the interrogation room where the other withdrawing drug addict was sitting.

"Whitey, I hate to break this to you, amigo, but you've been fingered just now. She said you weren't the one that shot that guard, but unless you start talking to me, you're going to face murder charges along with your friend in there." O'Reardon pointed into the cell area, where Junior was.

"I don't know what you're talking about, there are plenty of *Whiteys* out there. Like I said to the other guy I'm a small-time user. I sell pot to support my habit. That's where the money you found came from."

O'Reardon kept at it. "Your wife, or whatever, is also being held." Whitey picked his head up and looked at the detective. "Your kid is going to wind up in foster care."

"What the fuck did *she* do?"

He leaned in and said in a low voice, "If you yell at me again, you'll be spitting out more teeth. What was she arrested for; you ask? Possession of 2.5 grams of heroin; that's possession with intent."

"The woman never used dope in her life, that's my shit and you know it."

"I do?" O'Reardon turned and walked out, shrugging his shoulders.

He walked over to Falco's desk. "We'll need more if we're going to convict them of anything serious."

"Yeah, I know, about a quarter-million more," Falco answered.

CHAPTER 8

Sal and Laura were very familiar with Dr. Stefanski's office. They were seated in one of the treatment rooms waiting for him to come in. Laura was straightening her husband's hair when the doctor walked in. The youthful looking cardiac specialist was looking over Sal's latest tests as he sat down.

"Mr. Marchetti, I'm not liking what I'm seeing here."

Sal was calm as Laura fought to compose herself and squeezed Sal's arm. After a pause Sal said, "Well then, Doc, whaddya think, I shouldn't be buying any unripe bananas?"

Laura laughed nervously, then teared up.

They bantered for a while longer before Stefanski finally put it out there. "You're a very sick man, Mr. Marchetti. Your arteries are clogged, and your heartbeat is minimal."

"What would you suggest, doctor?" Laura asked.

"Honestly? That you folks get your affairs in order."

After further explaining the lack of solutions he tore a prescription out of the pad and handed it to Laura with a sad expression.

Sal helped Laura up and they headed out. "What do you say we go over to the Ship's Inn for dinner," Sal suggested.

Laura thought about how ironic life is. Getting him to take her out to dinner had always been a monumental task; now, when the furthest thing from her mind was food, the man wanted to dine out. "Great idea, Salvatore."

After dinner, Sal dropped his wife off in front of the house. He continued to drive east, as planned, to see his eldest son. He told Laura the purpose of the visit was to advise his oldest son about his condition. He arrived in East Meadow around seven.

Mike greeted him at the door.

"Hi Dad, hit traffic?"

"Of course."

"Come in, give me your coat, have you eaten?"

"Yes, your mother and I just had dinner at the Ship's Inn."

"Nice." Mike handed him a beer and they settled onto the living room sofa. "So, how'd it go today?"

"Stefanski had the usual good news," Sal answered sarcastically.

"How do you mean?"

"Well son, according to the doctor, my heart has no business beating.

Michael's shoulders slumped as he got up to shut off the TV.

Sal looked around. "Is Patricia home?"

"She's at the library, should be home soon," Mike answered, sensing that something else was up.

"Michael, I need to talk to you."

"Sure, Dad." The son shuffled off the armchair and sat on the rug with his back against the sofa his father was sitting on.

"My doctor told me two hours ago to get my affairs in order."

After a moment of silence, Mike started, "That doesn't necessarily . . ."

"Just listen, when I'm gone, all your mother and your brothers and sister will have to live on is eighteen hundred dollars in our savings account, a ten-thousand-dollar life insurance policy, and a small pension. That's not going to go very far, and it's certainly not getting anyone through college."

"Well, Mom could always work, and I could—"

"Let me finish. Listen carefully; what I did, I did only for the survival of my family. I knew I wasn't going to be around, and it was *my* choice, my *only* choice, Mike."

His son didn't even blink as his fidgeting father continued. "I misreported the amount taken in the holdup."

Mike sat back and swallowed as his father went into the kitchen for another beer. "How much money did you, uhh, misreport?"

"Roughly two hundred and fifty thousand dollars."

Mike gasped. "WHAT!"

"You are the *only* one who knows about this, son."

"Dad, this is *crazy*," Mike said as he leaned his head back and looked at the ceiling.

"Believe me, the last thing I wanted was to get you involved in this, but as long as you follow my instructions, I can promise there will be no risk to you or any family member."

Mike couldn't resist asking, *"How did you do it?"*

Sal held his palms up. "It wasn't planned, it just fell into my lap. We had a large delivery the night before that we were unable to secure in the safe."

"Unable to secure?"

"Yeah, I never told you guys this, but I wasn't entrusted with very much at the bank. I only had access to the safe on rare occasions, usually when the manager was unavailable. I'm surprised he didn't fly up on his vacation to handle the delivery. Anyway, to make a long story short, Chubby and I wound up locking the money in an office cabinet until we could tinker with the safe's combination and get it open."

While his father was telling him the rest, Mike was becoming not entirely uncomfortable with the notion of this much money in the family.

"Where is it now?"

"In our cellar."

"How in the *world* are you going to explain it to Mom? She'll never allow it, Pop, you know that."

"Sure, I do. That's where you come in, Mr. Wall Street." Sal felt his top pocket. "Want a cigarette?"

He shook his head. "What is it you want me to do?"

"Nothing. Say nothing, do nothing. After I'm buried and Hartford pays your mother the ten grand, I want you to convince her to let you invest it for her, which shouldn't be difficult since she's been after me to invest money since day one."

"Go on."

"After six months, or longer, keep an eye out for what took off on the market and simply tell her that's where her money is. Then, and only then, you start paying her dividends from the bank money." Mike was squirming in his seat. "Son, I really need your help to get them off Flushing Ave. Nothing good ever comes out of that neighborhood. Buy a house for them, ideally out here near you. I know there's enough money there to buy ten houses, but it must be made to look legitimate, to both her and everyone else. This can only be done by moving slowly."

Mike again looked skyward and ran his hands through his hair and paused for a long while.

Sal watched his son while he lit the cigarette. "Mikey, I realize there is risk involved in this and I will understand if you don't want to get—"

"No, no that's not what I'm thinking, I just have a better idea."

Just then his wife Pat came in.

"Hi, Dad! What a nice surprise."

Sal got up, a little unsteady from the beers, and kissed her on the cheek. He was feeling better. It felt great finally speaking to another person about this. He was also encouraged by his son's reaction.

"Good to see you again, Patricia."

"What brings you out here on a weeknight?"

"Pat, Dad received some bad news from the heart guy and wanted to tell us in person."

"Oh damn."

"Yup, Patti, your old father-in-law should have taken better care of himself and yeah, quit these." He held up his Chesterfield. Sal surprisingly was matter of fact about the whole thing. They spent a half hour talking about heart disease and even death.

Finally, Sal slapped his thighs and sprung to his feet. "Well, kids, I gotta get going."

"I'll walk you out," Mike said.

Outside Mike started to speak about his idea when his father cut him short. "Patti's coming behind you. Listen, forget whatever you're thinking and please just focus on what I laid out."

"Oh, Dad," his daughter-in-law moaned and hugged him and began sniffling.

"Now, now, don't you worry about me, you just look after my boy here and keep him out of trouble."

Michael smiled nervously.

On the way home Sal was feeling uncertain again. He began wondering, What the hell am I doing? Am I going to get my son locked up?

* * *

The phone rang just before eleven at O'Reardon's apartment.

"Hello Lieutenant, this is Sergeant Sangenito. I know it's late, sir, but I thought you'd like to know we found a handgun and cash in Junior Saez's apartment."

"How much?"

"Eleven thousand, four hundred."

"That's all? What caliber was the gun?"

"Twenty-two short."

"That's probably the gun we want. Try to get a hold of someone from ballistics tonight; failing that, see that they run it first thing in the morning."

"Sure thing, Lieutenant, but it doesn't appear to have been fired recently."

"Hmm, all right, thank you."

That's not what O'Reardon wanted to hear. *Where the fuck is all the money?* he wondered.

* * *

Junior was about an hour away from making bail when the new charges were brought up. Sandy's bail was fifteen hundred dollars, which was gathered up by her family and paid. Junior's bail went from five thousand to fifty thousand after the gun and cash charges. His was now the same as Whitey's. The District Attorney argued for bails of a hundred thousand each, given the amount of money they figured these two had stashed.

Junior Saez was shipped off to the Brooklyn House of Detention where Whitey had been since yesterday. Luckily, they both wound up on the same floor, the eighth. They'd both been here before, except not on the eighth floor with the guys facing *hard* time. Usually, the fifth or sixth floor was the level they were held in, where they housed the small-time offenders. During the lockout period Whitey was surprised when he spotted Junior approaching him in the corridor.

"What the fuck! I thought you made bail, June."

"Whitey, if my fucking brother had come an hour sooner, I would be out on the street. They found my gun and money too."

"What! I thought you said you got rid of the piece."

"I was going to, bro, but I didn't get the chance."

"They found the whole fourteen?" Whitey asked.

"I guess so. Those fucking thieves reported only eleven thousand though."

Whitey couldn't help laughing through the sniffles and coughs. "No shit! Damn Junior, everyone is making money off this job but us. Fuck, we needed that money for a lawyer. I already told that dumbass Legal Aid I didn't think we'd need him anymore."

"Well, looks like we might need him."

Whitey got serious. "What did you say to them?"

"I didn't say nothing. After they found my stash and brought me back down, I told them that I have three brothers who also live there, and they have friends coming in and out. That shit could have belonged to anybody, man."

Junior told that story so well he almost had Whitey believing it.

"Then they started in again on that three hundred-thousand-dollar bullshit."

Whitey shook his head. "I swear, Junior, when they hit me with that shit I was going to confess to EVERYTHING, just so I could tell the dumb asses that we only got fifty thousand and the bank screwed the insurance company out of the rest."

"Yeah, like they're gonna believe *you*?"

"How you feeling? Doc hook you up?" Whitey asked.

"Yeah, this morning. He gave me some Dolophine. Still feel like shit though."

"Yeah, me too, he's supposed to be back here again tonight for sick call."

Junior looked at his noisy surroundings and shook his head. At this place were guys who couldn't make bail and were awaiting trial or sentencing. There were card games going on as well as dominoes. Most of them were just sitting on the corridor floors rolling cigarettes and shouting over one another. Junior heard four black guys at the very end harmonizing Drifters' songs. "They sound pretty tight."

Whitey ignored him, then said, "Wonder what Hector is doing right now."

"Whatdya you think? Shitting in his pants."

Whitey then shook his head. "Nah, he knows we won't give him up."

"*I* might though, if he doesn't get us a lawyer," Junior half-joked.

The guard then yelled down from the catwalk. **"Okay, sick call! Junkies form a separate line on the window side of the corridor!"**

"Bout time."

CHAPTER 9

Laura tried to get her husband to eat some of his breakfast before going to work. They had been up a bit later than usual last night going over their finances. She was certain things were going to be even tougher in the future. Sal always handled the bill paying and major purchases. Laura wondered, *could she be expected now to hold it all together with even less money coming in?* Her husband assured her that Michael would handle the family finances, and everything would be fine. It still didn't comfort her. If only she could manage a good night's sleep.

Angela, while leaving for school, paused at the door then came and sat alongside her father. He looked at her and smiled. "How's my little princess?" was all he could manage. The fourteen-year-old kissed him on the cheek and hurried out before she started crying.

That didn't stop Laura though. She moved into Angela's vacated seat and held his arm.

Later that morning, upon Sal's arrival at the bank, Manny called him into his office.

"Sal, the head office called. To save you a trip into Manhattan they're sending someone from personnel here this afternoon to get you processed."

"That's great, thanks."

Manny also told him he could use his remaining sick days, so it won't be necessary to drag himself in the last two weeks if he didn't want to. "What are your plans now, Sal? You're gonna have a lot of free time."

"I just want to spend my remaining time with Laura and the kids."

"Why don't you take Laura on vacation or something?"

"Don't think so, Manny, it's going to be pretty tough as it is, without spending hundreds on a trip."

Sal was using every opportunity to cry poverty.

"Are you planning on remaining in Queens?"

Sensing an odd demeanor with Manny, he replied, "Yup, including burial at St. Charles. So, I guess you could say even my remains are remaining."

They both grinned, although Manny had to force his. Sal was learning that people around him weren't very comfortable with the subject of his demise. The tellers, sensing that this was probably Sal's last real day there, sent Dana out to buy a cake and they put together an impromptu retirement party. By afternoon they were done with all the tears and speeches. His retirement would be effective in two weeks according to the personnel department woman, who officially severed his thirty-year banking career with her thirty-minute visit.

All went according to plan that day, that is, until Chubby Werner's wife Marie called.

* * *

"Brian, ballistics came back," Falco said.

"Let me guess, no match?" O'Reardon replied.

"That's correct." The two detectives reasoned the shooter and the person holding the bulk of the money were still out on the streets.

"Let's go ahead and get Saez charged with the shooting anyway," O'Reardon said finally.

Falco expected that. "You think that will shake him enough to talk?"

The lieutenant shrugged. "It would *me*." O'Reardon was once again combing through the list of known felons in the area. "There is something about this case that really baffles me, Brian. How is it that these two guys can't make bail with all that money out there?"

O'Reardon shook his head. "You would think this third guy would do his best to get them out of there, if nothing else to save his own ass."

"Exactly. Why piss off someone who can screw you back ten times over."

About then, their boss, Captain Rogers, came over. "Guys, where do we stand on this Morgan mess?"

"This is a real *enigma*, Captain," Falco answered. "There's a lot here that just doesn't add up."

"Such as?"

"Well, we know we got two of the guys but only ten percent of the money and one weapon."

The captain was staring out their window. "Damn, you can see all the way down Myrtle Avenue from here. Yeah, I just heard your one handgun isn't the one we want."

The other cops in the area were looking over, surprised the captain had ventured out from behind his blinds and walked among the mortals.

He turned from the window and looked at his lead detective. "I just got off the phone with Mayor Wagner's office. His deputy says the old man wants results. First of all, this guy Werner is a retired cop. Secondly, his widow, who apparently was a good *friend* of the mayor during his councilman days, has been calling his office non-stop for information."

Falco smirked. "I met her. Good looking woman, Miss New York State something or other, back in the day . . ."

The captain interrupted him. "Let's get this fucking case nailed, alright?" He then started back to his office before turning back. "If this becomes too much of an *enigma* for you two, let me know, we can bring guys in from Brooklyn North to take it over."

He again turned and walked out.

O'Reardon grabbed his crotch. They all smirked.

* * *

"Hello, Salvatore, how are you?" said Marie Werner.

"I'm fine Marie, all things considered. You missed my little retire-ment party today."

"Oh, so you *are* leaving, can't say that I blame you. No need to work now, is there?" He noticed her speech was slurred.

"Well, no need since it would be best to spend my remaining time with Laura and the kids. Are you drinking again, Marie?"

"Drinking again? Yes, I guess you could say that. I drank this morning and this afternoon I'm drinking *again.*"

"I don't think Chubby would approve of your method of coping with all this."

"Funny, my drinking during that afternoon we spent at the St. George Hotel was never an issue, and I don't believe old Chubs would have approved much of that either."

"Christ, Marie, that was twenty years ago, why must you bring it up now? Is that why you called?" Sal was whispering now and glancing around.

"Not exactly, Sal. I called because I managed to get hold of a copy of the police report."

"Yes, and?"

"Well, pal, I think it would be a good idea if we had a little talk."

Sal was now feeling uneasy. "Marie, what the hell are you talking about?"

There was an eternal pause.

"I found it peculiar that no mention was made in the report of those gunmen entering Manny's office."

Sal sprang to his feet, then lost his breath.

"I have no idea what you're talking about. Listen, Marie, you're obviously stoned and making no sense. Call me when you've sobered up."

Stunned, he hung up before she could reply. Sal walked back into the lunchroom where two of the women were cleaning up.

"Sal, you alright? You look like you've seen a ghost."

"I'm not feeling well, Rose, I think I'm going to head home early."

Rose kissed him on the cheek. "You better not be a stranger, Marchetti."

He went through the goodbye process with the others. More tears and hugs from the women and a debilitating handshake from

Manny. In a fog, Sal Marchetti walked through the big doors of Morgan Trust for the last time.

He arrived home with no recollection of his drive. Sal then slowly walked once around the block to settle down and get his bearings before facing his wife. He felt weak and nauseous. *Maybe that walk was a bad idea.* He walked in the door, rushed past Laura, and *just* made it to the bathroom to throw up.

So much for getting my bearings, he thought, while brushing off his knees.

"Are you alright?" she asked when he finally came out.

"I think my ticker is looking to retire as well."

"Honey, you look pale. It might be best if you get off your feet. I'll call you when dinner's ready."

He passed on his favorite dinner, spaghetti and red clam sauce, and went to the couch to lie down.

Paulie was sitting nearby when he woke up. "Hey Dad, how are you feeling?"

"Better, Paul. What are you watching?"

His son started humming the *Bonanza* theme song.

"Oh, *Gunsmoke*?" Sal grinned, and Paulie groaned. "Where's your sister?"

"Inside on the phone, where else?"

"So hotshot, you gonna be ready for next season? Coach Handley expects you to be his top scorer."

"Make you a deal, Dad, I'll do just that if you're there to watch."

Laura, who hears everything from *anywhere* in the apartment, whirled her head around from the kitchen sink. There was a pause, then she heard, "You got yourself a deal, son."

* * *

"Hey man, what happened in the chow hall?" Whitey asked.

"Nothing man, that spook Jefferson kept fucking with me, so I hit him upside his head with my tray."

"Looks like he hit you back, bro."

73

"*Yeah, he did,* ain't that some shit!" Junior laughed. "The swelling finally went down from the nightsticks, now the *other* side is fucked up."

"Lucky you're not in isolation."

They walked over to a secluded spot further from the noise and sat on the cold cement floor. Junior had a serious look on his face.

"I don't think I can take much more of this place, Whitey," Junior said as he buried his face in his hands to hide his emotion. He then lifted his head and asked, "No word from Hector?"

"Nope," Whitey replied while lighting two cigarettes.

Junior took one and shook his head. "I don't trust this Legal Aid dude Silverstein; I was really hoping that skinny fuck would come through and get us a lawyer."

"Forget him, he's probably in San Juan by now. What don't you trust about Silverstein?"

Junior's whisper got louder, "You know these motherfuckers make deals with the DA. You get this one, you give me the next. I don't wanna be the *this one!*"

Whitey shrugged. "Why do you think *you're* the gift?"

"When I spoke to Silverstein this morning, he said he may want separate trials for us."

Whitey looked surprised. "*He said that?* Why?"

"Get this shit—they're talking about charging *me* with the shooting."

Whitey moved away and looked at him sideways. "**Bullshit,** no way dude! Hector is thirty pounds skinnier than you, and his high-pitched voice is unmistakable. *You* even said he reminds you of a Puerto Rican Don Knotts. Those people could never confuse you with him."

"I don't know, man, I've seen crazier shit happen in a courtroom."

Whitey shrugged and offered, "Listen Junior, first of all, I don't see no Jew lawyer allowing his client to go to jail for icing a dude from Germany named Adolph."

"Hey, ya know, fuckin' A, *and* if the judge has a beanie on his head, we definitely walk!"

Early that evening the ringing telephone woke Sal up from his second nap.

Laura answered it and looked befuddled. "*Hold on.* Sal, it's for you."

"Who is it, at this hour?" he asked as he walked toward the kitchen.

"Sounds like Marie Werner to me."

"Hello?"

Laura stood three feet away with her arms folded.

"I didn't want to call you at home, but you gave me no choice."

"What do you want, Marie?"

"I don't think you want me to say it over the phone. Meet me."

He thought it best to do so, and asked, "Where are you?"

Laura's brow turned down.

"I'm on the pay phone outside the cigar store on your corner."

Sal exaggerated an annoyed tone and said, "All right, I'll be right down." He slammed the phone down. Laura waited for the explanation. "She's outside drunk. I don't know what the hell she wants, probably feeling sorry for herself."

He grabbed his coat and headed out the door before putting it on.

Laura was bewildered. She went immediately to the bedroom window and saw her husband below briskly walking to the corner tangled in his overcoat. She strained to watch him, then finally opened the window wide and stuck her head out into the frigid air. She then saw him bending over talking while Marie sat in her parked car. After a minute or so he got into the front seat. Laura waited, expecting them to pull away, but they never moved.

"Okay, you wanted to talk, so talk."

Marie picked up the manila envelope that was between them.

"Any idea what this is, Mr. Marchetti?"

"My guess is the police report you spoke about. I still don't understand where you're going with this."

"Sal, Chubby told me."

"What are you talking about, *told you what?*"

She slowly lit a cigarette then turned her upper body and looked straight at him. "Thursday night, Chubby joked about the armored car delivery and how you were unable to open the safe. Ring a bell?"

"Sure, but we did manage—"

She interrupted, "He also told me you locked the money away in Manny's office for *temporary safekeeping*. Hmm, which *safe* word do you suppose came first, the noun or the adjective. What I'm saying is, is the stuff safe if it's not in a safe . . . for safekeeping?"

Her laughing sounded raspy. It was a booze and cigarette voice. While she was rambling, Sal was groping for an answer.

Marie continued. "Now hear me out, Mister Sal. According to your statement to the police, the thieves entered the bank upon opening Friday morning, which would leave no time for you to figure out the combination and get that money in. I see no report stating any of these guys entered Manny's office during the holdup, leaving, how should I put it . . .a shitload of cash unaccounted for."

"It's **freezing** in here, Ma, why's the window open?" Tuddy yelled.

He reminded her she was also shivering. She hurried into her closet and grabbed a sweater. "I'll close it in a second, honey," and went right back to her post.

Sal wouldn't relent. "Marie, you know the alcohol is clouding your brain. Are you suggesting *I* have that money? That I would take money from the people I've worked for most of my life? I thought you knew me better than that. Marie, I don't think you know how sick I've been. I haven't even the strength to walk two blocks let alone plan a heist." *He* now started rambling. "I'm not going to be around much longer, why would I do something like that? That goes against—"

She again interrupted. "It's obvious you have health issues by the way you're breathing. I'm sorry for you. Even *more* reason you'd do this."

"Marie, do you think the police would believe you even if it *were* true. Which it's not."

"Sal, I'm just saying the police would be very interested if I was to tell them what Chubby told me."

That's the last thing he wanted. He put his hand on Marie's shoulder and started massaging it as he spoke. "Marie, we go back a long way . . ."

"You're about twenty years late for that, Buster." She jerked her shoulder away.

He stared straight ahead. "What is it you want?"

"I want half."

It occurred to Sal that Chubby probably didn't tell her how much was in the Wells Fargo delivery.

"*Fifty thousand dollars! Are you crazy?*" He took a shot.

She bit. "This thing cost me a husband; did you forget? It's only right."

After a pause he turned to her. "If I agree, you'll disappear?"

"Gone!"

"Swear?"

"On the twins."

He closed his eyes and exhaled through his mouth in a kind of whistle. "Okay, wait here."

He got out of her car. Laura saw his outline in the dark heading toward her. She darted her head back inside and closed the window, watching him through the blinds as he entered their building. The harried woman then took her place in the kitchen and awaited his arrival and explanation. She realized she still had her sweater on and quickly removed it and tossed it into the living room.

Her husband never arrived. Instead, he went straight into the cellar, rushed over to the bin, reached on top of the crossbeam finding the key. He then grabbed an empty paper bag that had once contained comic books and quickly counted out the money. It didn't all fit in the bag, so he stuffed some into his coat pockets and headed back to the corner.

Laura, in the meantime, was at the top of the steps in the hallway wondering where he went. She heard him scamper out of the cellar and head back outside. Without hesitation she rushed down the steps and into the cellar not knowing what she was looking for. The light was still on, and she found the bin door wide open. Laura knew he was coming right back. She looked around for whatever it was he had down there and gasped at the sight of two large bank satchels sitting in the old carriage. She could see they were filled with neatly wrapped currency. The bewildered woman turned and fled back up the stairs into her apartment. She was trembling. *Am I dreaming? Could this be real?* She wondered. *Were Sal and Marie behind the bank robbery? Oh, God forgive me. No way. When he gets back, he'll explain the whole thing.*

Sal watched as Marie counted the bundles.

"I must confess, Sal, I really didn't think you actually *had* this money. You're just not capable of this." She snickered. "I expected you to tell me when and how you managed get it in there and I would just go away!"

"As long as you *just* go away now, Marie. You *do* understand now this is all my family will have after I'm gone."

"*All they would have?* I'd say they'll be damn well off with fifty thousand cold cash. Anyway, it was nice doing business with you, partner."

"Remember, Marie, I have your word. I'm denying my family half their amount in return for your secrecy."

She smiled and winked, "Just another of our secrets, sweetheart."

Sal again exited the car. He hurried up the block breathing very heavily. Before going up to his apartment he went into the cellar to lock up. While heading up the stairs he thought how lucky he was to have a wife with a trusting, naive demeanor, certainly a stark contrast to the woman he'd just left.

Because Tuddy was sitting in the next room, Laura managed to remain composed. The longer she was sitting there thinking, the more absurd the notion was of Sal being involved in a bank robbery, resulting in murder, no less.

He finally came through the door and was hyperventilating as if he was going into cardiac arrest. She reached into his pocket and took out one of his nitroglycerin tablets and he popped it under his tongue while Tuddy rushed for a glass of water.

Angela heard the commotion and she emerged from her room. "Dad?"

He regained his composure. "I'm okay."

Angela and Tuddy went into the living room and Laura leaned in and said simply, "Sal, what in heaven's name is going *on*."

"Oh honey, I don't know *what* the matter is with that woman. She's been drinking continuously since Chubby's death and has now totally lost control of her faculties."

He glanced at his wife expecting a response, but she said nothing.

"Know what she just told me? She hears Chubby's voice at night calling her and now she refuses to go back to her apartment. That's why she called here. I convinced her to go to her daughter's apartment and spend a couple of days with the twins and dry out.

All Laura could manage was, "I see."

She then got up and went into their bedroom and slumped onto the bed. Sal went straight for the telephone and called his son.

"Mike, I can't say much right now," he whispered, "but it's **imperative** you drive in tonight and get that stuff out of the cellar."

"Dad, I'm getting ready for bed."

"I know it's late, Michael, *trust me*, there's no alternative. There's no traffic at this hour, you'll be back in bed in an hour."

"What am I supposed to tell Patti about me suddenly leaving the house at this hour? I'm Clark Kent??"

"Just make sure no one sees or hears you down there. Remember where the key is?"

"Are you all right, Dad?"

"I'm a little out of breath is all. Don't worry, everything's fine, I'll call you tomorrow."

"Okay then, meet me down there when I arrive."

"No, I can't leave. I gotta stay up here. Your mother is already wondering what's going on."

Lying down on her side, even without her glasses, Laura could still see her husband in the kitchen through the rooms. He was talking on the phone with his back to her. She then saw him reach up and hang up the phone. She watched while he stayed in the same position for what seemed an eternity, probably five or ten minutes. Laura was lying there trying to make sense out of everything that had gone on tonight. She blamed Marie for getting her husband involved in this. Her head was scattered.

She and Sal must have convinced a couple of neighborhood drug addicts to carry out a risk-free robbery. How else would they know that was the perfect day to pick? Did Marie purposely want her husband dead? Or worse—did both Marie and Sal want her husband killed? Is Sal even as sick as he says? She started praying.

Tuddy suddenly yelled, "Mom! **Mom!**" She sprang to her feet and now heard Angela yelling. She saw her husband on the floor clutching his chest. Angela was screaming, **"Mommy, call an ambulance!"**

CHAPTER 10

"Saez, you got a visitor."

Junior knew it was his legal aid Silverstein, since it was way past visiting hours. The lawyer was escorted to the lawyer/client area where he sat on the bolted-down stool. Junior was on the other side of the table waiting for him. "You're here on a Sunday, this can't be good."

"Mr. Saez, how are you feeling?"

"Been better."

"I'll get to the point. The D.A. just announced you are being charged with the shooting death of Adolph Werner and your bail has been raised to three hundred thousand dollars."

"I had *nothing* to do with that robbery; what evidence do they have on me?"

"Well for starters, they have the money and a gun, though not the one used on the guard, I found out."

"It's bullshit."

"Listen to me, Mr. Saez, they're spitting fire. I've not often seen motivation like this coming from those people. For some reason they moved your friend Wilfredo this evening down to the seventh floor. They want you two apart."

"They moved Whitey?"

"Yes, and if I were you, I'd meet with this Detective O'Reardon and see what he has to say."

"Why?"

"Where and when should be your reply, *not why*! Listen to me—this can be a good thing. I'm setting it up for tomorrow afternoon—you alone."

"I'll talk to him, but don't expect anything to change."

Junior went back to his cell and thought about his new bail. *Three hundred thousand, what a joke. Fuck, I can't even come up with three hundred dollars.* He felt empty knowing his friend wouldn't be with him on the tier. He also knew something shady was going on for Silverstein to be up here at this hour, on a Sunday, no less.

When the Legal Aid exited the jail, the familiar black Dodge was parked outside. The lawyer walked over to it. Detective Falco rolled down the window. "Well?"

"Tomorrow, two o'clock."

"Thank you, Counselor," Falco replied as he and O'Reardon drove off. Silverstein walked to his car thinking what he'd just done to his client could easily get him disbarred.

* * *

Laura and the kids were in Cumberland Hospital waiting room for what seemed an eternity. Angela dozed off and Tuddy was absently turning the pages of *Look* magazine. It was way past midnight. Laura had been shaking in dismay this entire evening. She was again trying to make sense of what she'd seen in the cellar.

"Mom, where's Paulie?" Angie asked.

Her mother didn't reply, just stared into space.

"He's staying at Luke's house," her brother answered.

Laura wondered why Michael hadn't arrived yet. She'd left word with his wife Patti over an hour ago. There was a sobbing woman sitting opposite them and a younger one carrying an infant having it out with the disinterested receptionist.

Finally, Michael arrived. It was his third trip in today, counting work. He hugged his mother.

"How is he?"

"He's still in intensive care."

The four of them sat there for another hour before a haggard-looking young doctor approached.

"Mrs. Marchetti?"

"Yes?"

His face saddened as he sat beside her. "I'm *so* sorry, we did everything we could. His heart was just too weak."

Laura popped up, put her hands to her face, and started crying loudly while slumping into her chair. Angela did the same. Mike thanked the doctor and her two sons kneeled in front of their mother and were hugging her. All four were now crying. As sick as he was, they all expected him to rebound and walk out in three days. Why should this one be different than his previous episodes?

After an hour of sitting there talking and crying, Mike finally said, "Let's go home."

* * *

On Monday afternoon at two o'clock, Junior was brought down into an administrator's office on the second floor of the detention facility. He was handcuffed behind his back waiting for the detectives to show up. Two correction guards were standing alongside him.

"Hey guys, no more beatings; your boss is watching," Junior said referring to the portrait of Mayor Wagner on the wall. They ignored him. He looked around the wood-paneled room. There was a portrait of the '61 Yankees as well as boxing figures adorning the walls. After ten minutes the detectives walked through the door.

O'Reardon looked at the taller guard. "Please remove the cuffs." The guard obliged and the two went outside and closed the door.

Junior rubbed his wrists and settled back into his wooden chair. "Got a cigarette?"

O'Reardon handed him a Lucky Strike while Falco plugged in a small tape recorder and placed it on the table.

O'Reardon did the talking. "How's life in here, Saez?"

"Just fucking peachy."

"Well, that's great, amigo, because if you're lucky that's what you'll get, life in here, or actually up in Sing Sing. If you're not so lucky you'll still get to go to up there, but only for a short time, say . . . until your appeals run out and a sad old padre knocks on your cell door."

"For doing what?"

"Well, how about for holding up a bank and murdering the bank guard? Funny how that seems to annoy judges."

Now it was Falco's turn. "Listen Roberto, uh, I mean Junior, that's what Whitey said you like to be called, you appear to be an intelligent guy. Now your friend Whitey, there's a very smart man."

Junior quickly looked at Falco, then caught himself and looked back up at Joe Louis.

"What are you saying?"

"I'm just saying he is a smart man, who doesn't plan on rotting away inside a jail cell. Now you—"

O'Reardon interrupted loudly, "Saez, your friend's not facing a death sentence, you are." He lowered his voice a few notches and shut off the recorder. "Are you telling us you weren't the triggerman?"

"I'm telling you I wasn't *there*."

"Listen to me, the bank already identified the cash found in your apartment as theirs." He lied.

Junior looked at Falco, who nodded in agreement. O'Reardon continued, "They're not happy because you still have two hundred and fifty thousand more of theirs and they have to break in a new bank guard to boot."

"Two hundred fifty thousand dollars?"

"Excuse me?" O'Reardon said, fumbling for the start button. Junior straightened up and ran his hands through his hair.

"First of all, let's get one thing straight, I didn't shoot nobody, you know that! You guys found my gun. Secondly, let's say I might have an idea who did shoot the man, will that make me *smart*?"

"A genius," Falco said.

"C'mon you know what I mean, will I be offered a plea?"

"I know exactly what you mean Saez, but plea bargains are up to the district attorney; however, as the lead detective of this case I might have something to say in the matter," O'Reardon said.

Knowing that Junior wasn't looking at him, Falco raised and lowered his eyebrows.

"I think I can trust *you*," Junior said, turning toward Falco.

"I *said* you're an intelligent man," Falco answered.

Junior buckled. "His name is Hector."

"Okay that narrows it down to a thousand guys on Bushwick Avenue alone."

"Hector Maldonado."

Falco jerked back and squinted. "Tall, skinny guy?"

O'Reardon turned toward his partner. "You know him?"

Falco asked again, "Is he a tall skinny guy . . . with a weird voice, kinda like a girl?"

Junior hesitated, somehow rationalizing that he wasn't *really* ratting him out if the cops already knew who Hector was.

Falco didn't wait for an answer, he looked at O'Reardon. "I busted him last year, no, musta been two years ago, 'cause I was still with Narcotics. It was a street sale if I remember right. Plea bargained it to possession and got probation."

"He from Greenpoint?" O'Reardon asked.

They both nodded. Falco took his notebook out. "Where's he live, Junior?"

"Over on Powers Street."

"Got a number?"

"I don't know the number, corner house near Bushwick Avenue. It's covered all with ivory and shit."

Falco looked up from his notebook. "Do you mean ivy?"

"Yeah, *leaves*. He's on the first floor."

"Is that where the rest of the money is Saez?" O'Reardon asked.

"There *is* no rest of the money. Maybe ten thousand, if that, is all you'll find there. That is, *if* he doesn't already have it in his arm."

Falco leaned closer to Junior Saez. "Listen, Junior, no cash, no plea bargain. So, if I were you, I'd say where it is."

O'Reardon chimed in, "You'll be too old to know what to do with it even if it's still there in the year *two thousand* when you get out."

"Hey guys, we got fifty-one thousand, four hundred dollars from that bank. We each got a third, which is why you found what you did. I swear on my mother."

O'Reardon called out, "GUARD!"

"Yeah?"

"He's all yours."

"Remember, Saez, no cash, no plea."

Junior shook his head as the handcuffs were put back on. While the guards were walking him out, Junior turned and yelled in at them, "You guys are being scammed. Probably by one of your own." Then out of sheer frustration, he slammed the side of his head against the door buck.

A grinning O'Reardon looked at his partner. "It's a good thing you clarified that, Rich."

"Clarified what?"

"*The ivy*; otherwise we would have been looking for a house with goat horns sticking out."

Falco put his notebook in his pocket and laughed. "Hey, with the Haitians in that fuckin' neighborhood we mighta found one."

* * *

"Who's there?"

"It's me, Sandy, Hector."

She thought she was hearing things. "Hector?"

"Yeah, open the door."

He was stoned and walked into the living room and sat down like nothing was amiss. It was as if Whitey and Junior were sitting there waiting for him.

"Are you *crazy* coming here?"

She went into the back room and peeked around the shade. "They have been driving by here every hour. Where you been the last three weeks?"

"I went to PR and stayed with my aunt in Ponce. Then she made me leave her house. I came back to New York to score some real dope. The shit they got there is garbage."

Sandy didn't want this junkie in her house. She didn't like him showing up when Whitey *was* home.

"You been to see Whitey?" he asked.

"Yeah, yesterday."

"What's going on with them?"

"Well, the cops found their money and Junior's gun. They're facing a lot of time, Hector."

"Is that right?"

"Whitey said if I saw you, to tell you they need four thousand for a lawyer."

" Shit, Sandy, that money is just about gone. I had to use a lot because I'm moving out of Brooklyn next week, and the plane fare to PR."

"You had fifteen thousand dollars!"

"Yeah, I know. I also bought some weight. As soon as I get set up and start dealing some, I'll get you the money for them."

Junkie promises, she thought. Will she ever stop hearing them?

"Listen Hector, you gotta go. I'm out on bail myself and if they find you here I'm screwed. **Hector** wake up! **You have to leave!"**

He was startled by her forceful shaking, and he pushed her. "Get out of my face, bitch."

"You better get the fuck out of here!" Sandy yelled.

He got up as if to hit her and thought better of it.

"You hit me, junkie, and Whitey will kick your skinny ass all over Greenpoint."

"Yeah, when?"

He stumbled out the door. She had to restrain herself from pushing him down the stairs.

* * *

"Manager in Bank Holdup Dead At 56, Gunman Still At Large," was the *New York Daily News* page five caption.

They misidentified him as the manager. Sal, in death, finally got the promotion he always wanted. The article suggested his heart attack was a result of the holdup. Laura noticed the same guy that had interviewed Sal last week had written the article. She was glad it didn't mention the funeral parlor by name. The fewer people attending the better.

Michael handled all the arrangements. There was still a large turnout at the wake. All the people from the bank were there, including Marie. She took her place alone in the same spot in the rear each evening. She never spoke to Laura. She avoided speaking to anyone.

Laura and the kids spent the last three nights out at Mike's house even though their apartment was only a half-mile from the funeral home. The kids never left Laura's side during the wake's three days.

It was an unseasonably warm morning at St. Charles Cemetery as the solemn Monsignor Tucci delivered the eulogy. At the end of the final tributes Laura watched as the dirt was shoveled onto his casket.

During the drive home Mike looked at his mother in the rear-view mirror. "Why don't you and the kids spend another night with us?"

"No, Mike, the kids missed enough school. We'll be fine, thanks."

"Are you sure?" Patti said.

"Yes, three days away from home is long enough."

Laura was always a homebody, and she couldn't wait to get back to her apartment. Now that the funeral was behind her it was time for them to get on with their lives. It was also time to figure out what to do with that money in her basement. She already thought out what her options were: turn it in and face a scandal; use it to move them to a nicer place and risk going to jail; leave it alone for the time being and risk someone dangerous coming to look for it. There was a fourth choice, tell her son Mike about it and let him decide. She quickly dismissed that option. *I could never let Michael, or any of the kids, know what their father did. They would never forgive him. I must somehow handle this alone.* Laura's first attempt at making decisions on her own would be a whopper.

* * *

"I'm spending more time in this neighborhood now than when I was assigned here," Falco said.

"Yeah, well, I was actually *born* on this block," O'Reardon said.

"St. Catherine's?" Falco said pointing his thumb at the towering old hospital they were passing.

"Yup, except I doubt it was such a shithole then. Make a left here."

It was ten a.m. on Tuesday.

"Ya know, I still don't know what to make of this, Brian. You have these two sitting in jail, they have a *Legal Aid* handling their case and the other day Saez had to bum a cigarette off you."

"So?"

"So, where's all this money?"

"Rich, these two are full of shit. Either this other guy Maldonado has it and is too scared to come out of his hole or they stashed it and now can't get to it."

"I think it's the next block, yeah, hang a right here."

The two drove down Powers Street and the house that Junior described was on the next corner and aptly named Judge Street. It was a five-family house, and as described, covered with ivy. O'Reardon drove past and headed back to the precinct. They knew Hector's apartment was on the first floor and they could have gone and kicked the door in. The trouble with that was, if the person wasn't there, he surely wouldn't be returning any time soon.

There was no getting around it. They had to catch him outside. It was smokeswagon time again. O'Reardon again set up a schedule with teams of two staked out in the van. Hopefully, like the last stakeout, it wouldn't take long.

"I'm betting there won't be much cash recovered there either," Falco said.

The lieutenant ignored him.

CHAPTER 11

Laura woke up at her normal time. Angela and Tuddy were headed back to school for the first time in nearly a week. She made them a breakfast of bacon and eggs. This was normally a Sunday treat, but she felt they needed a little extra care, and the usual way Italian mothers interpret that is, *extra food*.

"Mom, what are you going to do today?" Angela asked, sensing her sad demeanor and realizing her mother was going to be left alone for the first time since dad's heart attack.

"I'm just going to rest this morning and go to the grocery store and maybe the butcher later on." Laura recognized the knock on the door. "Tuddy, let Lina in."

The landlady had her arms full of fresh bread and pastries from downstairs. "This is for your family."

"Oh, thank you Lina," Laura said.

"You husband was a good man, lika my Joe. If there isa anything I could do for you tell me, okay?"

Laura couldn't hold back her tears and when Lina hugged her the two started sobbing.

"Lina, now I know what pain you felt when Joe died. I feel so lost!"

"You musta try to be strong for your children's sake. Did he leava you money?"

Laura was taken aback by her directness. "Yes, Lina, he had a life insurance policy."

"How much?" she persisted.

"Well, enough, I think, to get us by for now."

"Okay dear, if there's anything I could do to help, you leta me know."

She felt oddly comforted by Lina's words. Laura couldn't wait to go down into the cellar and find out how much was in those bags. She had grown used to the idea of having the money over the last few days. Getting past her landlady was going to be no easy task.

"Mom, do I need a note for school?" Angie asked.

"No, I don't think that will be necessary. They all know about your dad."

As usual, she watched them from the window as they headed off to school. She never saw them hold hands before. It was while watching her children that very morning below her window that she decided she was keeping the money. She *had* to move them out of here! Laura knew *now* was the best time to get down there unnoticed because the bakery's busiest time was the early morning hours. She put on her slippers and headed down. She'd always hated it down there. She could hear the mice scampering when she turned the light on.

Nervously, she reached over the door of their bin and felt the key in its usual spot. She listened for Lina then opened it and went in. *The bags were no longer there.*

Laura started moving things around, then throwing things over as she became distraught. *Was I dreaming that? Certainly not. Someone took that money out of here!* Numb, she went back upstairs and began to cry again. *This is all for the better*, she tried to reason. The tears kept flowing. She hated her reaction to it more than the loss itself. She prayed for forgiveness and strength. She jerked her head up with a sudden realization. *Marie! Of course, Marie Werner took it. Perhaps it was hers all the while. Did Sal talk her into returning it? That would make more sense than him stealing it. Why, then, would he lock it in the cellar and not tell me?* Somehow, she wanted to find an answer. She also wanted to find the money.

* * *

Blown up mugshots of Hector Maldonado were taped to the van's dashboard. It was Friday, day two of the stakeout. The team of McLaughlin and Davis were in the van. Bill Mclaughlin had been twenty-five years in radio cars before finally making detective third grade. Because of his callous manner, being paired with Mac was an assignment everyone dreaded. Willie Davis was the unlucky guy. He was much younger and the first-ever black detective in the precinct. They were sipping their morning coffee when Davis called to the rear of the van, "Mac, that's him!"

They watched as a tall, thin Puerto Rican walked down the front steps of the ivy-covered house. He walked to Bushwick Avenue and headed toward the subway entrance. The plan called for them to radio for backup but that was if he went *into* the house. There was no time now. He was only a block from the M train entrance. The street was crowded with the locals heading to work. The van pulled up behind him and they hurried out. They were pretty sure he was carrying a gun, hopefully *the* gun. They came up behind him at the top of the subway entrance steps.

Without warning Mac knocked him to the ground while Davis, with his knee on his neck, waved his badge and shouted, **"Police."**

This was directed more to the crowd, who stopped cold in their tracks, rather than to their startled prisoner lying beneath them. They quickly cuffed him and got him up and into the van before they had another Ellery Street scene. He was bleeding from a nasty gash above his eye.

"What do you want with *me*, I'm going to work, I DIDN'T DO ANYTHING," the trembling man said in a high-pitched voice.

"Hector Maldonado, you're under arrest for murder and bank robbery," Mac announced. He then dragged him into the van and tossed the handcuffed man onto the floor, slamming his already bloodied head against the rear wheel well. He groaned and lost consciousness.

"You trying to kill him, McLaughlin?" Davis said angrily as he pulled out the man's wallet and found his driver's license.

"Fuck!"

"What is it?"

Davis flicked the license at Mac.

"*Miguel* Maldonado, meet Detective Asshole Bill Mclaughlin."

"Listen, spook, I'll put your fucking lights out next you talk to me like that."

Davis ignored that; this was not the time nor the place. He kept thumbing through the wallet until he reached a picture-ID card. He read it aloud. "Associate Professor, Mathematics Department, St. John's University. Looks like you beat the shit out of a college professor, Detective, or should I say, *Officer*?"

"Let me see that! Why the fuck did he fight with us if he was so innocent?" Mac stared out the van window awhile. He then purposely banged his own forehead against the back of the seat making a huge lump.

Davis shook his head. "Now I fuckin' seen everything."

Mac picked up the radio. "Lieutenant O'Reardon, this is Caterpillar Four."

"Go ahead, Four."

"We have in custody one Miguel Maldonado, for 733 and assault."

"Where are you?"

"Bushwick and Grand."

"Stay there, we'll be there in two minutes, we're just east of you."

"I think we're making a mistake, or should I say *another* mistake?" Davis said, looking at the still unconscious Puerto Rican.

"Did he say *Miguel* Maldonado? Falco asked, as they pulled alongside the van. Falco motioned to them to follow him. O'Reardon turned onto a small side street and pulled over. The van pulled up behind them. They quickly went into the van and saw the handcuffed man just waking up and moaning.

"What happened to your head?" Falco asked MacLaughlin.

"This fuck hit me when we were cuffing him."

"What the hell happened here?" O'Reardon wanted to know.

Davis stood quiet. Mac replied, "This guy is probably Hector Maldonado's brother, Miguel. When he emerged from the house, we stopped him for questioning because of his resemblance to the suspect."

"They beat me up and dragged me in here for no reason. I was on my way to work. I teach at St. John's."

O'Reardon jerked his head toward the two detectives. Falco looked down and shook his head.

Mac said, "Why did you fight us?"

"FIGHT YOU! You two knocked me over and handcuffed me! How the hell was I going to *fight* with you?"

Falco, while holding his handkerchief against the dazed man's head, asked him, "Are you related to Hector?"

"Yes, he's my kid brother. **I want to know why these guys assaulted me.**"

"Is your brother home now?"

"*Yes*, he is. My brother is a heroin addict and needs help."

O'Reardon motioned for Mac to follow him outside the van.

"I want you to take him first to Greenpoint Hospital to get bandaged then down to the station and wait for us." He put his index finger on Mac's chest. "There better not be another mark on him."

Falco called for two radio cars to meet them. O'Reardon leaned in the window of the van and asked Miguel, "Does your brother have a gun in the house?"

"A gun! Hector? I seriously doubt it. Why are you arresting him?"

"Is anyone else home?"

"My sister already left for school, my mother's there."

"Any dogs?"

"Yeah, a little one."

The lieutenant waved his hand and the van drove off.

"Fucking stupid."

"Who's that?" Falco asked.

"*Me*, that's who. I should have never had two third grades paired. Where's those cars?"

"There's one now and the other should be right behind him. I know Mac is a disaster waiting to happen, but Davis is a good cop."

O'Reardon was steaming. "Yeah, well, they really fucked this one up."

The four uniformed cops got out of their cars and O'Reardon briefed them, summing it up with, "Don't forget there's an old woman in there." The six of them drove to the house and the two detectives went first followed by the two uniformed guys. The other two went around the back to block any escape.

Falco hammered on the door and yelled, **"police, open the door!"** They could hear the woman talking in excited Spanish along with the barking of the Yorkie. He repeated, **"policia, abrir la puerta!"** They were about to break it open when they heard the latch moving. She opened it and they pushed their way in, guns drawn.

"Where's Hector Maldonado?"

They headed into the back rooms where he was yanked out of a clothes' closet three minutes into the search. His mother was screaming as he was dragged to the ground protesting his innocence. O'Reardon saw how the other two could have mistaken the brother for him. They looked and sounded very much alike.

"Hector Maldonado, you are under arrest for murder and bank robbery!"

He was too stoned to comprehend what Falco was saying.

"How'd this guy ever make it *into* the closet?" one of the cops snickered. Falco grabbed an overcoat, and they got him into it.

"Take him in *your* car," O'Reardon ordered one of the officers.

"Is he gonna puke back there, Lieutenant?"

"Don't worry, junkies only vomit when they're not high," O'Reardon impatiently replied.

Falco then motioned out the kitchen window for the other two to come up and the four of them began searching the place. They ignored the protests of the mother. She finally sat down at the kitchen table quietly moaning in Spanish, while reciting the rosary. It wasn't long before one of them found a .22 revolver stashed behind boxes on the top shelf of the same closet he'd been hiding in.

"Here ya go, Lieutenant."

O'Reardon took it from him and looked in the cylinder. "One missing, where was the gun?"

"Up there."

He pulled the boxes down and felt around. "Um hmm, thought so," O'Reardon said as he produced a brown paper bag. Thumbing through it he looked at Falco. "Not even five thousand."

Falco was sporting his *I told you so* look. They spent another half-hour searching the apartment and turned up a small amount of heroin. During the ride back to the station house O'Reardon was silent. By his demeanor you never would have known they had made a major arrest and recovered the probable murder weapon.

O'Reardon broke the silence. "Shit, I forgot. Now we've got to deal with his brother."

As soon as they arrived, Captain Rogers called them into his office. "Good collar, anything turn up in his apartment?"

"A loaded .22, 'bout five thousand in cash and his wakeup shot," O'Reardon said.

Then the captain's expression changed. "Brian, what the hell happened with Mac and Davis this morning?"

"Captain, did you look at the two brothers? They're identical. They thought they had the perp."

"For Christ's sake, man, why is he all banged up? What the hell did your guys do to him? He's a fucking college professor!"

O'Reardon sided with his men. "Did you see Mac's forehead; this guy didn't want to be taken."

"Listen, I don't want him charged."

"But Captain, if we do that, we're going against the word of our men. What kind of precedent will that set?"

"Lieutenant, you know Mac's a nutjob. I spoke to them both and I could tell by Davis's body language that this was all McLaughlin's doing and you know it too, so don't bullshit me. Drop the charges and release him; get him a ride home, and you better hope we hear nothing more from him."

* * *

"Yo! Children of Jesus! If you're going to Catholic mass stand at your door. Leaving in 10 minutes."

Whitey was dressed and ready. They were escorted to the chapel down on the fourth floor. Sunday church services were very popular at the Queens' House of Detention. Not for the worshiping aspect in most cases, but because it was the only opportunity to get off the tier and maybe communicate with friends held on the other floors. Whitey knew Junior would be there for the same reason. As they filed into the pews the guards made only a half-hearted attempt to keep the various floors seated together. Whitey saw the eighth-floor hard-cores entering and spotted Junior. He waved, as did five other worshipers. Junior and others weaved their way toward their friends from the sixth floor. The priest started the Mass amid a chorus of excited whispering and hand slapping.

"Hey, my man! How's it going?" Whitey asked.

"Fucked up, Whitey. I'm still sick and they stopped the meds."

"Yeah, mine too," Whitey said. "They only give you the shit for ten days then you go cold turkey. You knew that. Did you hear? Hector got busted."

"What!" Junior faked his surprised response. "When?"

"Yeah, with the gun, too."

"Fuck!"

"What is it with you two dumb asses not getting rid of the pieces like I told you?"

Junior, who wasn't about to tell Whitey that he'd given up their friend, replied, "At least mine didn't kill nobody. When did they bust him? Is he here?"

"All I know is what I heard on the radio last night. He was arrested without a struggle and a handgun was confiscated, is all they said. Oh, and five thousand dollars."

"Which probably means ten," Junior said.

"In the name of the father, the son and the holy ghost." The priest was trying to speak over his murmuring parishioners.

"When did they start saying Mass in English?" Whitey asked.

"I dunno, why? Was it in Spanish?"

"Latin, you moron." They both laughed aloud, annoying the few serious Catholics around them.

"Oh."

CHAPTER 12

Mike and Patti went to his moms for Sunday dinner. Laura had just returned from the nine o'clock Mass when they got there. Angela and Paulie were already out with friends.

"Did you hear, Ma? They got the last guy," Mike said.

"Yes, I know, there's a big article in the *Sunday News*," she answered.

"Oh yeah? What's it say?"

Laura was getting the meat for her sauce out of the refrigerator. "You know, about the arrest and all. They think they got the gun that shot Mr. Werner. It also said something about the guy's brother, who's a teacher, getting mistaken for him and beaten up by the police."

Patti reasoned, "He must've done *something*."

Her husband shrugged and said matter-of-factly, "He did something alright; he was related."

Patti sighed. "Was the money recovered?"

Laura fixed her eyes on her garlic dicing. "What kind of pasta you two want, I have ziti, shells, and spaghetti."

"Doesn't say if it was. Ziti sounds good to me, how about you, hon?" Mike replied.

"Uhh, sure, ziti."

"Have you been sleeping well, Ma?" Mike asked.

"Not really, I just have to get used to sleeping alone is all. I never realized your father's snoring was so soothing." She changed the subject. "How are you feeling, Patti? I see you're showing pretty good now."

"I'm fine, Mom," she replied, rubbing her stomach. "Ask me again in June."

Laura groaned, remembering what it was like carrying in the summer in the hot apartments.

"At least come June, you'll be out in the country where it's cooler."

Mike walked over to his mother and started twisting the can opener over the cans of tomatoes and asked her, "Did you hear from the insurance people yet?"

"Yes, I got a letter yesterday saying the check will be sent within seven days."

"Good. Dad said he spoke to you about me putting it to use for you."

"Yes, he did. Are you sure that's the best way to go, Michael?"

"Believe me Ma, I guarantee the ten grand will double in six months. I have information on a stock that's going to go through the roof. I'd like to get that money into it before it does."

Patti gave a puzzled look at her husband. Laura also looked up.

"Really! Okay then, as soon as I get the check, I'll call you . . . Oh fudge, I'm sorry, there's not enough ziti."

"Spaghetti sounds good, Mom."

* * *

"Morning, Sergeant."

The front desk officer replied, "What's so good about it, Richie? It's Monday and your guy in there had quite a night."

"What's he sick?"

The sergeant looked down at Falco. "Let me put it this way, we were never so happy to see the cleaning guy as we were this morning. The guy threw up everywhere but in the fuckin' toilet bowl. He must've finally fallen asleep because I don't hear him in there now. When the hell are we getting rid of him?"

"The lieutenant wanted him to stay put until we finish talking to him."

Falco went up the stairs to his desk. He had thought his days of dealing with sick junkies were over when he'd left Narcotics.

"Hey Falco, how's it hanging?"

"Just fine, Mac, how's your *head*," he asked sarcastically.

"A lot better than that spick's head, I guarantee ya."

"Yeah, well, if that reporter Williamson continues harping on that beating you gave him, the captain may add a few lumps on top of the one *you* already put up there."

"Listen, you fucking wop, you don't know what happened out there!"

Falco started to move around his desk when the other guys stepped between them.

"That's *enough* you two," O'Reardon said as he entered the room. "You know, McLaughlin, I stuck my neck out for you Friday. First of all, you got the wrong guy; secondly, you were supposed to call for immediate backup; third, you rendered the **wrong** guy unconscious; and fourthly...."

"Lieutenant, you know those two look alike . . . and there was no time for backup. As it was, we caught up to him just as he was entering the subway. My right, Davis?"

"You're right, Mac, you're always right." Davis' voice trailed off.

O'Reardon motioned for Falco to come with him into the empty interrogation room. Once inside, Falco, still worked up, said, *"He's such a fucking asshole."*

"Forget him. Listen, our friend downstairs is not getting any better and I can't put off his arraignment any longer so we'll have to see what we can do to *get* him feeling better."

"Do you mean get him a hit?"

"We'll let him do a line off the desk in here, I think it will make him a lot more talkative."

"Okay, I'll go and get him up here." Falco felt they were stepping over the line but went along with it.

"MALDONADO, WAKE UP!" Falco winced from the smell. He brought the bent-over Puerto Rican into the interrogation room where O'Reardon was already seated and sat him down on the opposite side.

"Rich, you know where it is, not too much."

"Maldonado, you're going to be arraigned this morning. I know you're sick and I've got a proposal for you."

He waited. Hector said nothing.

"You hear me?"

"Falco walked in and slipped O'Reardon a glassine envelope. Hector caught a glimpse of it and thought he was seeing things. O'Reardon didn't want to risk his partner's career. "Stand outside the door and don't let anyone in." He then opened the contents of the envelope and rolled up a dollar. "You know what this is, amigo?"

"Smack?"

"Not just ordinary street garbage, but pure shit."

He now had his attention.

"You know we have all the evidence we need on you, and you won't *ever* be seeing the money you have stashed. Tell me where it is, and your puking stops." He spilled some powder onto the desk, arranged it in a long straight line with one of his calling cards, then looked at his prisoner.

Hector looked back at him, bewildered. "What money?"

"Don't LIE to me or I'll scoop this shit into the ashtray. Both your friends said you have it." Another lie.

"Officer, I shot up most of my share, you took what's left from the closet. Can I *please* have that?" he said pointing to the makeshift straw.

O'Reardon wanted the shit off the desk anyway, so he handed him the dollar bill. He was amazed how quickly it was gone. The lieutenant got up and called Falco in. They watched Hector transform into a human as the narcotic took hold. He straightened up and said, "This whole thing was supposed to be a simple robbery. I never meant to shoot him. The gun went off by accident, I swear. Hey, this *is* good shit. Next time bring *works*" He clowned referring to a hypodermic needle. Can I have a cigarette?"

O'Reardon handed him one and said, "Tell me something, Maldonado, how much money did you guys walk out of that bank with?"

"The exact amount, you mean? I think forty-eight, something. Hey, where'd this dope come from?"

O'Reardon pounded his fist on the table.

Falco spoke for the first time. "Hector, did you expect to get more than forty-eight thousand?"

"Hell yeah, we expected a *lot* more."

"Who told you how much was supposed to be there?" Falco asked.

"Whitey."

"How'd he know?"

"I asked him that and he wouldn't say. Can I have another cigarette for later?"

O'Reardon seemed to ignore his request. "I saw at the rap sheet of each of you. Petty shit. I'd have to say you three were way over your heads holding up that bank. It's a huge step from shoplifting and purse-snatching. Now you're facing a murder charge. If I were you, I'd do whatever I could to keep from getting fried."

He then tossed over another butt which Hector put behind his ear.

"The only thing I know that would help you is cooperation."

"I thought I *was* cooperating. What else do you want to know?"

"Who drove the getaway car?"

"Some strung out junkie chick we all used to bang. Inez something or other. Whitey threw a couple of bags of dope her way and she drove us. She didn't even know what we were gonna *do*."

Falco chimed in again. "Why did you shoot the guard, Hector?"

"*I didn't mean to, man!* He moved suddenly and scared me, and the gun went off. I swear to God, that's the truth."

O'Reardon said, "See, you're lying about the driver, you're lying about the gun firing by itself, and you're lying about the money. How am I supposed to help you, Maldonado?"

"No, I'm *not*. **What money**?"

"Listen, amigo," O'Reardon snapped, "don't feel the need to protect anyone, especially your so-called friends. They're the ones who gave you up."

Hector looked up at the lieutenant with the *you're-full-of-shit* look.

"Don't believe me? How the fuck you think we got your address, dumbass?"

His face turned stoic. He glared at the detectives. "*Which one gave me up?*"

"You got all the answers, you figure it out."

* * *

"Luuucy, I'm hoome!"

"I'm up here, Mike," said Patti, ignoring his over-used impersonation.

"I don smell dinner, you haf lot of splaining to do, Lucy."

Patti smiled and shook her head. "I told you this morning, I wanted to go to the Half Moon tonight for dinner."

"Oh, please refresh my memory on the reason?"

"Sure, two actually. First, I have a craving for clams on the half-shell. Second, how often are we going to be able to get out once the baby is here?"

"Okay, half-shells at the Half Moon it is. I'm not even going to change. Let's go, I'm starving."

After dinner they had another glass of wine. Mike decided it was time to let his wife know what's going on.

"Patricia, there's something I need to tell you."

She sat back and gazed at her husband.

"My father did something crazy."

"*Your* father did something crazy!"

"Hear me out. He knew he wasn't going to be around much longer and suddenly an opportunity to leave a little something for his family was dropped into his lap." Mike added to her glass of wine. She was glued to his every word. "He . . . *exaggerated* the amount of money taken in the robbery." Mike paused briefly and looked for a reaction. His wife didn't blink. "Understand it didn't cost his bank a cent since the money was insured and *especially* understand that he knew his family was going to have a very difficult time making it on his pension."

Patti finally spoke, slowly. "So, the robbers didn't get the entire, what was it . . . three hundred thousand?"

He was beginning to have second thoughts about telling her.

"Uhh, correct, they didn't."

"How much of that did your father . . . exaggerate?"

He glanced around the bustling restaurant and leaned closer. "Two hundred and fifty thousand," he said point blank.

"Michael, you're not funny."

Her husband just stared at her and said nothing. She put her hand to her mouth. He sat back and sipped his wine without taking his eyes off her.

"Believe me, I know it's hard to comprehend. My father is the last person on the planet who would do something like this."

"Oh, myyy God!" is all she could manage.

"Patti, I didn't want to get you involved but I also didn't want any secrets to—"

"Wait. How am *I* involved?"

"Well, you aren't really, uh, but you sorta are . . . The money's in our house."

"WHAT!"

"I was gonna tell you sooner . . ."

"How could you do something like this without first talking to me?" she said in a strained whisper.

He sighed. "I'm talking to you about it now."

"Okay, let me get this straight. We have a quarter-million dollars that your father embezzled from Morgan Trust Bank *in our house?*"

Mike grimaced and meekly replied, "In our attic."

"What does your *mother* say about all this?"

"She doesn't know. Are you kidding? She'd never be part of anything like this. I'm the *only* person that knows, well, and now you."

"Wrong! Three bank robbers also know it."

"That's probably true, but don't worry about that. Even if they admit to the holdup, which isn't likely, who's gonna believe a bunch of thieves and murderers. Patti, you know my father was by no means a reckless man. He put a lot of thought into this; he wouldn't jeopardize his family if he thought it wasn't infallible."

"Tell me, genius, how are you planning on giving your mother all this money without her knowing it?"

"Simple, make her think we earned it. Remember on Sunday when I was telling her about investing Dad's life insurance money?"

"Yes, I do, and I remember you telling her she was guaranteed to double her money in six months. I thought that was unrealistic when you said it. *OH, I see*, you're going to give her the money letting her think that her son is the greatest investment broker since Andrew Carnegie."

"Exactly, except Carnegie's money came from steel."

"Oh. And this didn't."

Mike smiled for the first time while he placed his elbows on the table and put his slightly spinning head in his hands. "You know, Patricia, sometimes I underestimate you." He then got serious. "I do have a bit of a dilemma though."

She raised an eyebrow.

"Dad made me promise I would do nothing with the cash that would trace it to our family."

"So, *that* makes sense."

"Honey, I'm an investment man, *it's killing me* this much money is sitting in the attic collecting dust while a bull market is running wild."

"Michael, first of all, when this wine wears off and I come to my senses I'm going to flush the money down the toilet bowl. Failing that, I think you should heed your father's advice and not raise any red flags by showing up on Wall Street with bundles of cash. Michael, you *can't* get reckless with this."

"Honey, I know the business inside out. If I invest it in small amounts at different times in different places, it will go undetected. There's no rush to do anything right away. Let's just see how the investigation plays out. In the meantime, let's get out of here, I want to get home and see what a quarter-million dollars looks like!"

"Check please," Mike called, suppressing a grin. He stood up and finished the last of the wine in one gulp.

He left a nice ten-dollar tip and headed out the door. Driving home, Mike was weaving in and out of the sparse traffic that was in front of him.

"Slow down, dammit! How about we keep today's felonies down to a minimum. Also, let's not get the baby killed before it's born."

At home, Mike drew the shades before dropping down the attic stairs.

"Heads up!"

Two plump Wells Fargo bags came down with a thud into their hallway. Patricia's eyes lit up. They were emptied onto the kitchen table. The two of them counted out the bundles of tens, mostly twenties, and some fifties. "Two hundred thousand, one hundred forty-five", she announced.

"Not right, let's count it again," Mike urged.

This time slower and more precisely they arranged the money into stacks of ten thousand.

"Seventeen, eighteen, nineteen, twenty. I don't get it, honey, why would Dad say there was two hundred and *fifty* thousand?"

"Looks like someone is getting greedy."

"It's not that, I'm wondering if someone else knows about it and has been into it?"

"Well, you said your brother Tuddy hides his cigarettes down there. You think maybe he found it and took some?"

"No way, he would have gone right up to my mother with it, and she would have surely called me. No, it's something, or someone, else. I should've told you—my father called me the night he died and sounded nervous. He wanted me to rush in and remove the money from the cellar right away. I tried to ask him what was up, but he cut me short, warning me not to speak over the phone."

"Ya know, Mike, that makes six."

"Six what?"

"People, who know about this money. This is sounding less and less, how did you put it . . . infallible?"

Mike shrugged. "Let's put it back in the bags and bring it back up. We'll just ignore it for now and see what happens."

"Yeah, *ignore* it."

* * *

"Captain, got a minute?"

"Yeah guys, come on in."

O'Reardon and Falco did so and shut the door. Captain Rogers motioned for the two to sit on the battered wooden chairs behind his desk. "How much longer you got, Brian? Must be getting close?"

"April eleventh I'll have my thirtieth in, so what's that, three months?"

Brian O'Reardon had actually put in for his retirement ten years ago, but when his wife and only child, a teenage daughter, were killed by a drunk driver a month before his scheduled departure he'd decided to stay on the force.

"You finally going to take that boat out past Jamaica Bay after you retire, Lieutenant?" Falco asked.

The captain laughed. "Only if he gets drunk, passes out, and it drifts out of the bay."

O'Reardon had bought the boat ten years ago, named it *Mister Meanor* and spent most of his leisure time in the summer just lounging on it drinking beer while tied up alongside fellow beer drinkers at the Canarsie docks.

"You ever take anyone out on that tub, Brian?" Falco asked.

"Nope, no room, empty beer bottles take up most of the space."

"Christ, how much space can beer bottles take up?" Rogers asked.

"When rolling around, quite a bit!"

The captain finally got down to business. "Looks like the Morgan Trust case will be open and shut. You guys did a good job."

Falco spoke, "Except there's still more to do."

"Do you mean the getaway driver? I think we put enough man hours on this case. If you can get a name from one the junkies, fine, otherwise let it go. We're backed up and I want you two on the floater they fished out of Pier Seven Monday morning."

"It's not about the driver, Captain". O'Reardon said. "It's the money."

The captain hastened, "You know how that works, Lieutenant. The DA will offer a plea to the guy that turns it in; if no one accepts it, fuck it, let it stay buried. Personally, I don't give a shit if the bank or insurance company *ever* get their money back. We had a robbery/homicide to solve, and we did just that."

Falco coyly looked at his partner and waited for him to speak, mostly wanting to hear him, in his own voice, finally admit to it.

"Captain, we're pretty convinced those three walked out of that bank with only fifty thousand dollars."

"What are you talking about?"

O'Reardon stood up and closed the blinds, shielding them from the commotion outside the office, and returned and leaned on Rogers' desk.

"Okay, I've been around here quite a while and heard *all* the bullshit from these lowlifes there is to hear. You develop a sixth sense about when they're straight and when they're lying, I'm sure you're aware of all that. Now bear with me, sir. Each one of these guys were arrested with roughly fifteen thousand. Well actually, the last guy had less because he had more time to shoot up his share. Now these are neighborhood dope fiends that normally cattle rustle to support their habits. By no means are they professional bank robbers, or even amateur."

"Cattle what?"

"Cattle rustling, Captain, they shoplift packaged meat from grocery stores and sell it in their neighborhood."

"All right, so what does that have to do with the case now?"

"They all stated point blank they got fifty thousand from that job. None of them were able to afford bail, or a lawyer for that matter."

"Or even cigarettes," Falco chimed in.

"A plea bargain was already offered for the return of the money. All they would say repeatedly is, *there is no more money.* You know what . . . I believe them."

The captain looked at Falco. "And you, Rich?"

O'Reardon answered him, pointing at his partner. "He's the one who convinced *me.*"

Falco, loving this, just nodded. Rogers spun his chair around and stared out onto the avenue. The partners glanced at each other.

Without turning around, he said, "C'mon, are you telling me a quarter-million dollars vanished into thin air?"

"We're just telling you we would like a little more time on this."

"Brian, I don't *have* any more time! Fucking mobsters are floating ashore like seaweed, a hooker from the Navy Yard turned up in a dumpster just last night, and every Puerto Rican in Greenpoint is torching their house. Oh, and I'm losing you in a few weeks, you Irish bastard."

"I understand, but the reality of this case is the *real* thief is laughing out on the streets, with most of the money," O'Reardon said.

Rogers looked at his two detectives. "Let's walk through this. What are we looking at here? I'd like to hear what *you two* think the possible scenarios are?"

"Well, one is they could actually have the money and are major league bullshit artists," O'Reardon said.

"And be willing to wait thirty years to get to it," Falco added.

O'Reardon continued, "Another scenario is the bank is doing a number on their insurance company, but I doubt that, it's a *bank* not a liquor store. Then there is the mastermind possibility, maybe even an insider, and *he* has the cash."

The captain shrugged. "What if they missed the money and left it behind?"

Falco replied, "We thought of that, and I asked Saez if he was sure he emptied the vault and he said the only thing they left behind was the contents of the safe-deposit boxes, *only* because the alarm was sounded."

"Well, it looks like you two have a dead end. You have two employees dead and three junkies in jail. Where would you go from here even if you had more time? There's no one left to talk to."

"I want to go back to the bank and speak with the tellers again, and I also would like to pay a visit to both widows," O'Reardon said.

"I'm not surprised, Brian, I hear the guard's wife is a pretty hot dame," Rogers said.

"That she is, she's also a total head case," Falco replied.

The captain rose to his feet, went to the door, and opened it. "I'm giving you guys three days. If nothing significant, and I do mean *significant*, comes up, you're on the floater. Agreed?"

"How 'bout a week?"

"Three days, gentlemen, now I've got work to do and so do you."

"Thanks, Cap," Falco said as they exited.

CHAPTER 13

"Hi Michael, it's Mom . . . We're fine. Listen, I received the check this morning from Hartford. Yes, ten thousand, so whenever you want you can come over and I'll sign it over to you. I'd also like you to take Dad's car off the street here and sell it or something. It already has a windshield full of tickets. Tomorrow? Fine. Maybe you can take the train here after work and drive it home with you. Okay, I'll defrost the pork chops. Say hello to Pat. Yeah, see you tomorrow. Okay, luv you too."

Laura went into the living room and sat with little Paulie, who was watching TV.

"Was anything said in school about your father?"

"Mr. Russo, the assistant principal, called me down to his office and told me some dumb story."

"About what?"

"I don't know, about when he lost his father, how he became the man of the house and helped his mother and lived happily ever after."

"That was very nice of him. You know, the Lord has a way of getting his message to you so you might want to listen when you hear things of that nature."

"Ma, I don't want to miss the end of this movie so can we talk about God and his messages later?"

Laura sighed and went into Angela's room. "Still doing your homework?"

"Just finishing, actually."

"Oh, another Beatles poster I see."

"Yes, isn't Paul a dream in that one."

Laura picked up her daughter's hairbrush, went behind Angela, and started brushing her hair. "I remember buying this brush for you when you received First Communion. Of course, your hair was a lot shorter then."

"I know, Ma, I look like a freaking boy in my Communion pictures."

"Must you talk like that?"

"Well, I did. My girlfriends used to call me Angelo."

"That's because you were much prettier than them."

"Mom, can I ask you something?"

"Sure, dear."

"Are we going to stay here?"

"Do you mean in this apartment?"

"Yeah, can we move? I heard you ask Dad many times for us to move. It's your decision now, ain't it?"

"What about your friends?"

"It doesn't have to be far away, I just don't want to live on this block, above this smelly bakery. I *really* want to move."

Laura put the brush down. "I wish *my* hair was still that shiny. We'll see Angie, I think we may be able to do just that."

"Soon?"

"As soon as the good Lord answers my prayers, and he is sure listening."

"Mom, you've been on that God stuff a lot lately. You never used to, this much."

"Oh? Well, that's a good thing, honey. Besides we need him now more than ever, wouldn't you say?"

"Uhh, yeah, but I also think we could use more money now more than ever. Mom, I'm so tired of being poor all the time . . ."

"You are *not* poor, young lady, you have nice things, plenty of food, your own room . . . Now look at Mary and Joseph—"

"MA, FORGET IT, okay! Forget it." Angela got up from her bed and stormed into the living room.

"What's all the commotion about?" Paulie asked.

His sister lifted her tearful head from her folded arms. "I *really* wish Dad was still here."

* * *

The next morning was frigid. Laura looked oddly at the new bank guard as he unlocked the door without even acknowledging the three women waiting to come in. Chubby always had a huge "Good morning' for everyone when they entered.

Rose came out from behind the counter. "Laura how are you?" she asked as they hugged.

Laura waved at the other two girls. She looked over at her husband's empty desk.

"We're fine. I had to come down to get some *more* paperwork taken care of. Is Manny inside?"

"Yes, he is. Just knock and walk in." She was about to do just that when he walked out.

"Laura Marchetti, I thought I heard your voice. Come on in, how are you?"

"Fine, thank you. I received this letter from the main office yesterday. Apparently, you forgot to sign one of the forms on Sal's retirement statement."

"Oh, I'm sorry, let me see."

"There, on the bottom."

"Oh damn, I don't know how I missed it," Manny said. "I hope it didn't hold up anything."

"Don't worry Manny, it will all get caught up eventually."

"Laura, I hope it's not too personal but have you a savings account or bonds you can fall back on?"

She thought that was an odd question and for some reason it annoyed her. Perhaps it was her daughter's poverty declaration that made her over-react.

"Thank you, we'll be fine," she said curtly.

"That's good to hear. You know a detective called yesterday afternoon and said he would like to come down here today and talk to the girls again."

She felt uneasy now. "Is that so? Why are you telling me?"

"I just wondered if he contacted you as well. I *hate* for the women here to have to rehash that whole thing and I'm sure you aren't looking forward to it either."

"Oh, did he say he is going to be calling me as well?" She was trying to be nonchalant.

"Actually, yes. Oddly enough he asked me if I thought you and Marie Werner were sufficiently recovered to answer a few *routine* questions, as he put it. I wonder if they ever ask questions that aren't routine."

Laura forced a smile. For some reason she never felt comfortable around this guy. Sal used to tell her that Manny had a *grifter* way about him and shouldn't be trusted. She kept it short.

"Thanks for everything, Manny. It was nice seeing you."

"If you need anything . . ."

She shut the door before he could finish.

* * *

Just before closing, O'Reardon and Falco entered the bank and Manny escorted them into the lunchroom. The women didn't mind the intrusion into their mundane banking routine. The attention of the detectives was a high point for them. They freshened up and entered the room. Manny and the two policemen were already seated.

"Afternoon, ladies," Falco said.

O'Reardon never lifted his head from his notes. Finally, looking up, he smiled.

"Okay, we'll make this as quick as possible so you can go back to your work. The main thing we're interested in right now is if any of you noticed the physical size of the parcel the perpetrators carried out of the vault. For now, I'm not interested in the skinny guy who was in the front with you, just the guys in the back."

The women looked at each other for a while and shrugged. Dana then said, "I know they each had an empty shopping bag they took out from their jackets when they entered. When they came out it wasn't really bulging, kinda saggy, now that I think about it. *You* see it, Rosie?"

"I don't have a clue. I wasn't lifting my head to look either."

"How 'bout you, miss?" O'Reardon asked Paula.

"I was lying three feet away from a man bleeding to death, let's just say I was a bit distracted."

Her answer annoyed him but O'Reardon simply replied, "Of course."

After a pause Falco locked eyes with Manny. "Mr. Figueroa, bank records indicate a delivery of roughly two hundred and fifty thousand dollars the day prior to the holdup in small denominations."

Manny nodded.

"Would that amount of money normally be delivered in several satchels?"

"Yes, most likely two."

"How big would you say those satchels were?"

"In those denominations probably each about this big." Manny held the palms of his hands about two and a half feet apart, then about two feet off the ground.

Falco continued, "I'm sorry, dear, what was your name?"

"Dana Jankowski."

"Dana, of course. Dana, did that look like the size of the bags you described?"

"I would definitely say no."

O'Reardon, after digesting that, turned toward Manny. "When an armored car delivery is made, what is the procedure exactly?"

"Normally two armed guards bring the money in while one waits inside the truck."

"Yes, I know that. I mean once inside, what happens?"

"Well, one would follow the bank officer and our guard into the vault area where the seals get checked and it gets put away. Then I, or Mr. Marchetti in this case, would sign their ledger, hand over their empty bags from the previous delivery, and off they go. They usually have a tight schedule, and for obvious security reasons, they don't like their truck outside longer than necessary with only one guy in it."

"Is the money put in the vault in the same bags they arrived in?"

"Yes, they have a seal on them to prevent tampering."

O'Reardon continued, "At what point then is the money taken out of the bags?"

"Usually our head teller, Mrs. Marino, Rose, will remove the cash from the bags, count it by bundle, then stack the bundles on the shelves in the vault."

"Is this done right away?"

"It's normally done by the late morning because the flow of customer withdrawals is heaviest in the afternoon.

"According to Mr. Marchetti's statement, the cash was stolen while still in the bags. I assume that's correct, Rose? What I mean is, you didn't stack that money onto the shelves yet?"

"That's correct, it was delivered late on Wednesday and the robbery occurred first thing Thursday morning so there was no time for me to do so."

"One last thing, Mr. Figueroa. Are armored car deliveries *always* put directly into the vault?" O'Reardon said.

"Why, yes," Manny said, without hesitation.

Falco thanked everyone as he snapped shut his notebook. Manny walked them to the front door, stopping them midway, before they got within earshot of the new guard. He then said in a whisper, "I'm guessing from your questions you don't believe they got all the money that was reported stolen?"

Falco answered in earnest, "Let's just say we're not satisfied they"—

O'Reardon interrupted, "*Let's just say* it's too soon to tell."

They continued out. On the way back to his office, Manny noticed the women were all abuzz. He walked over and said, matter-of-factly, "Okay, let's hear it."

Paula spoke first. "Who do you think has the money?"

Then Rose chimed in, "I'll bet Mr. Bilkey told Sal to exaggerate the take."

"You ladies have been watching too much *Dragnet*. The fact is whenever the police can't recover something, they like to assume it wasn't lost in the first place. I guarantee these three guys have that money buried so deep in the ground Chinamen are spending it. Now let's get back to your drawers so we can get out of here today."

The women weren't convinced.

During the ride back, O'Reardon was staring out the window.

"You know there's something about that Figueroa guy that bugs me. He has a fucking annoying way about him."

"Could be because he wears more jewelry than Liberace," Falco said.

"Hey Lieutenant, you still think it's a waste of time to interview the Wells Fargo guys?"

"Probably, but since we're not far from their place, what do you say we swing by and see if they're around. It's just off Myrtle Avenue, take the Interborough one exit."

They arrived at the old brick building in fifteen minutes. If it weren't for the armored trucks parked inside the rear fenced area, one would have thought it was an ordinary warehouse. The detectives walked up to the only door not behind a barbed wire fence. A sign said *Visitors Please Use Telephone.*

"May I help you?"

"Detective Sergeant Falco, New York City Police, we would like to speak with two of your drivers."

"Stay where you are please."

A moment later a car pulled up and an armed guard got out. Falco displayed his gold shield.

"I also need to see a picture I.D. with that, Detective."

O'Reardon already was reaching for his, anticipating the request.

"Thank you, Lieutenant, how can we help you?"

"We would like to speak to the guys who have the Maspeth route, Morgan Trust Bank. Does your dispatcher have that information?"

"No need to speak to the dispatcher, I know who they are, Ralph Sweeney and Charlie Rodriquez. They're probably upstairs changing. Please come on in." He unlocked the door and led the two into a lounge area. "Sweeney is retired from the force; you might even know him. Have a seat, I'll go up and get them."

Falco was looking through the window into the hallway. "Quite an operation."

O'Reardon was more interested in the *Field & Stream* magazine he found. After a short while, the two entered the room. The older one had already changed into his civilian clothing.

"I'm Detective Falco and this is Lieutenant O'Reardon."

"How do you do, Ralph Sweeney."

"Charlie Rodriquez."

"I understand you're retired from the force. What precinct?" O'Reardon asked.

"Next one over, the eight three. As a matter of fact, I was there with Adolph Werner, the Morgan Bank guard."

"So, you knew him?" Falco said.

"Very well. It's a damn shame. I just heard the other guy died as well. Those bastards should be charged with two murders."

"The reason we're here is to find out what took place when you made the delivery to Morgan Trust on Thursday, January eleventh. That would be the day before the robbery," O'Reardon said.

"Well, it was pretty routine except the amount of money seemed more than usual, plus I remember the bank manager wasn't there. That was a first," Sweeney said.

"You mean he's *always* been there for deliveries?" Falco asked.

"In the two years I've had that route I don't recall him missing one," Sweeney replied.

"Are the managers of banks usually the only ones who oversee cash deliveries?" Falco asked.

"Depends on the bank. In most cases the assistant manager also does it. Some banks, like Morgan, the assistants have limited access to the main vaults."

The younger guard, Rodriquez, spoke for the first time. "That's probably why the poor guy had such a hard time opening it."

"Shit, that's right! You know, I forgot about that," Sweeney said.

"What guy? Are you talking about Salvatore Marchetti, the assistant manager?" O'Reardon asked.

"Uh huh." Rodriquez nodded.

"Did he finally open it?"

"I'm sure he did, we didn't stay."

"Didn't stay?"

"We were late and had other stops," Sweeney said.

O'Reardon quickened the tempo of the questions. "When you left him, where, exactly, were the satchels?"

"Where? We placed them at his feet, just outside the vault. He signed our ledger and we split."

The detectives looked at each other.

"So, you're positive he didn't get the vault open while you were there?"

Sweeney got defensive. "We're not required to be there for the actual placement of the money inside the vault. I suppose that's why the bank guard is back there."

"I get that. *Did* they get the vault open while you were there?"

"Nope, not while *we* were back there."

"*Was* the bank guard back there with you?"

"Yes, Werner was right beside us."

"Ralph," O'Reardon continued, "You said you knew Adolph Werner personally. Did you know his wife?"

"Sure, I knew Chubby's wife. She was quite a gal, Marie."

"How so?"

"Well, first of all, she was a lot younger than her husband. She was a local beauty queen, more than local actually, she almost became Miss New York State. Word was Chubby pulled her car over and gave her a ticket, that's how they met. They wound up married with twins, grown now."

"What else can you tell me about her?"

"I suppose one can say she had more than her share of male pursuers. I understand a few even caught up with her." Sweeney winked, then grinned. "Also, word is, she never met a bottle of gin she didn't like."

O'Reardon looked at his watch. "Thank you both for your time. You've been very helpful."

"Is this guy Marchetti suspected of anything?"

O'Reardon confided in him, one old cop to another. "We think the perps only got fifty grand from the bank."

Falco was surprised his senior partner revealed that to him, especially within earshot of the younger guard.

"Wow, you're kidding." Sweeney said.

"That's not to get out," the lieutenant said.

As soon as the detectives got out of the building, Falco hummed, "Hoooly shit."

O'Reardon smiled at Falco. "That just bought us another couple weeks, partner."

* * *

As time passed Laura struggled to accept the absent loot. She was becoming bitter about having all that money at her fingertips only to have it just disappear. She needed advice and the only person she could turn to was her father. She'd almost told him at the funeral home but thought he might overreact and do something irrational.

Laura knew her father's *bull in a China closet* manner could be lethal, but at the same time, it might be helpful. She had to take the chance. She decided tomorrow was as good a day as any to take a trip to Staten Island. She would take the kids. They usually went there only on Christmas Eve and maybe on one other occasion during the year. Sal used to find excuses for not going. He didn't mind the big family weddings or parties when just he and Laura used to go, but he always balked at their kids being exposed to too much of her family. Especially her father and brother Mario. The old man knew this and was bitter over it.

When the boys got old enough to read newspapers, they were tactfully told about their grandfather's mob ties. Better they hear it from Mom and Dad than the *Daily News*. They never really told Angela, but she knew anyway. Laura suddenly remembered Mike was coming over after work. At 6:30 the bell rang. Tuddy buzzed Mike in just in time for dinner.

"So, you three are going to Staten Island tomorrow. Better dress warm. You're going to freeze on that boat. Who's picking you up at the ferry?"

"I don't know, either your grandfather or Uncle Mario. You and Pat are welcome to come with us."

"No, I'm going with a friend from work to the Garden." Laura was glad he didn't take her up on the invitation. It would have been difficult for her to speak privately to her father with Mike there.

"*No way!* You have Rangers-Canadians tickets?" Tuddy bellowed.

"Well actually my company has season tickets, and they sometimes make their way down the food chain to me and Joel."

"See if you can get the Gump's autograph for me."

"Sure, Tud, Gump Worsley is going to come up to our section, skates and all, and sign autographs. How 'bout you, Angie, any requests?"

"Yeah, take me with you so I don't have to go to Grandma's."

"Young lady, you might as well get used to it. I promised your grandfather we'd be making a lot more visits to them," Laura said.

Mike looked surprised and said simply, "Oh?"

"And why not, they're not getting any younger. They won't be around forever, you know."

Mike recouped. "Sure, I get it."

Laura went and got her purse while Angela cleared the table. She took out the envelope with the insurance check.

"What do I do, Michael, just sign the back?"

"That's all, Mom."

"How you're planning on doubling this in six months, is what I'd like to know."

"Three letters, Mom . . . IBM"

"Typewriters?"

"Yes, *electric* typewriters and more importantly, their new model 7094 office computer. It'll be the business world's most powerful."

"Oh, Michael, I hate those things. Didn't you see that Tracy/Hepburn movie where all the office workers lose their jobs when they got a computer?"

"Mom, that's only in Hollywood. Besides don't worry so much about office workers, worry about yourself and the kids, okay?"

He folded the check and put it in his wallet. Before he left, he pulled his brother Tuddy over to the side to remind him of the *your-now-the-man-of-the-house* talk he gave him at the funeral home. He also told him not to worry; things would be getting much better for the family soon enough.

* * *

"Did you see the article this morning, Lieutenant?" Falco asked.

"What article?"

Falco pointed at the desk. "Page three."

O'Reardon sensed trouble as he thumbed through the paper.

COPS QUERY REPORTED TAKE IN QUEENS BANK JOB. The article went on to say: *A reliable source told the Daily News yesterday that of the $300,000 reported stolen by Morgan Trust, police now believe "somewhere in the neighborhood of $50,000" to be the actual amount grabbed by the suspects. There is an ongoing investigation to determine the whereabouts of the remaining quarter million.*

The story went on to give more insight regarding the three suspects arrested and other details of the investigation.

"That little *rice vacuum* overheard me talking to Sweeney and went to the papers," O'Reardon said.

Wincing because even fellow uniform guys weren't immune to his racial slurs, Falco replied, "I don't know, Lieutenant; I'm thinking Sweeney would better fit their *reliable source category*. In any case I'm glad I won't be here Monday when Rogers gets in."

"Screw him, it was bound to get out anyway. Did you get the addresses of the two widows?"

"Yes, I did. They live within a mile of each other over in Maspeth."

"Okay, let's go see Marie Werner first."

Her apartment was in a quaint two-story brick building. The upper one of the two bells read Werner. She sounded like she'd just woken up when she answered the door. It was 10 am.

Falco held his badge up to the peephole and she let them in. "You guys are at it on weekends too?"

"Sometimes, Mrs. Werner. We're very sorry about your husband. It's our understanding he was a very good cop and a fine man," O'Reardon said.

"Thank you, he was that and more."

"If you're up to it we have a few questions we'd like you to answer."

"Sure, go ahead, now is as good a time as any, I suppose. I'm as half-awake as ever."

O'Reardon smiled.

Falco started, "Can you tell us how long your husband worked for Morgan's?"

"Well, from '59 to this year. Five years. I worked there fifteen years myself. Talk about a waste of good years."

O'Reardon looked around the apartment at the expensive furnishings. "Nice place, did it take long to collect these antiques?"

"Yes, it did, Officer. Chubby and I traveled extensively over the years and tried to bring something back from each trip."

"Fifteen years is a long time," Falco said, "I take it then you knew Sal Marchetti very well."

Marie surprised the detectives. "I guess you could say we had our brief little thing, but that was a long time ago, when I first started working there."

"I think you mighta misunderstood me, ma'am, I only meant you must have known him well as a fellow worker."

"Oh, I'm sorry, I assumed you spoke to Laura Marchetti, and she had her usual opinions."

"No, we haven't spoken to her yet. Can you tell us what sort of man Mr. Marchetti was?"

"Sure, he was a fine family man, a devout Christian, very active in the parish here. Let's see . . . I wouldn't describe him as a driven man, he just kinda lived day to day. He often complained about being overlooked for promotion.

"I notice you haven't mentioned the word *honest* in your description," O'Reardon said.

"I assume he's honest, I mean he's never taken anything from me. *Square* is a better description," she replied, forming the shape with her fingers.

O'Reardon continued, "Mrs. Werner, are you . . ."

"Please, call me Marie."

"Okay, Marie, are you and Mrs. Marchetti on friendly terms?"

Marie sat down and her long crossed legs were revealed through her bathrobe. "I wouldn't expect an invitation to her next Tupperware party, if that's what you mean." She smiled up at O'Reardon.

He nodded and folded his arms.

Falco sensed his partner's attraction to her. He was not surprised.

"Actually, we were good friends when we first met. We went shopping together a few times, usually to Macy's in the city. She was kinda frugal. I remember she would go from rack to rack looking for bargains and wind up leaving empty-handed. The Marchettis weren't exactly rolling in the dough. They had it pretty tough with four kids in school on Sal's salary. I think she never really got used to their bargain-basement lifestyle."

"She came from money?" Falco asked.

"I'd say. You might have heard of her father."

"Who's her father?"

"Well, her maiden name is Paparelli, ring a bell?" The detectives looked at each other,

O'Reardon shook his head. "No, it doesn't, what's his first name?"

"John." Marie was enjoying herself.

O'Reardon's eyes widened. "Is she from Staten Island?"

"Uh huh."

Falco looked puzzled. The lieutenant turned toward him smugly. "Johnny Papa."

Falco's head jerked. "As in Gambino underboss Johnny Papa? Holy shit."

Marie added, "As in Carlo Gambino's next-door neighbor Johnny Papa. She told me she used to play in his house with his son."

"Small world, theirs," O'Reardon replied.

Marie leaned back again and recrossed her legs. "I swear, if you knew the woman, you'd be more inclined to think she was Billy Graham's daughter."

O'Reardon watched Marie as she got up and went to the refrigerator.

"I'm sorry, fellas, can I get you a cup of coffee, or orange juice perhaps?"

"No thank you, we have to get going."

"Okay, Detective O'Reardon. By the way, do *you* have a first name?"

"Yes, you may call me Brian."

"Okay, when may I do that?"

O'Reardon reached into his jacket and handed her a card. "Whenever your heart desires."

Falco put his coat on. "I'll go warm up the car, thanks for your help, Marie."

He exited.

"Your partner seems very nice."

"That he is. There's something I'd like to ask you, off the record. How well do you know Mayor Wagner?"

"My goodness, stories do travel. Bob and I go back to his council-man days. I'd say I knew him quite well then, we've been mostly out of touch since."

"His loss. Did you two date or something?"

"Or something. It was before I was married. Are you always this inquisitive off the record, Brian?"

"Only when I'm genuinely interested."

"I get it, Bob Wagner is a very compelling man."

O'Reardon smiled and looked her up and down. "Anyone ever say you look like Rita Hayworth?"

People used to say that quite often, eons ago. Not lately though."

"That's only because she no longer looks as good as you."

Marie laughed then sprang to her feet and wrote something on a piece of paper. O'Reardon also got up. "Here, take this. Hopefully, Brian, you'll call me before our next encounter, so I'm not in a bathrobe when you arrive."

O'Reardon beamed as he headed toward the door. "No bathrobe. Now *that's* something worth coming back for."

Falco was sitting behind the wheel lighting a cigarette when his partner came down. They were silent for a while as they drove toward the Marchetti home on Flushing Avenue. Finally, Falco spoke, "So *Brian*, you remember what happened the last time you screwed a potential witness?"

He'd expected Falco to say just that. "Are you referring to that broad from Williamsburg?"

"Why? Were there others?"

"First of all, that was a mercy fuck."

"A what?"

"Her old man was doing five years in Louisville, and she was in need of a little comfort. Hell, and I thought you were a compassionate guy, Rich."

"Oh, but I am. From what I remember, though, Internal Affairs wasn't."

"Marie Werner is different. Tell me she isn't the sexiest woman in all of Maspeth."

"She just may be, but she's also trouble. I know you see that. I also know she's not your type."

"Hey, I'm a few weeks from retirement. I'll be on my boat stumbling over beer bottles before Internal Affairs gets halfway through their investigation."

Falco laughed as they pulled up in front of the Rannazzisi bakery. "This is the place. Now if you get the urge to comfort *this* woman, her father will cut your balls off and cook them in his sauce."

"It'll be the best sauce those wops ever had."

Falco just shook his head as he exited the car. They rang the Marchetti bell and waited for an answer. There was none. Lina emerged from the bakery to ask them their business.

"We're looking for Laura Marchetti, know if she's home?"

"You justa missed her. She tooka the kids to Staten Island to see their Nonno and Nana. You know, you shouldn't park there, you'll get a ticket."

"Thank you, Senora," Falco said. "We'll come back another time."

Lina eyed them as they got into their car and drove off.

CHAPTER 14

The Eldorado, with Laura, the kids, and her brother Mario behind the wheel, pulled up to the massive Tudor-style house. Its southern-facing facade looked regal, basking in the bright sun.

Angela looked at her Uncle Mario and said, "It looks different."

"Grandpa had an addition put on a year ago. See, it only shows how long it's been since you and Tuddy have been here."

Laura's brother Mario, just turned forty, was divorced and living here with his parents. His prior address, as of six months ago, was Attica Correctional Facility in upstate New York. He'd served eighteen months of a three-year term for an attempted hijacking of an electronics shipment out of Idlewild Airport. His wartime Bronze Star kept him from getting the same five-to-ten year sentence his co-defendant received.

"Angelina! Paulie!" Their grandmother greeted them with kisses at the door. "Laura, how are you, honey?"

"I'm doing well, Ma. Where's Dad?"

"He went to the butcher. He should be back any minute."

Rosa Paparelli was a small woman in her mid-seventies who, despite their money, did all the cooking and, until recently, all the cleaning as well in their oversized house. She and John Paparelli had come to New York from Sicily as newlyweds in 1910.

"Did Mikey have the baby yet? What's taking so long?"

"Pattie's not due for a while, Ma. They said to say hello."

"Mom, come and look!" an excited Angela called out. Laura and Tuddy went into the sunken living room and found Angela gawking at the TV.

"*It's in color!* Watch this." Angela pointed the remote control and changed the channel.

"Wow, cool. Let me do it," Paulie said as he wrestled the gadget from his sister.

"You're gonna break it!" Laura shouted.

Paulie found a football game and that was the end of his channel hopping.

"Uncle Mario, I never knew Southern Cal's uniforms were maroon. I always thought they were gray."

"I'll bet you thought the grass was gray too."

"Mom, can we get a color TV?"

Laura ignored her son's request.

"Where the hell are my grandchildren?"

Everyone flocked to the front door. The robust old man with a full head of gray hair put the brown bags on the floor and began hugging the kids. "Where's Tuddy?" Angela cringed as his two-day-old stubble tore at her cheek. She could also smell the cigar smoke embedded in him.

"How are you, Dad?" Laura asked.

"Aside from my sore back, enlarged prostrate, and bum knee I couldn't be better."

"But the flu's all better, right?"

"Yeah, Laura. I'm sorry I missed Sal's funeral. I couldn't get out of bed that morning, even if the house was on fire."

"It's okay, Pop, as long as you got to see him at the wake. It was probably those ferry trips that made you sick."

"We won't *have* to take that shitty ferry, if they ever finish the goddamn bridge," Mario said.

"Did you get the veal cutlets, Giovanni?"

"I told that fat bastard to save me a good cut, Rosa, but all he had left was the shoulder."

"That's alright, the shoulder makes better gravy anyway."

Laura was reminded of her late husband's incomprehension of her father's simple lifestyle. She too, found it bewildering that a man of such power in the underworld was just a simple elderly man at home. He kicked Tuddy out of his chair and watched the football game with the kids. Laura went to join him in the living room while her mother got busy with the cooking.

"I'll be right back to help you, Ma."

"Grandpa, this TV is awesome," Tuddy said.

"I wanted to send one to your house, Tud, but your father . . ." The old man saw the look on Laura's face and stopped mid-sentence. "But they're not so great, you have to get up and adjust the color every time you change the channel."

"They watch too much television as it is," Laura added.

"So, how's Mr. Wall Street doing?"

"Mikey's doing fine, Dad, you and Mom should see their new house."

"They like Long Island? There's nothing but farms out there."

"It's getting built up a lot. You remember it from the forties. It's not like that anymore."

"I like Staten Island better. What are you and the kids gonna do now, Laura, stay in Maspeth?"

"I'm not sure, Dad . . . Kids, go help Grandma in the kitchen for a few minutes."

Tuddy and Angela grumbled as they made their way out of earshot.

"You know, Laura, I never interfered while your husband was alive. I knew he was an honest, hard-working man. I also knew he didn't agree with *our thing* and kept the kids away as much as possible." He shrugged his shoulders. "Eh, whadya gonna do, he's their father. But now it's different. He's gone and his . . . what do you call it . . . *legacy*, is less than adequate. At the funeral home you mentioned the life insurance policy, how much is it for?"

Laura didn't hesitate. "Ten thousand. Mike is going to invest it for me, and he says we'll do very well."

"Okay, that's good except I don't see how ten thousand dollars is going to make you do *very well*."

"Mike seems confident that his plan will take care of everything."

"Well, if there's anything you need, you just let me know."

"Thank you, Dad, but I know you're already burdened with this FBI stuff and lawyer fees." Laura was aware of the heat being brought upon her father and the Cosa Nostra in general. First with the turncoat Joe Valachi congressional hearings and more recently with Attorney General Robert Kennedy's crusade against organized crime.

"Don't you worry about that. Lawyers are bloodsuckers but the good ones are worth every nickel. But that's neither here nor there . . . like I said, if you need anything . . ."

"There *is* one thing I need, Dad. Advice." Laura looked behind her to make sure the kids weren't nearby. "I have a dilemma and I just need to talk to someone about it."

Her father, sensing the urgency in her voice, lowered the TV and leaned in. "What is it, Lauri girl?"

"I don't know where to begin . . . Remember that problem Sal and I had when the kids were little?"

"No, what problem?"

"When I brought the kids, and we stayed here for a week."

"Oh yeah, that thing with the *putana* from his bank."

"Yes, her name was Marie Werner. I remember how you told me that it's natural for men to occasionally stray and it means nothing. You and Mom even convinced me to return home."

Angela called in from the kitchen. **"Mom, can we come in now?"**

"In a minute honey -- The night Sal died; the craziest thing happened."

Laura went on to explain the whole incident, starting with the phone call and his meeting outside with Marie, the money in the cellar then gone in a flash. She told him how distraught Sal was that evening, just before his heart attack. After telling the entire story to her stone-faced father, she said to him, "I've kept this inside of me without telling a soul for weeks now." She started to quietly sob. "I have no idea what it means. Was he back with her? Was he with her all along? Was the money part of the robbery cash? Where did it disappear to? *Dad, it's all driving me crazy!*" Laura let it out. Her crying got a little louder as her father moved alongside and put his arms around her. Paulie saw that something was going on in there but stayed put in the kitchen. His sister and grandmother were pre-occupied rolling meatballs.

The old man hadn't held his daughter like that since she was twelve.

She composed herself and looked at her glassy-eyed father. "Does any of it make sense to you, Dad? Sometimes to me, it makes more sense to think it never happened, that I imagined the whole thing, or it was a crazy dream, or something . . ."

"Laura, knowing your husband all these years I probably wouldn't believe it ever happened either, but did you see today's paper?"

She lifted her head from her hands and said, "No, why?"

He walked into his den and got the *Daily Mirror*. He started, "'The police suspect most of the loot was taken by someone beside the—'"

Laura snatched the paper from him before he could finish. It was already folded into the article. She slumped into her seat as she read it.

"Have the cops been to see you?" her father asked.

"No, no one has," the trembling woman replied. "Dad, what could possibly have happened?"

"It sounds to me that Sal and this . . . broad, pulled a job. They could have somehow set it up, maybe even got her husband bumped off, who knows, honey? What else could explain it?"

"I thought about that, Dad. The only thing that doesn't make sense is if Sal knew he was so sick why would he plan this with *her*. It's not that they were going to run away together."

"Do you think that money was supposed to be for you and the kids, or at least some of it?"

"I did, but I thought if that money was supposed to be for us then why on earth wouldn't he tell me about it? I could see him not wanting the kids to know but he would *have* to tell me, don't you think?"

"I don't know. What I *do* know is that this woman has what belongs to you. You give me her name and address and we'll see if we can convince her to be reasonable."

Angela walked in on them. "Ma, I'm going out for a walk."

"It's freezing out there, where are you going?"

"That park Dad used to take us to. It's only two blocks."

"Paulie, go with your sister. I don't want her walking in a strange neighborhood by herself.

Grumbling, he put his coat on and walked out with her. Rosa called to her grandchildren, "Don't get lost, you two, we're going to eat soon, and button those coats! Tuddy go with them." He looked up from his magazine, "Uh, uh Nana, it's freezing out there."

Laura turned her attention back to her father. "Pop, I must admit I was angry when I found out the money was taken out of the cellar, but now, after reading that article, I really don't want any part of it. The police are going to be looking everywhere and they're *not* going to find it in my house."

"Listen to me, Laura, just give me the information I need. I'll take care of the rest. *You* don't get involved, and don't speak a word about this to nobody."

Laura held her head back and sighed. "Okay, but promise you'll be careful, and also promise *no one will get hurt.*"

"Don't you worry about a thing, sweetheart."

CHAPTER 15

Brian O'Reardon spent his day off in the woodworking shop he'd set up in his garage. Building furniture was his favorite pastime when he wasn't on his boat. He had Marie Werner on his mind all day. After a few beers calling her made perfect sense.

"Marie, hi, it's your favorite public servant."

"Brian, what a nice surprise . . . *Or is it?* Is this business or pleasure?"

"Well, since my business visit was a pleasure, I don't know what you'd call this."

"How about a nice surprise then?" Marie said.

"Listen, have you had dinner yet?" Brian asked.

"Uh, no. It's only four o'clock. I've got a few years before I start having dinner this early."

He laughed. "Good, have you ever had the chicken parmigiana at Vitelli's?"

"No Brian, can't say that I have."

"Well, how about a nice quiet Sunday evening dinner with me?"

"Tonight? Ohhh, Sunday nights are my favorite time to just relax and watch Ed Sullivan and the Sunday Night Movie."

"All right, I wouldn't want you to miss Ed Sullivan. How 'bout I bring the dinner to you. What kind of appetizer would you like with it?"

"My, you are the persistent one."

"I recommend the baked clams."

"Are they breaded?" she joked.

"With the finest semolina this side of heaven."

"Well, I guess I can't pass that up, now can I?"

"Great, I'll see you around seven?"

"Okay, Lieutenant Brian, seven o'clock is fine."

O'Reardon hung up and pumped his fist into the air. This was not his usual get laid and go home date. He was genuinely looking forward to being in this woman's company. At 7:10 he showed up with the large bag of Italian food. Marie greeted him wearing a red dress that didn't hide any of her beauty pageant curves.

"I hope you're hungry, lady."

"Starving, please come in."

He watched her as she closed the door behind him.

"Can I get you a drink? Martinis are my specialty."

"That sounds good, with vodka please." O'Reardon unpacked the bag, and they sat settled in at the already-set kitchen table.

"So, tell me about yourself, mister."

"Okay, I'm fifty-four and retiring in three weeks after thirty years on the force."

"Married, separated, divorced?"

"Actually, I'm a widower. My wife and daughter died in a car accident ten years ago, April 3rd, '54, to be exact."

"Oh, I'm so sorry, that must have been awful. Are there any other kids?"

"No, Kelly was the only one. She would have been twenty-five last Saturday."

"I'll bet she was pretty."

He opened his wallet and pulled out a frayed picture of her.

"Ohhh, absolutely stunning."

"How about you, children?"

"Yes, twin girls, both recently married. They didn't make the same mistake I did, they waited until they were in their twenties."

"How old were you when you got married?"

"I was just out of high school when I met Chubby. We married when I was eighteen. He was thirty-two. I got pregnant, we got hitched." Her candor caught Brian by surprise.

"That happens. More common than you'd think," he said.

"I suppose. Ya know, we managed to have a pretty decent marriage considering we were never in love with each other. I must say though, the man remained faithful for twenty-seven years. Umm, this cheese is delicious."

"Did *you*?" he asked.

"Did I what?"

"Remain faithful."

"Oh. The first ten years I pretty much did. Sal Marchetti, of all people, was actually the cause of my first, shall we say, *indiscretion*.

"Let me guess, he seduced you on that couch in the bank lunchroom."

Marie laughed aloud. "No, *Manny* seduced me on the couch in the break room, Sal happened in the St. George Hotel . . . and you might even say I seduced *him*."

Brian now realized that the martinis were the reason for her candor. He found himself feeling disturbed by the Manny admission.

"How long ago did these things happen?"

"Well, first of all you're talking about apples and oranges. I really felt something for Sal. I guess I always have in some weird way. I could never understand why; the man was the epitome of mediocrity and not likely to get mistaken for Paul Newman."

"So, what happened?"

"After a couple of dates, he ended it. I think he caught himself straying too far from his mediocre lifestyle and corrected it."

"And Manny?"

"This is starting to sound like an interrogation, Officer." She got up and fixed herself another martini. "Can I get you another?"

"Actually, I'd like a beer if you have any."

"I have Rheingold?"

"Perfect! No, Marie, I'm not interrogating you, I'm just interested is all."

She returned with the drinks. "The Manny incident actually occurred *years* later, near the end of my employment there, a coupla years ago, yeah, in '62. The bank was closed, and he asked me to remain and help him with the quarterly report. We sat down in the back room with all the ledgers spread across the table and out of nowhere he started to rub my back and then my neck. Then his hands started to go elsewhere and when I briefly moved away, he got more aggressive. I soon gave up resisting and it just happened, in the blink of an eye. Before I knew it, he was on top of me on the couch. A few minutes later he was done."

Now Brian was totally unsettled. "He raped you?"

"Not really, I never screamed or resisted even."

"Marie, that doesn't matter. I knew I never liked that spick. I even told my partner so. I'm going to—"

"Forget it Brian, it was a long time ago, and honestly, nothing lost, and a lot gained. I got favorable treatment afterward. I know that sounds horrible."

"You know it's not too late, you can still file charges . . ."

"*Again,* forget it. I shouldn't have said anything. But I must say, finally talking about it strangely makes me feel . . . I don't know . . . somewhat relieved."

"Imagine how relieved you would feel if I locked up the bastard."

"Brian, *please*, it's not happening. I soon after left the job and erased it from my memory,

"Soon after? You mean *two years* after!

She shrugged.

He thought it best to drop the subject. They finished their dinner and O'Reardon started to help her clear the table.

"I'll get that, you relax," she said. "As a matter of fact, go inside and put on channel two. It's about time for Ed Sullivan."

Brian walked into the living room wondering what the meaning of his offering to help with the dishes was. He'd *never* done that before. He put on the television and settled back on the couch. After a few minutes Marie came in with another beer and martini. She sat next to him as Ed was introducing Eddie Fisher. The two engaged in a conversation about Fisher and Elizabeth Taylor. Brian thought about the similarity between Marie and Elizabeth Taylor, then remembered, nope, Rita Hayworth. During their talk Brian dropped his hand onto her shoulder and Marie instinctively folded her hands in her lap. He was about to move it off her shoulder, thinking she wasn't ready for this, when she instead began to stroke the top of his hand. O'Reardon felt like a schoolboy all over again.

"So, tell me, Brian, I still don't understand why you came over yesterday morning. Did you really want to question me about the case, or did you have ulterior motives?"

Her hand was now rubbing his knee playfully as she spoke. He assumed she knew about the new developments in the case.

"Truthfully Marie, with this so-called missing money we are expected to speak with everyone remotely connected with the case. It's just routine stuff."

Marie was trying to remain cool while her heart pounded with apprehension. "Oh? *So called missing money?*"

"I'm sorry, I assumed you read about it."

Marie was feeling the drinks and was not very clear-headed. She struggled to remain lucid. "I'm not much of a newshound. Tell me about it!"

She knew the money that Sal had given her was half of what they're seeking. She was feeling paranoid. She wondered if O'Reardon had found out she was given the fifty thousand and was just on this date to find out where it was. *Stay cool, don't blow it,* she thought. She began playing with his hair and then ran her forefinger along the length of his ear. Brian was short and to the point.

"We're pretty sure the holdup men only got fifty thousand from the job."

"Did you say *fifty* thousand?"

"Yes, and if that's true, that would leave a ton of money unaccounted for," he said.

"Uh, exactly how much is a *ton* of money?"

"Well, my guess it's about two fifty."

"As in two hundred and fifty *thousand*?" Marie gasped and again composed herself. *That bastard lied to me. A hundred thousand, my ass.*

"Listen lady, don't you concern yourself with any of this. I didn't come here to talk shop."

Brian leaned over and kissed her on the lips. Marie found his words reassuring and returned his kiss with the same eagerness. After the kiss he kept his eyes closed and exhaled with a slight smile. "There's something I'd like to tell you, Marie."

She braced herself, still feeling nervous, especially since the fifty thousand was in a drawer not twenty feet from where they sat. "I haven't felt this way about someone for quite some time."

She was taken by surprise by this declaration. "Brian, what a sweet thing to say," was the best she could manage.

He liked hearing her say his name, though disappointed she didn't return the emotion verbally.

They kissed again. This time his hands ventured to seek out new territory. Marie relaxed herself and allowed him to continue. Her breathing grew more rapid, and he knew they were beyond the point of no return when he felt her hand reach for his zipper. After a few minutes of clumsy clothes-tugging, Marie got to her feet, took Brian's hand, and led him toward her bedroom. He stopped in his tracks. "What about the puppet?" He deadpanned motioning toward the TV.

She laughed, "*That's Topo Gigio,* he's on Ed's show every other week."

"Alright, then I guess I could wait." Now they both laughed as she yanked him into her bedroom. His head was about to explode as he watched her remove her dress. She then sat on the edge of the bed and began to detach her garter from her nylon stockings. She looked up at him while unhooking the second one.

"Are you planning on joining me?"

He realized he was standing there still fully dressed watching her in a trance.

"You'll have to excuse me for staring. You are the most beautiful woman I've ever been with."

He began by unbuttoning his shirt. They both reached their underwear and stopped undressing for a few seconds waiting for the other to go to the next level. Brian, wishing he had stayed on that diet last summer, preferred to get under the covers before removing the rest, but remained standing. Marie took the initiative and removed her bra, then slid down her panties and paused there a moment, allowing him to take it all in before she glided under the bed sheets. He tore off his t-shirt and boxer shorts and slid in alongside her.

Her immediate reaction to his touch at first startled him. A few caresses later he was sure the folks downstairs were saying *"that didn't take long!"* She was the most amazing woman he'd ever been with. Some thirty minutes later they were both lying face up speechless. Her because she felt awkward and a bit guilty. Him because he was wondering if he could be falling in love with this woman. Brian leaned over and rested his cheek on her breast and held her.

She spoke, finally, "I hope you don't get the wrong impression of me."

"Not at all. I think you're amazing." He meant it.

She brushed her hand through his hair but again didn't return the compliment. After another period of silence Marie spoke in her most innocent voice and asked, "Brian, I'm sorry! I'm just bursting with curiosity, where do you think that money is?"

He was annoyed with the timing of the question but answered it anyway. "Well, the only logical person to suspect is your friend Sal. However, knowing what I do about him, I'm more inclined to believe that if he *did* misinform us, it was done on behalf of his bank."

"I don't follow you, why would he do that?"

"Just about every victim tends to exaggerate their losses by about twenty percent after a holdup or burglary. By the time they're done with the insurance company they'll even manage to turn a capital crime like this one into a profit. Banks are no different; the only thing that puzzles me in *this* case is the *thieves* got the short end."

"I tend to agree with you about Sal. He would never do anything like that for personal gain. That man was blindly loyal to those people and probably reported whatever amount they instructed him to."

"Yeah, that's probably what happened."

"Now that Sal's gone, Brian, how do you—"

He finally cut her short, "Marie I have spent the past weeks thinking about nothing but this damn heist. I'm now lying nude and aroused next to a very beautiful woman and the *last* thing I want to do is talk shop."

He started running his hand over her again.

She knew she'd asked one question too many. "I'm sorry, Brian, but I'm sure you understand my interest in all this."

"I do, gorgeous, and surely you understand my interest in all *this*."

His hand reached down along her thigh, and she involuntarily parted her long legs slightly while her breathing again grew rapid.

She closed her eyes and whispered, "What case?"

CHAPTER 16

The girls at the bank each brought in the same newspaper article. They all had separate theories. Only Dana thought Sal was directly responsible.

"I think Sal set the whole thing up. I know you ladies loved him but let's face it, if he wasn't in on the thing, those guys would not have left without taking *all* the money. Mark my words, his wife and kids are not going to be living on Flushing Avenue much longer. He left them quite a nest egg."

Paula spoke up, "Dana, if you knew Sal like me and Rose do, you would not believe *for a second* he would do anything like that." Manny emerged from his office just as the first few customers were let in. He motioned for Dana to come into his office. She nervously entered just as Manny was settling behind his desk. "Please close the door."

"I really would prefer it to stay open, Manny."

He impatiently got up and closed it himself. Dana remained standing beside the entrance.

"Dana, I'm sorry for what happened Friday. Things haven't been going well with my wife and I haven't been myself the last couple of days. I thank God you were able to make me see how wrong I was."

"It's *me* you better thank; I could have had you arrested for what you did. Just so you know, I spent the whole weekend contemplating going to the police. If you so much as touch me again, I swear to you, I will."

"Aw come on, you're making it a big deal, all I did was brush against—"

"*I mean it,* it better not happen again!"

"Okay, I really appreciate your understanding that it was merely an unfortunate mistake on my part and be assured it will never happen again."

Dana shook her head. "You never fail to amaze me, Mr. Figueroa." She turned toward the door.

"Oh, Dana one more thing, I heard you out there a minute ago. Do you *really* think Sal has that money?

"Yes."

"Is there anything you might have heard or have knowledge of that the bank might want to know about?"

"No, it was just my own thinking, however I *do* have *other* information I'm sure your bank would like to know about."

Manny grimaced as Dana abruptly exited.

* * *

"Let's try to avoid the old lady this time," O'Reardon said as they walked toward the Marchetti apartment building. The bakery was busy, and the detectives were able to enter the hallway unnoticed. Laura answered the bell, and they headed upstairs.

"Good morning, Mrs. Marchetti, I'm Detective Lieutenant O'Reardon and this is my partner, Detective Sergeant Falco."

Laura was not surprised by their visit. "Please come in."

They sat at the kitchen table. Falco looked around at the dreary wallpaper and faded linoleum.

"Would you gentlemen like some coffee?"

"No thank you," O'Reardon said.

"First off, we'd like to extend our sincere condolences to you and your family," Falco said.

"Thank you. May I ask why you gentlemen are here?"

"We just have a few routine questions; however, if you feel it is too soon, we could come back at a later date," O'Reardon said.

"No, it's okay, the sooner we put this whole thing behind us and get on with our lives, the better."

"Great. Then I'll get to the point. There appears to be a large amount of money unaccounted for. I suppose you've seen news reports of this nature."

O'Reardon knew he was walking a fine line and would have preferred not to further upset the grieving widow.

"Was your husband under any stress . . . or better yet, was his behavior during the time leading up to the robbery out of the ordinary in any way?"

"Well, his health was failing, and he should have been in bed instead of out in winter weather—other than that he was totally rational."

"How would you describe your financial situation?" Falco asked.

"Like most people these days, we go from paycheck to paycheck and try to keep up with the bills. Now with my husband gone it's going to be even more difficult to do it." She looked at the senior detective. "Tell me officer, is my husband a *suspect* in any of this?"

"Well Laura, may I call you Laura?"

She nodded.

"At this point we're certain of nothing, and we can't rule anything or anyone out," O'Reardon said.

Falco then asked, "We understand you have four kids, your oldest son, what does he do?"

"Michael works for a brokerage firm on Wall Street."

"Will he be handling your financial affairs now?"

"Yes, for the most part, what little there is . . . he's investing my husband's life insurance policy for us. With God's help, that will make the difference on whether we'll be able to sustain ourselves further."

O'Reardon leaned forward and rested his arms on the table. "How was your visit to Staten Island on Saturday?"

Falco spun his head toward his partner.

Laura was stunned and fought to compose herself. "Did you people follow me there?"

"No, we get seasick too easily," was all the lieutenant said.

Laura was now visibly upset. "My father, regardless of his lifestyle, is *still* my father *and* the grandfather of my children. Furthermore, I do not care for the nature of your questions. So, gentleman, with crime rampant in this neighborhood I'm sure you two have more urgent places to be."

Falco felt uncomfortable. "The lieutenant only meant—"

O'Reardon popped out of his chair. "You're correct ma'am, we do have a busy schedule ahead. Thank you for your cooperation."

Laura looked for Falco's reaction, sensing the disorder between them, but there was none. He simply put his coat on and the two headed for the door.

"Thanks again," Falco said before exiting.

In the hallway O'Reardon smiled at his partner. "I've been thrown out of better places."

Falco chose to ignore the remark.

A few minutes later in the car O'Reardon broke the silence, "There was a reason for that."

"Brian, that woman is a churchgoing widow. You *can't* really think she has anything to do with this. Why did you hit her with that?"

"Rich, I actually found her compelling. Ya know, she reminds me of Jenny, my wife . . . a lot! Not as much physically, but the way she carries herself. Weird. Anyway, the captain has been on our asses to find a direction with all this, and I can't say I blame him. I made it clear to him that we don't know where the fuck to go because it all dead-ended and I mean that literally. The only two people from the bank that were in that vault are dead and the three holdup men are facing life and still insisting on the fifty thousand-dollar take. That leaves two widows and three bank tellers. It's time to stir the pot and see what boils over. That's why I riled her up like I did."

"Expecting what?"

"I want her to wonder how we knew she was at her father's house. The old lady downstairs telling us was actually a blessing. Ideally, she'll think her father's house is bugged and we heard something incriminating." O'Reardon then looked at Falco. "Who knows, maybe she'll panic and point the finger at someone."

"Like who?" Falco said, impressed with his partner.

"The bank officials, the bank guard, the armored car guys, who the fuck knows?"

"Or her husband!" Falco said.

"*Yeah, or her husband!* By the way," O'Reardon said, "under that housecoat that woman has a decent body and not a bad face!"

Falco threw his arms up. "I knew that plain-Jane was more your type!"

"Well yeah, those are the ones that surprise you in the sack."

As they were pulling up in front of the precinct Falco asked, "So Brian, are you still planning on making a move on the other one, or is your attention now diverted?"

"By the *other one,* are you referring to Marie Werner?"

"Affirmative."

"Actually, the move was already made. I was there for dinner last night."

Falco looked up at the car ceiling. "Did you screw her?"

Normally, O'Reardon would simply answer yes, no, or almost. This time, however, he resented that Marie was referred to in the same manner as his other conquests, which included everything from gin mill pickups to vice arrests.

"Is that all you think I look for in a woman? We just had dinner and watched Ed Sullivan."

Falco sensed his partner's manner was out of character when talking about Marie. "Sounds like this one's got a hold on you, pal."

"She's just different from the others."

Falco tried to keep a straight face, "You mean she's different than say … Cockeyed Mamie?" He was referring to an older prostitute whose oral expertise Brian had succumbed to in the back seat of his unmarked police car.

"You'll never let that one go, will you?"

"I remember you said you couldn't tell if she was looking at your face or your dick."

"Do you remember me saying it was the best damn blowjob I ever had?"

"No, the only other thing I recall was you saying it was a mistake in judgment," the smirking Falco said.

"My only *mistake* was telling *you* about it."

* * *

"Yo, Junior! What the fuck you doin' here?" Whitey excitedly called out when he spotted his friend escorted past his cell carrying his linen and blanket.

"They sent me back down here. Fuck if I know why."

"*All right my man,* I'll catch up with you later," Whitey yelled.

As soon as the fifth-floor cell doors were opened for the lunch meal, Whitey hurried down the corridor and found his friend. They embraced and followed the crowd to the chow hall.

"How you feel, Whitey?"

"I gotta say, one good thing about this place is no fuckin' drugs. I feel truly healthy for the first time since my navy days."

"Yeah, me too, but you know what, if I had a bag of smack and some works, I'd do it in a heartbeat."

"Shit, Junior, that goes without saying. Heard anything from Hector?"

"All I know is he's still on the ninth floor. I didn't see him in church Sunday—you either. What happened, you two giving up God?"

"I wanted to go but Sandy came Sunday morning."

"How is she doin'?"

"I don't know man, she seemed weird. Put off, like. I don't think she's planning on waiting around for me."

"*Sandy?* Shit, you two been together since you were kids, there's no way she'd be with another dude."

"Junior, we're facing minimum ten to twenty. She really can't be expected to stick around that long. I just don't want to know shit about it when she hooks up with another old man."

"No matter what she does when you're in here, the day you hit the streets I guarantee her ass will be parked outside waiting for you."

"I won't be holding my breath."

Junior finished his sandwich. "Oh shit, I forgot! Did you see the *News* Saturday?"

"No!"

"We were in it again. They *finally* gave up thinking we got that bullshit money. *Conio,* I left the paper in my old cell upstairs."

"What did it say? There was no fuckin' three hundred thousand, right?"

"Wrong Whitey, looks like there *was* three hundred big ones. They just finding out now it wasn't *us* that got it, is all! The paper said something about them questioning the bank people and shit. You *said* those *ladrones,* are bigger thieves than us."

Whitey shook his head. "At least now they'll leave *us* alone about it."

* * *

"*Michael!* Why didn't you call me and tell me you were coming?" Laura asked.

"I wanted to surprise you. Where's Tuddy and Angela?"

"Angela's over at her friend Julie's house and I have no idea where your brother is. After dinner his friends picked him up and off he went. What brings you here on a school night?"

"This does." Mike reached in his jacket pocket and pulled out an envelope.

Laura saw the envelope was from his brokerage company, Lehman Brothers. From it she pulled out a stack of twenty-dollar bills.

"Oh my God, Michael, what is this?"

"One thousand, one hundred forty dollars. The first dividend on that stock you bought."

She unfolded the enclosed paper. Mike had even gone through the trouble of faking a receipt showing an IBM stock dividend for that amount.

"That's wonderful! I didn't expect it to pay off so quickly!"

"Hey, did I tell you it was a sure thing or what? Before long, there should be more where that came from."

Laura was beside herself. She popped out of her chair and hugged her son. "I've been so worried how we're going to pay the bills in the coming months. This is a godsend, Mikey!"

"Do me a favor, Mom, and don't say anything about this to *anyone.*"

"All right . . . Why?"

"Well, I wouldn't want it getting back to my company. I'm supposed to get family investments approved by my boss. I'd probably lose my job if they found out." Mike sensed his mother's change in persona. "Ma! You didn't say anything, did you?"

"Nobody that's going to contact your company. The police were here and—"

"The police? Why were *they* here?"

"Just routine questioning, they said. It's nothing really. Apparently, there's a discrepancy between Dad's bank and the police investigation." Laura was regretting telling him but thought he certainly would know. "I thought you must have heard about it by now."

Mike got very tense but hid it from his mother. "Ma, we get the *Long Island Press* out there. They report on smashed mailboxes." He wanted to ask her all kinds of questions about what the police said but decided it was best to appear unconcerned. Remarkably, his mother also had the same idea. He finally relented and asked, "So you told them about my investments?"

"Well, they asked if I had an alternate source of income, so I told them you'd invested Dad's life insurance."

"Mom, you really don't have to answer their questions. It's best if you don't because they're likely to find a glitch at some point."

"What glitches? We certainly have nothing to hide."

"I know that. But trust me, the less said the better. Again, the less said the better! Should you feel something is too personal, I'm sure they would understand if you chose not to discuss it." Mike nonchalantly leaned back and clasped his hands behind his head. "So, what's this *discrepancy* all about anyway?"

"According to the newspapers—"

"What newspapers, when?"

"The *Daily News* is married to this story and even the *Times* had something. They seem to have taken a special interest in all this and have a constant stream of follow-up articles. On Saturday they said there's a difference of two hundred and fifty thousand dollars between the amount reported by your dad's bank and the amount found in the robbers' possession."

Mike remained calm. "Well, whadya expect, the police can't recover the money, so it was never stolen. How convenient." Mike made a mental note of the two hundred and fifty thousand number, confirming what his father had told him that night on the phone. *Why was there only two hundred grand in the bags*, he again wondered. *Who could possibly have the other fifty?*

"Have you eaten, Michael?"

"I'm not really hungry, I had a late lunch. Also, Patti's planning on going out tonight for dinner so I better get home."

"You know, Mike, I don't think it's a good idea for her to be drinking alcohol while she's pregnant."

"Why do you say that?"

"I read something in *Readers Digest* that said drinking and possibly even smoking can be bad for the babies."

"That's ridiculous. Listen, I gotta get going. Give the kids a hug for me."

Laura again hugged her son. "What would I do without you?"

CHAPTER 17

John Paparelli arrived two hours earlier than his usual time at the "Democratic Club" on Victory Boulevard. The early start was because he had to go over to Brooklyn for a two o'clock meeting with Vito Genovese regarding the Joey Gallo airport fiasco last week. Before he made that dreaded trip, he wanted to tie up a few loose ends at home.

Fat Frankie Musselli greeted him at the door. "John, if I knew you were coming this early, I would have had the cold cuts already here."

"That's all right, Frankie, I can't stay long, I gotta catch that fucking ferry."

"Oh shit, that's right, you got that sit-down with Vito today."

"Yeah, what a pain in the ass Gallo turned out to be. Is the Monk here?"

"He's inside."

Enzo "The Monk" Distefano was a made soldier in the Genovese Family. Whenever Johnny Papa wanted a personal job done, he always entrusted it to him. Enzo had had a large bald spot in the back of his head since his twenties, earning him his hated nickname.

"John, how are you?" the Monk said as he kissed his boss on the cheek.

"Have a seat, Monk, I got something I want you to do for me. Where's Ragusa?"

"You forgot? Today's his hearing on that numbers thing; he should be around later though."

"Oh yeah. Okay, I want you and him to go to Queens and visit someone for me this weekend."

"Sure John, who's the lucky guy?"

"It's a broad this time."

"You're kidding? A woman? Who?"

"You remember that bank job in Queens a couple of weeks ago?

"The one where the guard got iced?"

"Yeah, turns out there's a ton of money still out there from that job and this broad either has it or at least knows where it is. I want you and Richie to *convince* her to give it up."

"Was she in with them?"

"No, word is they only got a small amount. I don't know what went down, the rest somehow wound up this broad's hands. This woman is the bank guard's widow. I swear to God, can't make this shit up! Her name is Marie . . . Warner or something." He handed him a slip of paper. "Here's her address."

"How the hell would she—?"

"Don't even ask, I just *said* I don't know what the fuck happened. I just have it from a very good source this woman has that money, and it should have gone to someone else. Someone more deserving."

"Okay, boss. The only thing is I never put the muscle on a woman before. Just how far do we take it?"

Paparelli thought for a while. "Fuck do I know, smack her in the mouth or something. That should be enough . . . just get it done."

"*Minchia*, this is one for the books."

The boss stood up and grabbed his coat. "Oh yeah, and another thing, this has nothing to do with *our thing*, you understand. This is a private matter. This money is not ours. Make sure Richie also understands this. I don't want to have to fucking explain in Brooklyn why the old man didn't get his cut. *Capeesh*? So not a word!"

"Sure boss, don't worry, we'll take care of it."

* * *

O'Reardon had been looking forward to this night all week long. He felt as if he was back in high school. He pulled up in front of Marie's brownstone and she motioned to him from her second-floor window.

"I'll be right down" is what he figured she was mouthing.

After ten minutes she emerged from the entrance wearing an exquisite fox coat that draped down to her knees. O'Reardon hopped out of his Thunderbird and opened the door for her. Before entering she paused and gave him a soft kiss. He could only smile as he watched her coat and skirt slide up her legs while she got in the car.

"You look stunning," he said.

"Thank you, Brian, you look mighty fine yourself, sir. So where is this secretive place you're taking me to?"

"You'll see, I hope you're hungry."

He headed into the Midtown Tunnel and emerged onto 33rd Street. Thanks to the twenty-five-degree weather the streets of Manhattan were deserted. O'Reardon pulled up in front of Sardi's restaurant. It was a no-parking zone, but he simply lowered his sun visor, displaying his NYPD credentials.

"Are we going in *here*?"

"Yes, you know this place?"

"Know it? Half the actors in *Screen Magazine* are photographed here. Oh, Brian this is so thoughtful of you." Marie put her arm in his and rested her head on his shoulder as they walked toward the front door. He felt like a million bucks.

Although the streets were empty, Sardi's was bustling.

"Do you have a reservation, sir?"

"Uh, yes we do." He discreetly flashed his gold shield.

"Sure thing, right this way, sir."

They were led to a small table along the railing. Settling into her seat Marie looked around for celebrities then settled for their caricatures that aligned the walls.

"That's Groucho Marx, Charlie Chaplin, Bette Davis. Who's that one?" she asked.

"That looks like Peter Lorre."

"I think you're right," she said.

Marie had two rum and Cokes before the appetizer was even brought out. O'Reardon waited for dinner prior to ordering her a third. They chatted about movies and life in the city while waiting for their sirloins.

During dinner he asked her, "Are you planning on ever returning to work?"

"Why would I do that?"

"Well, it might be good for you to keep busy."

"Oh! Is that what you think, oh wise one? Maybe I should call Manny and ask for my job back. Is that what you'd like?" Her remark caught him off guard. He saw that alcohol didn't agree with her as she finished the third drink.

He chuckled to play it down. "What is it they say, 'Idle hands is the devil's workshop?'"

She corrected him, "*Are* the devil's workshop."

"I'm sorry?"

"Idle hands *are* the devil's workshop, and the devil can kiss my ass." She whirled around. **"Waiter!"**

He was dismayed by this side of her. He also felt a bit intimidated, which was something no other woman had managed before. Had this happened with any other date she might have been on her way home before dinner was served, perhaps even on her own.

"Another Bacardi and Coke and a beer for my friend here."

"Schaefer, please."

"So, Brian, have you guys tracked down the loot yet?"

"Nope, not yet, Marie," he answered condescendingly.

Marie was getting frustrated with his responses to her inquiries. She had no one to help her get what she considered the rest of her half of the loot. She even considered confiding in O'Reardon, though wisely thought better of it. She was in this all alone.

"You mean after all this time the New York City Police Department has no idea where a quarter-million dollars disappeared to?"

"Seems that way. I find it interesting that you don't consider the arrest of the men who killed your husband more important than the recovery of a bank's insured money."

Even in her tipsy state Marie righted herself. "Most certainly, Brian. I think you guys did a swell job getting those bastards. I just hate the idea of them or even their families benefiting in any way from Chubby's death, that's all."

Brian answered, "It's not likely whoever has it will be able to conceal that much money for very long. I can't seem to make out that person up there. It's either Bing Crosby or Bud Abbott," he said, changing the subject.

"Niven."

He looked up again, then at her. "You're right. It's David Niven."

After dinner they headed back to Queens.

"Nightcap?"

"Sure," he replied.

* * *

"Ma, look who's finally awake," Angela said with a mouthful of toast.

"Tuddy, what time did you get home last night?" Laura asked.

"I don't know, Ma, it wasn't that late. Any rolls left?" Tuddy hobbled over to the closest chair and practically fell into it.

"Young man, I really wish I knew what goes on with you and those friends of yours all hours of the night."

Angela, not comfortable with someone sitting in her father's seat, especially her hung-over brother, sarcastically remarked, "Ma, do you suppose Tuddy now considers himself the *man* of the house?"

"Shut up, idiot," he replied as he slid over to his usual seat.

Laura couldn't resist. "His behavior lately hardly qualifies him to be the man of anything."

"Goddamn, I just woke up. At least let me get something in my stomach before you two start busting my balls."

His mother, choosing to ignore his language, said, "After school tomorrow we're going shopping for clothing for you two."

Angela shrieked. "Can we go to Macy's? They have the *best* clothes there. I saw this green dress there last week, no wait, can I get a *new coat* instead?"

Laura looked over from the stove. "You can have both and new shoes."

Tuddy lifted his head from his folded arms. "We get money or something?"

"As a matter of fact, we did, and hopefully there will be more where that came from."

"Where from?" Tuddy asked.

"Well don't go broadcasting but your brother invested some money for us, and it seems to be doing well, thank God."

"Why is that a secret, Mom?" Angela said.

"I didn't say it was a secret, I just don't want our business all over Maspeth."

The siblings looked at each other and shrugged.

"Mom, instead of buying clothes can we move?"

Laura laughed. "Angie, darling, I'm afraid moving will cost a bit more than a coat. First things first. If your brother Mikey's predictions come true, we should be able to move to a nicer block. Who knows, God willing we might even be able to buy a house someday."

"Where? In the country with Mike?"

"I hope so, Tuddy, I would like nothing better than getting you away from those friends of yours. I think out in the country would be good for you. Your sister too."

"Ma, I'll need a bicycle if we move there," Angela said excitedly.

"Sure, honey, how 'bout a Schwinn."

＊ ＊ ＊

After twice circling the block, Marie finally, luckily, found a parking space near her house. It was already dark and starting to snow. Both hands were grasping A&S shopping bags as she made her way up Lawrence Street wondering if the lamb chop she'd left out was fully thawed. Her street was deserted, and the old streetlamp was out as usual. Just as she was reaching for her keys, she heard footsteps.

Two men suddenly came up behind her and one calmly said, "Hello, Marie."

Oddly, she didn't feel threatened by the well-groomed men and replied to the taller one, "Do I know you?"

Richie Ragusa grabbed her firmly by the arm and said, "You do now."

"Down here." Monk motioned to the car parked just across the street.

Marie stiffened and was about to let out a scream when Richie grabbed her by the back of her neck and spoke firmly into her ear. "Just pick up your fucking bags and get into the car quietly and you won't get hurt."

She did as she was told. Richie slid into the back seat with her as Monk got behind the wheel. As he pulled away from the curb, she felt Ragusa's arm reach across her. She stiffened as he pushed the button down on her door. Her heart sank. She started crying. "Please tell me what this is about."

The Monk looked into the rear-view mirror. "It's about two hundred and fifty thousand dollars."

"What! I don't know what you're talking about."

Ragusa started stroking her long hair then jerked it, pulling her head violently toward him. "Do you know *whose* money you got?" He pulled again. "Have you any idea *who* you're fucking with?"

Marie had a very good idea now. She tried to compose herself. "Okay, you're talking about the holdup money. Hey guys, I'm a *victim* of that crime. My husband was killed in there. How the hell am I going to. . ."

She felt the car come to an abrupt halt and then the barrel of the Monk's handgun was six inches from her face. They were parked on Grand Street where she saw nothing but empty factories and abandoned cars. She thought that was to be her final vision.

"Listen bitch, we know you took that money from the cellar!" He was emptying her shopping bags onto the car floor while Enzo was screaming at her.

Marie quickly realized that she had better be up front with these two. "You are making a mistake." Her breathing quickened. "*Sal Marchetti* had that money! He gave me a small amount of it because of my husband. Fifty thousand dollars, I swear on my kids, not a penny more. He had me believe that was half of the take. You should speak to his wife Laura if you want the rest of it."

Marie had forgotten Laura's connection to these guys.

"Fuckin liar!" The Monk reached back and hit Marie on the forehead with the butt of the .32. A stunned Richie looked on as blood streamed down her face. Marie shrieked and covered her head. Crying loudly, she managed to utter, "I swear! I have forty-eight thousand dollars in a brown paper bag in my apartment. Come with me and I'll give it to you. I have nothing else."

She looked at Monk's contorted expression. "Please don't hit me again."

Enzo made a U-turn and headed back to Lawrence Street. They double-parked outside her house and led her inside. Ragusa handed her his handkerchief, which she held to her forehead. Her phone was ringing when they entered her apartment. She looked at the Monk.

"Don't even think about it. Get the money."

Marie went into her dresser and pulled out the bag. "This is practically every cent of it, still in the bag it came in!"

The Monk snatched it away from her as he looked around at her lavish furnishings.

"I know you're lying. We'll be back for the rest! Soon."

She was still crying as she dabbed the already drenched handkerchief to her forehead. **"There is no more!"**

Marie heard the door close as she slumped to the sofa. She knew she had to get to the hospital before she lost much more blood. She grabbed a small towel, wrapped it around her head, and headed down to her car.

In the Emergency Room at St. Catherine's a nurse helped her onto a stool and cleaned her wound while they waited for the doctor. Marie tried to look composed.

The youthful-looking doctor entered and went over to the sink and started washing his hands. "What happened to you?" he asked without turning around.

"I slipped on the ice in front of my house."

He walked up to her and started wiping the blood from the immediate area of her cut. Looking into her gaping wound he said, "Oooh, we're going to have to sew this up." He removed her coat and noticed the bruises on her arm. "Is this from the fall also?"

"Yes, I . . . landed pretty hard."

The doctor looked at the nurse then at Marie. "Okay, we're going to have to shave a bit of hair off the front of your head."

"How much hair—?"

"I can't stich the hair. As little as possible."

Marie was given a local and received sixteen stitches. Gauze was then wrapped around her head to hold the bandage in place. She caught a glimpse of herself in the mirror. "I look like a Civil War soldier. Is all this around my head really necessary?"

The doctor handed her extra bandages. "Tomorrow you can remove the gauze and use this tape to hold the bandage. Come back in six days and we'll take the stitches out. Hopefully there won't be too much of a scar. Listen, Mrs. Werner, if your husband did that to you, you should report it to the police."

"Doctor, my husband is hardly in any condition to do this but thank you for your concern."

Driving back to Maspeth, Marie was wondering how she was going to explain her battered head to Brian. She then remembered her bigger dilemma. *Did those two believe me or are they really coming back?* She also realized a third problem; her money was gone. Dismay, then anger, overwhelmed her.

CHAPTER 18

"Hey boss, how ya doin?" Johnny Paparelli was greeted by Fat Frankie as he entered the club.

"Frankie where the hell is everybody?"

"Inside. Richie's got his flicks going again. New one this time."

"Really, I hope these fucking broads are better looking than the pigs in the last one." Johnny Papa strode in and quietly sat down behind everyone.

"Hey, Ragusa! Isn't that your sister?"

"John, when the fuck did *you* get here?" Richie said, as he switched off the projector.

"Christ, where do they find these women, in a zoo? Come outside, I want to talk to you. You too, Monk."

They followed him into the street.

"Where's your coat, Monk? It's freezing out here."

"I'm okay, boss, this weather doesn't bother me."

The two of them were feeling tense, wondering if the old man was going to like what they had to tell him. Richie walked over to his car directly in front of a fire hydrant and pulled the brown bag from his trunk.

"Forty-seven thousand in there, boss," he said as he discreetly passed it to him.

"Okay, when is she giving you the rest?"

Monk chimed in, "Well, I don't think she got no more. We did a pretty good job on her and . . ."

"What the fuck you mean, she spent it, lost it . . . what?"

"She said your son-in-law Sal gave her the fifty G's because of her husband getting iced and all. Believe me, after I opened her head, she would have handed over her kids, she was so fucking scared."

Paparelli looked at Enzo, then at Ragusa. He spoke slowly, "This woman has *at least* another two hundred grand. What do I gotta do to get you to listen? I want you to wait a couple of days then go back there. How hard did you hit her?"

"I hit her a pretty good shot with my piece," the Monk replied.

Ragusa nodded in agreement.

"Then hit her harder! Get that fucking money from her! Capeesh?"

"Yeah, sure thing, boss," Richie said.

Paparelli re-entered the club shaking his head, while they remained outside. "Enzo, how did *we* get stuck with this shit? What are we supposed to do, kill this broad to satisfy that old fuck? You know as well as me she ain't got no more money."

"Don't worry, kid, I know you got no stomach for this. Leave the head banging to me. You know, the old man usually knows what he's talking about with shit like this. Remember the Jew on 47th Street? Turned out he had those diamonds all the while, just like John said. Joey Fingers was ready to ice the poor fucking courier."

"Yeah, I know, still, this is a broad! I'd feel better offing the *wrong* guy with a bat than the *right* woman."

"Hey Rich, what could I tell ya? Eh!" He lifted his hand. "We gotta do what we gotta do. Come on, let's go in and get an espresso. I'm fucking freezing."

"Any sambuca left?"

**

It was unseasonably warm for a February day and O'Reardon was not happy about having to work on Saturday, overtime or no overtime. "Rich, let's get the hell out of here. We can still catch the twelve o'clock boat out of Howard Beach. Striped bass are swarming off Buoy 19. They're hauling in their limit in two-hours' time."

Falco would have liked nothing better than taking the afternoon off except fishing was probably the last thing he wanted to do. Besides, Captain Rogers was also there, and would not be keen on the idea of them leaving considering the slow progress of their investigations.

"Because it's forty-five degrees outside today it doesn't mean it's that warm out over the water. You'll freeze your ass off."

"Who you kiddin Falco, if it was eighty you wouldn't go out there."

"You're right, not fishing with a bunch of old army guys. I heard enough about the war."

"Hey guys, can you come in here a minute?" The captain was standing in the doorway wearing his Franklin K. Lane High School jacket.

Falco lit up. "Is that where you went, Captain?"

"Yup, class of '41, almost twenty-three years ago."

"So *you're* the guy they graduated that year," O'Reardon chided.

He had it buttoned to emphasize his unchanged waistline.

Falco said, "I went two stops west of there. East New York Vocational."

"Yeah, I know," Rogers replied, "class of '51. Think I don't read the personnel files around here? Your partner O'Reardon there went to Canarsie High, class of 'kicked out on his ass with three months remaining.'"

"Very good, Captain, you did your homework. Did you also find out why they kicked me out? And it was with one month remaining."

Falco was enjoying it all.

"Yeah, you nearly killed a basketball ref in the school gym."

"He had a glass jaw, I tapped him once and he hit his head on the floor."

"He spent two days in a coma," Rogers reminded him.

"Holy shit, how did you get on the force with *that* on your record?" Falco asked.

O'Reardon smirked. "Remember when I told you about my cousin Charlie, the queer?"

"Yeah?"

"Well, besides being a movie theater pervert, he was also a criminal lawyer. He represented me on the felony assault charge. The guy convinced the DA, who was probably a fag himself, to drop it down to simple battery, which is a *misdemeanor*, thus enabling me, with the help of an equivalency diploma, to become one of New York's finest."

Both Rogers and Rich Falco in unison called out "*Mister Meanor!*"

O'Reardon grinned. "That's right! That's where she got her name!

"I get that, but why would you name your fuckin' boat *that*?" Rogers asked.

"Because that wonderful lesser crime statute made me eligible to land this gig!"

"Now I heard everything! Let's get serious here. What do you two got on the bank job?" Rogers asked.

O'Reardon spoke first. "You think it was confusing before, guess who's the latest player in this little drama of ours?"

"Lee Harvey Oswald!"

"Close, John Paparelli."

The captain folded his hands behind his head and moaned. "Shit, why did I even ask? Tell me, how does Johnny Papa get involved in a bank heist in Greenpoint? It's way out of his territory."

Falco stood up and started pacing. "Believe it or not he's Laura Marchetti's father!"

"Wha—"

"Wait, there's more . . . She went to see him on Staten Island the other day and when Brian mentioned the visit to her, she seemed to get unsettled."

"How did he know she went *there*?"

"Ah, an old baker lady."

"What do you make of all this, Lieutenant?" Rogers asked.

"Well Cap, that, coupled with the armored car guys' statement and everything else, I'm guessing our bank nerd isn't quite the Walter Mitty everyone makes him out to be."

"And you, Falco?"

"I think we're starting to make people nervous. We gotta keep stirring the pot and see what boils over. If we're dealing with amateurs, it shouldn't be long before something breaks, but if the mob is an ingredient in our stew, then we got a different ballgame."

Rogers remembered Marie. "What about that Miss New York gal? Get anything from her?"

Falco did his best to keep a straight face. "Not really," he replied. "Things seemed pretty normal when I spoke to her. How 'bout you, partner, you *get* anything from her?"

O'Reardon chose to ignore Falco's wisecrack and replied, "With Marie Werner, what you see is what you get. It's all pretty *straight up* with her. I don't think she's hiding anything."

Captain Rogers shrugged. "I find it baffling that you guys trust a woman like Marie Werner over a church-going respectable woman. I don't get it. I'm really tempted to shut this thing down. If there weren't so many untied ends I would. Keep stirring and be certain that I'll be sniffing your pot. Don't screw it up."

Upon exiting the office, Falco asked, "Was that an actual joke you made in there?"

"What's that?"

"Your 'straight up' remark."

"Uh . . . no."

"I didn't think so."

* * *

Whitey and Junior were taking their seats in the chapel. Most prisoners attended the Catholic services each Sunday for no other reason than a change of scenery from their cells, others to get news from their friends, and a few even prayed occasionally. A few minutes into the Mass the duo noticed they were the topic of conversation of the group of guys seated in front of them. The mostly Italian thugs were looking back at them while laughing amongst themselves.

The shortest one finally shared the humor. "Is that true you guys come here to pray that nobody digs up your stash?"

"Stash? Don't believe everything you read," Whitey answered.

"Listen, my man, I'm getting outta here in a few days. I'll tell you what I'll do for you. Let me know where that load is, I'll get it dug up or whatever and have you both bailed out in twenty-four hours."

"Really, you'd do that?" Whitey said.

"Word of honor, bro."

Whitey leaned in closer. "It's in your mother's mattress with the rest of my loads."

The little guy was about to climb over the bench when his hysterical friends held him back.

"So that's where she got your bail money from, Mario," one of his friends touted.

The guards didn't notice the almost-altercation, but the nearby seated churchgoers grumbled their displeasure. Things settled down for most of the Mass. Later, it was during the receiving of Communion, while the truly faithful were filing up to the altar, that a louder commotion sprang up. On the opposite side, where the ninth-floor hard-cores were seated, two Puerto Ricans had each other in headlocks while their friends around them were yelling in Spanish. All six guards positioned in the aisles ran toward them. They let go of each other just before the first baton was about to come down. The guards were in their midst pushing everyone around for no reason other than re-establishing authority. When things calmed down the winded guards remained standing near them outside the aisle. They were whispering and even laughing together when a piercing scream came from the side of the original disturbance.

"Motherfucking rats!"

Whitey was holding his chest, gurgling.

"Hector, noo, was all Junior could manage before the same make-shift shank was punched into his neck.

It was done with such force that only a small part of the crudely shaped handle was not imbedded inside him. Those around them cleared out, some tracking blood. Junior dropped straight down. The only movement from him was a convulsing leg. The two pools of blood became one and slowly rolled toward the alter. The guards knocked anyone down who happened to be in their path, and even some who weren't. Horns were blaring.

Hector was screaming at the moaning Whitey as he was slammed to the ground by two of the guards. **"I thought we were brothers! You gave me up!"**

Whitey had his thumb inside his breast, attempting to plug the spurting blood. He was down on both knees struggling to lift himself up with his free hand. Before shock had totally engulfed him, he was squinting up into the slow-motion maze of blue uniforms and swinging clubs, trying to determine who had stabbed him. Finally, he saw Hector's contorted face being lifted off the ground by his hair. Two other newly arrived guards scooped Whitey up and rushed him right past the group beating on Hector. The once best friends locked eyes. Whitey's showed disbelief against Hector's scornful glare. The rest of the prisoners were hustled out while his floor-mates shouted their appreciation of Hector's revenge. They felt a sense of accomplishment their diversion was successful.

Junior's lifeless body remained while a guard tried to locate the vanished priest. He found him hidden behind the podium in the Protestant portion of the revolving altar.

"Father, we need Last Rights out there."

* * *

Laura exited the ferry with her daughter in tow. Angela had been unable to beg out of this visit like her brothers had.

"Ma, we were just here last week."

"That was two weeks ago, and I told you to get used to it. Again, your grandparents are not getting younger, and we need to spend more time with them."

The only blowing horn in the busy terminal parking lot had to be her brother Mario.

"How's my favorite niece?"

"Fine, Uncle Mario, and I'm your *only* niece."

"Dad home?"

"Yeah, Laura, he's watching the game with Richie. Where's Tuddy?"

"Who?"

"Tuddy, your son."

"No, who is *Richie*?"

"Oh! Richie Ragusa, one of his guys."

"I know him?"

"When you see him, you'll remember. He's from the old neighborhood. He was in all my classes . . . well, before I got left back."

Angela laughed.

"Nice."

The Caddy pulled up to the Paparelli home. Walking up to the house Laura was reminiscing about the time her father taught her how to ride a two-wheeler on this very sidewalk. The house had been a lot smaller then and the sidewalk somehow seemed larger. She tried to share that memory with her daughter, but Angie's focus was on the snacks always waiting in the house. Mario motioned as he led them in.

"Mom's in the kitchen, Dad's downstairs, take your pick."

"Angela, go say hello to Gram, I'll be right up."

Laura headed down into her father's den. She remembered this area as a damp, spider-infested cellar as a kid. It was finished years ago with wood paneling, rugs, and a dropped ceiling. The old man had built it so as not to have to watch another episode of *Lawrence Welk* with his wife. When he was home, in the basement was where you found him. He had even moved his office down there.

"Laurie girl, come on down. You remember Richie?"

"Sure, from the old days." She didn't.

"Jeez, I'm sorry 'bout Sal."

"Thank you. Sorry to barge in on you Dad on such short --"

"Don't be silly, sit down, sweetheart."

"Go and shut the door up there," he said to Ragusa, pointing to the top of the stairs.

When he came back down Rich lit up a cigar and sat on the couch facing his boss. Laura formed a right angle with them where she was seated.

"Laura, Richie here, along with Enzo, paid your friend Marie a visit a couple of weeks ago."

This caught her off guard as she turned and faced her father with a troubled expression.

"Minga! What a night that turned out—"

The old man subtly held his hand up to Ragusa while still looking at his daughter. Richie stopped his sentence mid-syllable.

"Laura, I told him everything. If I'm sending these guys out, they have to know what's goin' on if they're expected to do the job. Capeesh?"

"Yeah sure, Dad, it's just that I didn't expect to have to talk about this to a . . . stranger."

"Wha? What's this *stranger* stuff?" Ragusa exclaimed. "I'll have you know I used ta play ringolevio with you and your friend what's-her-face at the Monsignor Farrell schoolyard."

"Listen, you must have been nine years old when me *and what's-her-face* went to Farrell, which is probably why I *don't remember you*."

Laura never had patience with these guys.

"Laura I'd be more respectful to this gentleman if I were you. He recovered nearly fifty Gs for you."

Laura surprised everyone when she quickly asked, "And where's the rest?"

Her father raised his eyebrows and motioned Ragusa to answer.

"We're pretty sure she gave us all she had," he said with an air of certainty. "We did a pretty good number on her. She would have given us her first born if that's what we were looking for."

Laura winced at that. "Did she say how she got the money?"

"She says your husband, may he rest in peace, gave her that amount because of her old man being wacked and all," Ragusa replied.

Her father spoke, "You said she called him that night. I think she was putting the squeeze on him, Laura. She musta known something." He looked at Ragusa. "I'd give anything to know what went on inside that bank."

"You got that right, boss."

"Dad, you *know* Sal. I ask you, could he have possibly pulled this off on his own?"

He shrugged then leaned forward. "Laura, I remember during the war, the *first* war, there was a guy in the neighborhood, just off the boat, Vito . . . something or other . . . anyway, he used to regularly get his ass kicked by anyone and everyone. Every time you looked up somebody was chasing him down the block. He was just that kind of kid, a real annoying pain in the ass. I remember his mother used to give him a beating, right in front of us, for not fighting back. About a year later there was a one-man crime wave. Someone was holding up stores up and down the avenue. The cops finally caught up with him coming out of a liquor store after a job. Two cops were shot before they killed him. I was just a kid, but I still remember the blood stains in that sidewalk, right under the El. Those stains were there for months. We'd always walk over there to see if it washed away."

"Let me guess, it was Vito?"

"That's right, Laura. He wasn't even eighteen yet. And that's only one instance off the top of my head. So, when you ask me if Sal was capable of this, I say anyone is. *Anyone!*"

He then got up and walked over to his roll top desk. He pulled a large brown envelope out of a drawer.

"Here. There's forty-seven thousand in there. If I were you, I'd be content with that, sweetheart. Don't you forget this is a murder case . . . Need I say more?"

"Listen to your father," Ragusa added. "Believe you me, you don't want this investigation on your doorstep."

Annoyed at the prospect of conceding two hundred thousand, she squeezed the envelope into her purse. "Thank you—both—I'm going upstairs to see Mom."

Before she got to the staircase her brother Mario appeared at the top. "Holy shit, just heard on the radio that two of the guys from the holdup were stabbed in the joint."

The old man looked up at his son. "They dead?"

"One is, I think they said the other guy is critical."

Laura put her hand up to her mouth.

Ragusa shook his head and said in a low voice, "This is getting fuckin' crazy."

"Hey, your mouth! Mario, call our friend at the *Mirror* and see what you could find out," the boss said.

"On Sunday?"

"*Stunad*, it's a newspaper not a grocery store. They work every day. Use this phone."

Laura sat back in her seat.

Mario dialed the number. "Yeah, gimme the crime office. Yeah, let me have Mike DiRobbio . . ."

"Mikey? Mario, how ya doin? Wha? I'm interrupting the Knicks game? . . . How much they paying you there. I want that job! . . . Bullshit, I read better than you. Tell me something, douchebag, what went down this morning at the Brooklyn House of D?"

Four pairs of eyes were on Mario as he spoke.

"Wow, in the chapel? One of the partners did it? No shit? What hospital they got him in? . . . What else? . . . Nah it's okay, that's good enough. No, I'm not telling him that, he's cranky enough. Okay thanks."

"Tell me what?" the old man demanded.

"Knicks are getting killed."

"Did I hear right?" Richie asked. "He said the *third guy*, his amigo, did it?"

"Yeah, some shit huh?"

Laura again got up. This time she went up the stairs without speaking.

"What's wrong with *her*?" Mario asked.

"Your sister's got a lot on her mind, she'll be all right," his father answered.

He now turned his attention to Ragusa. "Go visit that broad again."

Ragusa took a deep breath.

Johnny Papa snapped, "What?"

"Nothing boss, I'll hook up with Enzo and we'll go this week."

Mario had a perplexed look on his face. Ragusa put his hand on his shoulder on his way out. "You don't wanna know."

CHAPTER 19

O'Reardon had his customary coffee and cigarette in his hands when he walked under the large 104 engraved in the crumbling precinct wall. Falco had already been there half an hour.

"Why is it freezing in here?" he asked.

Falco was sitting at his desk with a topcoat on. He didn't even look up from his newspaper. "This place is falling apart. We're waiting for engineering to get here and fix the burner."

O'Reardon shook his head. "You know when this place used coal, we never had this problem. They should have left it alone."

"That's your fuckin' Mayor Wagner for ya!"

"Instead of tearing these old shithouses down and replacing them, they waste money trying to fix them up," Detective Mclaughlin said from across the room.

"You hear something?" O'Reardon sarcastically asked Falco while looking around.

Falco didn't hesitate. "I think it's that old queer from across the street complaining about our cars again."

"Fuck you Falco, fuck both of you," Mclaughlin yelled, now standing up.

"Be careful, asshole, we're not college professors." O'Reardon sneered, referring to Mclaughlin's latest beating victim.

"No shit! You don't even have a fuckin' high school diploma."

Falco stood up and got between the two, expecting his partner to react violently. He then looked straight at Mclaughlin. "I wouldn't if I were you!"

"Wouldn't what? Listen, you two think your shit don't stink. You've been dickin' around the same bullshit case while the rest of us are breaking our asses out in the streets. And don't think I'm the *only* one here who feels this way either."

Falco looked around and the other detectives looked down at their desktops. O'Reardon was ignoring the whole conversation, casually reading Falco's newspaper.

McLaughlin wouldn't let up. "Give it up already. Who's left to investigate? They're all dead. The guard, the manager, the perps . . ."

O'Reardon shot his head up. "What perps?"

Falco looked at O'Reardon. "I didn't get a chance to tell you—"

"He don't even fuckin' know," Mclaughlin interrupted. "Our *lead* detective!"

"What happened?"

"There was a stabbing at the jail. Saez's dead. Aparicio is critical," Falco said.

"Yeah," McLaughlin said, "and guess who iced them? Pancho number three. An *educated* person would have had them **separated.**"

O'Reardon was still facing his partner. "Rich, in a minute I'm going to shoot this cocksucker."

Falco believed him and ushered Brian out of the room. Passing McLaughlin, Falco bit his lip and opened his eyes wide. "You came close."

They silently entered their Dodge and Falco headed west. Falco heard his passenger murmur "Three more weeks," to no one in particular.

"Where we going?" he then said in a slightly louder voice.

"Cumberland Hospital," Falco answered.

"That where he is?"

"Yeah. In the Intensive Care Unit."

It's common practice for thorough detectives to visit hospitalized prisoners. A heavily medicated suspect about to meet his maker often provides information that could break a case wide open. More importantly, judges and juries love deathbed stuff.

"That shithead McLaughlin's right. We *are* running out of people worth interviewing."

"Speaking of which, when was the last time you saw Marie Werner?"

"That night we went to Sardi's," O'Reardon replied.

"Seriously, not since?"

"No, for some reason she's been avoiding meeting me. She calls now and then, but when I want to get together it's always something like . . . My daughter this, my lawyer that, maybe tomorrow. I'm reaching the end of my rope with her. I'm too old for this shit. I can do without turbulence."

Falco felt Brian's angst and felt grateful for his 16 stable years with his real estate agent wife and their two straight A teenage sons. "Ya think I should try to call her again Rich? "

"Well, we do have to go back there so you have your reason."

"Screw her, I think I'm going to try to keep it business like for the sake of resolving this case. I'm not going out with this shit still on the books.

They arrived at Cumberland. The sprawling nineteenth century hospital dwarfed the neighborhood. After leaving their car outside the Emergency Room the duo hurriedly walked through the biting wind.

"ICU is right through there." The uniformed security officer instinctively knew he was talking to cops.

They knew they were approaching his room by the sight of another uniformed officer sitting outside it. This one was from the Bureau of Corrections.

Falco displayed his gold shield. "Is he able to speak?"

The guard shrugged, "*I* haven't heard him. There's a doctor in there with him now."

The doctor was startled when they opened the door.

"Visiting hours are not until . . . Oh, sorry, is there anything I can do for you, Officer? I'm Dr. Gupta."

"He coherent?" O'Reardon asked.

"Barely, he drifts in and out. He's heavily sedated."

"Sedated? I'll bet he's loving that. What's his chances?" O'Reardon asked.

The doctor winced and led them to a corner of the room. "He *can* hear us," he whispered. "The knife entered his chest and punctured his lung. He's not responding well to treatment. Does he have any family we can notify?"

"A girlfriend in Greenpoint is all I know of," Falco said. "Got a kid with her."

"We'd like to have a few minutes with him," O'Reardon said.

"All right, but don't get him too riled. He's very weak."

O'Reardon gave a short nod and the doctor left.

"Why the hell do they always say that?"

"Don't know, I think Ben Casey started it."

Falco leaned down. "Aparicio, can you hear me? **Whitey… can you hear me?**

O'Reardon tried, **"Hey, wake up!"**

He half opened his eyes. "Fuck you want?" he whispered.

O'Reardon turned to Falco. "What's he saying?"

"He wants to know what the fuck do you want."

"I *want* you to speak with us," O'Reardon answered.

"Maybe tell us a few things you might have remembered since we last spoke."

"You tell *me* something, fuckface. What bullshit did you feed Hector that made him do this?" Whitey was straining to get the words out.

"We didn't tell him anything that wasn't true," Falco said. "One of you gave him up. His mistake was thinking both of you did, unlucky for you."

Whitey realized right there that Junior had betrayed Hector. He closed his eyes and shook his head from side to side. "You're saying you didn't tell him it was me who ratted him out."

"That's what I'm saying. Why would—"

"What the fuck is the difference?" O'Reardon barked. "If I were you, I'd be worried about your girlfriend and kid. You left her facing jail time and the baby facing a foster home."

The morphine the doctor had just given him was reaching its full effect. His voice grew stronger. "What is it you want from me, Irishman?"

O'Reardon remained calm. "We know you guys are small-time junkies who couldn't plan a circle-jerk let alone a well-timed bank job." Pointing at his heart-rate indicator, O'Reardon continued, "I'm gonna be very frank with you. Your doctor who was just here said it won't be too long before those jagged lines up there get straight." When the recorders were off O'Reardon would say anything, *truth* was never a priority."

Looking at the scope, then at the detective, Whitey said, "What do you want from me?"

"How did you know to pick that very morning to do the heist, when there just happened to be five times the usual amount of cash, all unmarked, in that bank?" O'Reardon asked.

"You gonna start that bullshit again? I thought you were over it. *Again,* there wasn't all that much in there."

Falco moved to the other side of his bed and leaned down. "That's no bullshit, amigo. The good news is, we no longer think *you* guys walked out with that much. What we want to know now is who *did*."

"I want to see Sandy and my son."

"You know she's not your wife; therefore, not an authorized family member for visitations," Falco said.

"You can make it happen?"

The cops looked at each other.

O'Reardon spoke, "I don't know, that's no easy task. You have something useful for us?"

"You know, O' whatever, I just might."

"O'Reardon. Spit it out, whaddya got?"

"Whoa! Not so fast. For what I have you should at least let Sandy walk. I'm talking charges dropped."

The detectives again looked at each other. Falco raised an eyebrow. "That good, huh?"

"Yes. That good."

"So, let's hear it," a skeptical O'Reardon snapped.

"I want to see her first."

"You must think we're fucking stupid."

"Listen, O'*Reardon,* my old lady is the last one out on the street. If I give you any names, then she's the next target. I need to try to get her out of this shit before I blow the lid off this."

The guys paused at this. Falco nodded slightly to O'Reardon, hoping the senior partner would give Whitey the benefit of the doubt.

O'Reardon was losing patience. "*You* want to guide her to safety? She'd be safer with General Custer's guide . . . Listen, we'll bring her up here but if you're bullshitting me, boy, I will come down on your ass with everything. Your kid will be raised by nuns dressed in leather."

"I know how you guys work. I'm not stupid," Whitey said.

Falco was stroking his chin. "We'll have her here in a day or two."

"With my boy!"

"Yeah."

CHAPTER 20

"Marie, are you there?" O'Reardon spoke into the phone.

She thought about hanging up but finally spoke, "Yes, Brian, how are you?"

"I'm doing okay. Hey, are you avoiding me?"

She didn't know what to say. Her physical wounds had healed in the two weeks since Ragusa and the Monk visited her. She'd done a lot of soul searching during that time and had been struggling to rearrange her life.

She also stopped drinking and being sober was not one of her favorite pastimes.

Marie associated Brian O'Reardon with the heist money, or at least the trail to it. However, now that the risks involved had reached a new plateau, she wanted no part of it and no part of Brian either for that matter. His call caught her off guard.

"I'm not avoiding you, Brian; I'm just trying to come to grips with everything going on and it hasn't been easy."

"You mean with your husband dying and all?"

"Yes, that, and a lot more." Suddenly she burst into tears. It was as if all the weight on her shoulders became too much, and her strength gave out.

"I'll be right over."

He hung up before she could object.

Marie paced through her apartment wondering what to say when he arrived. Normally, she would have been in front of the mirror refreshing her makeup and fixing her hair. That was the old Marie, she wanted to believe. She oddly felt a sense of relief with the thought of someone caring for her as Brian did. The more she paced, the more she looked forward to his arrival. Stopping in front of her dressing room mirror she finally reached for a hairbrush.

The ringing doorbell jolted her. He must have been around the corner when he called.

She let him in and there was a moment of silence before he spoke.

"What's going on?"

Marie tried to remain in control. "Nothing really, I just overreacted to a lousy day."

O'Reardon became annoyed with her attitude change. He'd come prepared for a damsel in distress whom he could comfort and maybe even get their thing back on track.

"You seem different."

"I don't think you've seen me sober before," she half-joked.

He chuckled. "Except that first morning when we woke you up . . ."

"I really need to get my life in a positive direction. I was married for so many years and now making important decisions is kinda stressful to me."

"And?"

"And I just . . ." She started to lose it again.

He took her in his arms and Marie buried her head on his shoulder and cried aloud.

"Brian, I'm so stupid. Why did I get involved with these people?"

He held her closer. "What people?"

She lifted her tearstained face to look at him. She wavered.

"What! Tell me!"

Marie sat at the small kitchen table. "Please sit." She motioned to the chair opposite her. She turned toward him. Their knees were against each other's as she grasped his hands.

"What people?" he asked again.

"Brian, what I'm going to tell you is something that I wanted to tell you from day one, but I didn't want you to become entangled in this mess."

He loosened his grip and righted himself.

"Believe me, I'm a good person. I just got caught up in—"

He cut her short. "Are you involved with any of this bank shit goin' on?"

"Yes . . . sort of." She now wondered about her legal situation with him. *Will he arrest me?* "I'm telling you this because I care for you, and I hate keeping secrets from you."

O'Reardon somehow wasn't buying that. "Marie, stop babbling and tell me what this is all about."

"Wow, where do I start?"

"How about from the beginning."

"Okay. Sal Marchetti had the missing money."

"How do you know that?"

"Well, Sal and my husband were unable to open the vault when the money was delivered. Actually, Sal was unable, Chubby had nothing to do with handling money. He was just standing alongside him."

"And?"

"Well, as a result the satchels were locked in an office cabinet overnight on the afternoon prior to the holdup. I know this because—"

"Because your husband told you."

"Yes, that night. He found it quite amusing actually."

O'Reardon was jumping out of his shoes but he was able to keep his poker face.

"So that's the extent of your involvement?"

"I wish. Sal called me and wanted to give me some of it to help with the funeral bills and all. I tried to decline but he said he would feel better if I took it. He was very close to my husband."

"How much did he give you?"

"Fifty thousand. I just left it in the bag and put it in my dresser. I never so much as looked at that blood money." Marie avoided eye contact while speaking and grizzled O'Reardon doubted the accuracy of her story by her demeanor.

"So, you have it here?"

"Well, I did until a couple of weeks ago, then the shit hit the fan. I was accosted out front here and beat up by these two *Italian* guys." She made quotes with her fingers. "They brought me up here and I gladly gave them the bag of money. Somehow these goons think there was even more here and threatened to come back. These guys, no doubt, were her father's goons. I wound up in Cumberland Hospital with sixteen stitches. That's why I avoided you. Seeing me wrapped up like that would have plunged you into this mess and that's the—"

He finished the sentence for her, "*Last thing you wanted. So, I heard. But what you *don't* seem to understand is that's... *what I do*—plunge into messes. It was my actual job description when I joined the force."

"Yes but . . ."

"But nothing!" His voice got louder. "This is a capital murder committed during the act of a bank robbery, of which I'm the lead investigator and you don't want to get me *involved*?"

She broke down again. "Oh, I know it's such a mess. I *so* wanted to tell you about it."

This time he didn't comfort her. "Did Sal Marchetti mention to you how much money he had?"

"He told me he was giving me half, but I later found out that he had much more than a hundred thousand."

"How?"

"Well actually, you told me. You said two hundred and fifty thousand was unaccounted for."

"When did I say that?"

"Uh, that night we were, you know, together."

He paused then rolled his head back. "Oh, *now* I get it. You were with me to get information. What a jerk I am."

"Brian, that is so far from the truth. I really care for you. I do."

Her still beautiful face soulfully looking up at him had the desired effect. The embrace she followed it with put the cap on it. He held her tightly for a minute without saying anything. She could sense he was struggling with his feelings. He leaned his shoulders back while still holding her.

"Tell me something . . . you say Sal had the money. Why then, is his family coming after you for it?"

"I've been trying to figure that out for weeks now. I have no idea, whatsoever. All I *do* know is I want no part of these people and that damn money."

"Did Sal ever mention to you where he kept the money?"

"He had it inside his house."

"He told you this?"

"I watched him from his corner go inside his house and come out with the bag of money and hand it to me."

Marie realized she might be giving more information than necessary.

"Hmm. Straighten me out on this. You did say, a little while ago, he came to you with the fifty thousand dollars, and you *reluctantly* accepted it. Now you say you were *outside his house* accepting it, still reluctantly, of course. Came down to meet you, did he?"

Without hesitation she replied, "Yes, he said it was necessary for me to drive to his block and phone him from the corner when I arrived. He was feeling weak and dizzy and couldn't drive. He *did* die that night, you recall. We spoke a few minutes, and he went and got it."

"Yes, I do. So, in his weak and dizzy state he walked to the corner to meet you without having the money with him, then he had to go back to his house a second time, climb the stairs *again* and return with your cash."

Marie suddenly felt uncomfortable. "What am I, in court? Am I trial here?" She was shaking her head. "What made me think I could confide in you with all this."

O'Reardon backed off. "I'm sorry, Marie. This damn case has me so twisted I don't know what to think anymore. We both need to take it down a notch." He rested his arms on her waist. "How 'bout we go out to dinner Friday and just relax."

"Sure, okay. If you promise not to talk shop."

He chuckled. "*Me* talk shop!"

* * *

"I don't believe we're doing this," O'Reardon said as they walked up the flights leading to Whitey's apartment. "I know this guy is scamming us."

Sandy already had her coat on, holding baby Victor, when they knocked on her door. She and the baby left with them before they even entered the apartment.

"These nice men are going to take us to see Daddy," she said to the frightened child. There was a freezing rain outside to deal with.

They arrived at Cumberland Hospital in less than fifteen minutes. The same guard in the lobby nodded to them and pointed down the corridor toward Whitey's room. "Still in there."

A different uniformed officer was sitting outside his room. Sandy looked at Falco. "He can't even get up to pee and you guys have a guard here twenty-four-seven like he's going to bolt out of here and sprint down Myrtle Avenue."

"When he's not breathing for more than two hours, we'll consider removing the officer," O'Reardon cracked.

Sandy mumbled something in Spanish to him, suggesting a difficult physical chore for him to perform. Whitey was awake when they entered his room. Sandy showed no outward emotion while the detectives were there. His bewildered little son didn't recognize him lying there with tubes in all directions and his face swelled up.

O'Reardon looked at Whitey. "You have thirty minutes."

As soon as the two exited Sandy rushed up to Whitey. He grimaced in pain as she hugged him.

"How are you, baby?" he asked.

Ignoring his question, she barraged him with questions about his condition.

"I don't know, the doctors say I should be okay, but their body language tells me the opposite. Whatever, what's more important is that you and my boy do good. Bring him closer."

She held baby Victor close to Whitey's face. The boy started crying.

"No, Poppy, it's okay. Don't cry," Whitey whispered.

The one-year-old latched onto his mother, while she laugh-cried at the frightened face the child displayed.

After ten minutes of catching up with events Whitey got serious. "I've got to talk to you before they come back. You're going to need money to get through this, so I want you to listen carefully. Don't roll your eyes! I know my plans aren't always the best, but this is the only one I got, and I can't see it going wrong."

"I'm listening."

"Remember the guy we met at your sister Gloria's party?"

"Which guy?"

"The tall Puerto Rican guy. I was talking to him in the back room then we went outside for a walk. You got pissed. Remember?"

"No, they were all Puerto Ricans at that party."

"The guy I was talking to in the other room."

"You mean the guy that kept talking about his girlfriend, *Natalie Wood*?"

"Yeah, that's him, and the girlfriend only was mentioned after he got high."

"Mentioned! He never shut up. She looks just like Natalie Wood. She wants to be a model. She's this, she's that."

"Okay, just listen to me." His voice lowered. "There's a diner on Flushing Avenue where he has lunch almost every weekday, the Empress Diner. I guess around noon."

"Let's see, *almost* every day, I *guess* around noon. What am I supposed to do, spend my days there until he finally strolls in?"

"Yes, if that's what it takes! First thing I want you to do is get a picture of him."

"What for?"

"I don't have time to explain. Just do as I say."

"With what camera?"

"Damn, baby, I don't know, borrow your sister's, you know, that one she had at the party. You can catch him outside while he's walking in or even better you take it inside. Just make it a good one and *don't* get caught. I want you to be friendly, act surprised to see him. Remind him who you are if you have to."

"Oh, *he'll* remember me! Sure did enough glancing in my direction that day."

"Yeah, well, that also must have been after he got high." Whitey laughed. She didn't. "Then lay it on him. Tell him you're out on bail for the Morgan Bank holdup. Then tell him you want twenty thousand or you're bringing the whole story to the police."

"What's his name, this friend of yours?"

"I don't know, that's the purpose of the photo. He was supposed to contact me after the job but when the old dude got iced it became a new ballgame and I don't think he wanted to play anymore!"

"Well, how does this whole story I'm *spilling* to the cops affect *him*?"

"Do you think snorting dope was the only thing we did outside that night? *This whole job was his shit.* He told me it would be a piece of cake. He said he would do it himself but one of the tellers would recognize him."

"Did a bank teller tell him about it?"

"I don't know, probably."

"Why didn't you tell me about him before?"

"Well, for one, *nobody* knew but me, not even Junior or Hector. The *less* people that know shit, the better. I always tell you that."

"Okay so who is he?"

"That's the weird part. I really don't know. Says he's from Bushwick. I'm pretty sure he works in the area. He must have money, drives a new yellow car, and wears nice suits and shit."

"You think this guy is going to say, *oh sure here's twenty thousand, let me know if you're going to need more.* Whitey, where do you get these dumbass ideas? Listen, I don't need any more trouble . . ."

"No! *You* listen. This guy is a faggot. I mean it, *you* could kick his ass. Tell him you got his license plate number. He's not going to want this murder rap coming down on him. Most important, *don't* let him know you're doing this alone. Tell him your people know about him and if anything happens to you, which it won't, they *will* be looking for him."

"Whitey, I don't know . . ."

"Baby, it's worth a shot. If he doesn't go for it, you walk away. Done. But I'm thinking anyone in his right mind wouldn't want even the possibility of getting involved in this death penalty bullshit. Also, you have to act fast because I'm giving him up next week to those two *pendejos* standing outside."

"You're what? Why?"

"So you could walk on that accomplice charge--" Before he could finish the sentence, the door flew open and O'Reardon said, "Okay people, we gotta go."

She leaned down and kissed Whitey. She saw tears running down his cheeks. Sandy sobbed quietly. She held their now sleeping baby to him and he kissed his son goodbye.

Falco looked over to Sandy. "We gotta leave. You're not legally here and we don't want to push our luck." O'Reardon, with no sympathy for the situation of a father probably saying his last goodbye to his son, turned around at the door and said to his distraught prisoner, "We *will* be back to talk."

CHAPTER 21

It was the time of the week when Captain Rogers got his briefings on the open cases. O'Reardon and Falco arrived at the precinct late afternoon, so they were his last meeting for the day. Their case was the one Rogers was most anxious to hear about.

"Well, gentlemen, where are we standing or should I say, *are* we standing? Or are we flat on our asses?"

O'Reardon spoke first. "Well, for starters we know what went down in the bank that morning."

"Yeah, me too! Three hundred grand and a guard saw the inside of that bank for the last time," the captain remarked.

Falco walked farther into the office and sat down. "Here's what we got. The bulk of the money never even made it into the vault. Sal Marchetti put it in the office cabinet when he couldn't open the safe. It was in there when the hit was made. Not being the sharpest pencil in the box he thought he could simply take it home, kinda like a piece of leftover birthday cake."

O'Reardon took over. "What we have now is everyone, that's family, friends, and lovers, going at each other, all thinking the next person has the money."

"Okay, explain to me," Rogers said, "who exactly is everyone?"

"You want the list?" O'Reardon said.

"Please."

He sat down. Without consulting his notes O'Reardon said, "Okay, stop me if I'm being redundant. There's Whitey Aparicio lying half dead in the hospital. He's offering us up the mastermind for his girlfriend's freedom. She was probably the wheelman. His two accomplices are out of the picture. One dead and one soon to be fried, facing two murder raps. Sal Marchetti, the bank assistant manager, winds up with the cash, then drops dead after giving a portion to Marie Werner, the dead guard's wife. Turns out she knew, from her husband, that Marchetti had the delivery bags in a cabinet. When the discrepancy became public, she probably put two and two together and wanted a piece, or he just offered her some, whatever."

"What about Marchetti's wife? Seems logical to me she would have it," the captain said.

"That's where it gets weird. Remember, I told you his wife Laura, is the daughter of a captain in the Genovese family. She must've gone to him for help in finding the loot because he sent two goons to put the squeeze on the Werner gal to give it up." He held his palms up "It all makes you wonder."

Rogers was scratching his head. "What makes me wonder is why, when we have custody of the robbers and the other thief, Marchetti is dead, are we putting so much time on this fucking thing? After all this time and effort, the only thing remaining to solve is *where can we find missing money?!* So why not let the insurance company worry about that so we all can go back to working on other crimes."

O'Reardon looked angry. "Captain, this is blood money! A good man, who was one of us, gave his life to protect it. No one, and I mean *no one*, should profit from his murder."

Falco cut in, "Cap, we're almost there, let us finish this. Remember, the newspapers are all over this. You can come out looking good."

"Yeah, and don't forget Mayor Wagner's interest," O'Reardon added.

"Oh, like I give a shit! . . . How much more time you need?"

"Two weeks."

"You said that two weeks ago."

"We're there, Cap. Let us have this," O'Reardon said.

"Then get it done. You know O'Reardon, I'm going to throw a big party when you retire. Don't expect to be invited."

Outside his office, a smiling Falco asked his partner, "What now, brown cow?"

O'Reardon looked down at his brown suit and shoes and also smiled. "Now, I guess we go back to Marchetti's wife. The money was in her house the night he died, presumably with her."

"Of course with her. Who else?"

O'Reardon reached his desk and plopped down. "Who else, you ask? There *are* other family members you know. I remember one of the women said he had a married son." He started flipping pages in his notebook. "Ah! Michael. Twenty-four years old and living out on the Island with his wife. Shit, how'd I forget this . . ." He looked up at Falco. "The kid's a stockbroker."

"*And?* You say it like he's a Mafia hitman. So, he's a stockbroker?"

"Rich, if you look up *money launderer* in the dictionary, you'll find a picture of a Wall Street trader."

"Hmmm, true, how dumb are *we*? Why would Marchetti entrust all that money to a naïve housewife when he's got a slick college kid in the perfect spot?" Falco said. "You see, Brian, and they say you've lost your touch."

"They say that, huh. And whaddayou tell 'em?"

"You *know* I don't let anyone badmouth you. I straighten them *right* out. I tell them, he may have lost his hair, and his waistline, his way around the harbor, and maybe even his sex drive. But his touch, never!"

O'Reardon laughed. "My sex drive too? What say I take you down to Williamsburg and we'll ask Cockeyed Mamie 'bout that."

"Wow, Cockeyed Mamie. You think she's still out on the street? That was almost ten years ago."

"Why not! *I* am."

* * *

"Mommy, I won't be long. I'll be back at one-thirty. Victor needs to be changed before his nap."

"Okay, *no later.* I mean it, Sandy, don't get lost, I have a lot of shit to do this afternoon."

Sandy waved without turning around. Her suspicious mother watched her walk down the street from the window.

She headed down Grand Avenue to Flushing Avenue and two blocks down Flushing, she came upon the Empress Diner. As luck would have it, the yellow Ford was already parked outside.

Sandy had never thought she would find him there on the first shot. She was not quite ready for the confrontation, but her legs carried her up the four steps and into the mostly empty diner. She saw him sitting at the counter in a three-piece suit and sat down one stool away from him.

"Coffee and a corn muffin, please."

After a while, Sandy placed the Kodak Instamatic next to her purse and without looking in the viewfinder kept snapping pictures in his direction. She stirred her coffee loudly to drown out the shutter clicks. After half dozen shots she slipped the camera back into her purse.

"Would you like anything else, Manny?" the waitress asked.

Manny Figueroa answered, "Just a check, Mary."

"May I have the sugar, please?" Sandy asked.

He looked up from his newspaper. "Sorry?"

"The sugar." She pointed.

He slid the glass jar over to her and went back to reading. After a few minutes he looked over. "I don't recall seeing you here before. You from around here?"

"Yup, born and raised, I just don't come in this place very much though."

He slid over to the empty stool between them. "Don't I know you from somewhere? What's your name?"

"Sonya Torres, what's yours?"

"Manny."

"Manny what?"

"Just Manny."

"You *do* know me, Manny. You know my boyfriend much better though. Remember the birthday party over on Devoe Street a couple of weeks ago. I was there with him. I'm sure you remember him; his name is Whitey."

"No, doesn't ring a bell. He quickly lifted his newspaper."

"Maybe this does, Morgan Trust Savings Bank. The one way down the block." Sandy was gaining confidence.

"What the fuck you talking about? Who are you?"

"I'm talking about a holdup you set up."

"*I* set up a holdup? Do I look like a bank robber?" Manny said, sweeping his hand alongside his sharkskin suit.

"No, you don't."

"I didn't think so."

"You look like the faggot who sends other people to do it for you. Whitey said you shit your pants when you heard about the guard and became a ghost!

"Listen, I don't know who—"

"No, *you* listen! I'm sure you already know that my old man is facing some hard time for this. Bad news for him. The bad news for *you* is the D.A. is offering him a plea if he gives you up."

"Gives *me* up! Are you on drugs or—"

The nosy waitress brought his check. "Who's your friend Manny?"

"No friend, just a lost soul who wandered in."

Sandy ignored him and continued her memorized speech. "Even with the copout he's looking at minimum ten to twenty. Not a great offer . . . He'd rather see his family get set up with enough pesos to start a new life. Whitey thinks you screwed him by saying there was hundreds of thousands sitting in there. I don't know where you got that from, but it was bullshit. You know they would never have done it for fifty split four ways, that's for fuck sure."

Manny suddenly realized something. This woman and probably her friends don't know he *works* at the bank.

"I hate to break it to you, but you got the wrong guy, mommy. I've never been inside that place."

"Enough bullshit, I want twenty thousand in cash by Friday, or you go down. Masterminding a bank robbery/murder will surely get your ass fried in this state. By the way, I got your plate number off that fancy little car out there."

"You're out of your fucking mind, girl."

"I will be here at noon this Friday. Either you give me the cash, or you will be giving it to a bail bondsman next week. Oh, and I'd like it in hundreds." Sandy got up to walk out, then turned and said in a low voice, "We know where to find you."

She lied, there was no *we*, just her, and she had no idea where to find him except this diner.

Manny watched from the huge window as Sandy walked up the avenue. When she was out of sight, he gritted his teeth and slammed his palm against the side of his stool. He then buried his head in his hands while his mind started churning. *What's the big deal? There is absolutely no evidence I was involved . . . I was in fucking Mexico. Twenty grand is my life savings. No way.*

* * *

"What do you want to do, call him in here or do we go out to East Meadow uninvited?" Falco asked.

O'Reardon peered at him over his coffee. "As much as I hate that drive, I would like to have a look around, see how he's living."

"You think we could get a search warrant?"

O'Reardon shook his head. "On what? He's the son of a banker? There's nothing. Even Evans won't sign it." Judge Stanley Evans was so easily swayed on search warrants that he gets most of the requests from the precinct, even if it meant driving out to his vacation bungalow in Rockaway Beach for his signature.

"Going to his house and catching him unprepared may give us some insight if we're on the right track. I also want to see how his wife reacts; they're usually the weak link."

Falco suggested dinner at Angelo's before they headed out there.

"You know I hate that place."

"Yeah, but when was the last time we paid for anything there?"

O'Reardon smiled. "You know, it's not the food so much. It's just the mob scene is why I don't go there."

"Yeah, I know. What's that saying? Nobody goes there anymore, it's too crowded."

On orders from Angelo, the waitress made sure their beer kept flowing. They waited until after six before hitting the road, giving Michael ample time to be home when they arrived. The traffic wasn't as heavy as they expected, and they were in East Meadow in half an hour.

"Number nineteen should be the second one down. Yeah, here it is. New Impala in the driveway, good start."

Michael answered the door.

"Good evening, I'm Detective Falco and this is Detective Lieutenant O'Reardon. We're from the 104th Precinct in Queens." Putting his badge back in his pocket, O'Reardon noticed Mike's wife, who was standing behind him, bite her lip.

"Please, come in. Honey, would you get these gentlemen something to drink?" Michael remained poised.

"Coffee would be great. Don't make fresh, what's in that pot is fine." O'Reardon answered.

"Sorry about your father," Falco said.

"Thank you, we miss him already."

O'Reardon watched Patti in the kitchen as her hands trembled a bit when she took the cups out of the cupboard. He then turned his attention to Michael. "We have some questions that are sensitive in nature. You might not want your wife in the room. Up to you."

"I have nothing to hide. I'd prefer my wife by my side."

Patti rushed into the room with their coffee so not to miss anything.

"Okay, as you wish. May we sit in here?"

The foursome seated themselves in the living room. O'Reardon surveyed his surroundings. "What kind of work do you do Mr. Marchetti?"

"Please call me Mike. I work for Lehman Brothers in lower Manhattan. I'm a stockbroker."

"And how long have you been working there?" Falco asked.

"'Bout a year and a half."

"And he's one of their best traders already," Patti said, putting her arm into his.

"Have you ever been arrested Mike?" O'Reardon asked.

"Uh, yeah, in '57 for carrying an illegal switchblade. That was during the days when the Chaplains from the Marcy projects were around . . ."

"Yeah, I remember them, busted a few," Falco said.

Patti looked at him. "You never told me about any arrest."

"It was bullshit. It was under four fingers. The judge suspended the—"

O'Reardon interrupted him. "Mike, your father has been implicated in a criminal act. There is evidence that leads us to believe this may be so."

"*My* father?" Michael and Patti made an expression of humor, as if it was part of a private joke. "I take it you guys didn't know him . . . Of course not, why would you?"

"No, we didn't. How 'bout you tell us," Falco said.

"Okay, he was the most goody-two-shoes man I've ever known. I would actually be embarrassed when he came up to my school. The guy makes Howdy Doody look like a mobster."

Patti forced another chuckle.

"Just what might this criminal act be, Lieutenant?"

"Embezzlement and falsifying a police report to start," O'Reardon said. He again glanced at Patti. She grasped her husband's arm a bit tighter.

Falco pulled out his notebook. "How many times have you visited your parents in the last two months?"

"Seven or eight times. Once a week, actually."

"How would you categorize your father's relationship with Marie Werner?" O'Reardon asked.

Patti furrowed her brow.

"Well, that depends on which year of their twenty-year friendship you're referring to. The one year, when I was in grade school, the two of them *supposedly* had a brief fling."

"As far as you know it never became serious?" Falco asked.

"I think my mom threatened to cut him off *Lawrence Welk* and that put an end to it." Mike and Patti again nervously laughed in unison.

O'Reardon became annoyed. "You seem to take this lightly. Let me remind you that this is a serious matter. Fact is, there is an enormous amount of missing money last traced to your family's apartment. It belongs to Morgan Trust Bank. I don't suppose you noticed anything out of the ordinary at the house?"

"No, the only thing out of the ordinary was my dad's failing health," Mike snapped. "We were told out of the blue, actually the same week as the holdup, that his heart was pumping blood at about fifty percent efficiency. He was too weak for an operation and should get his affairs in order, if you know what I mean."

"Your point is?" Falco asked.

"My point is, where would he find the time or strength to be planning anything other than his funeral arrangements?"

"Affairs in order." O'Reardon remarked. "Exactly what are his affairs, the financial ones, I mean."

"He had some insurance, and a savings account. Probably not enough to take care of my mom, brothers, and sister in the long term."

"Doesn't sound like much of a legacy," Falco said.

Michael saw where this was leading. "Their *legacy*, as you call it, will be provided by me, my trading abilities in the stock market."

"Oh, how so?" O'Reardon asked.

Mike, and Patti as well, judging from her expression, knew he'd misspoken. If his trades were monitored, there'd be hell to pay.

"I just plan on helping my family benefit by my good fortune. As long as the market stays healthy, we *all* should be all right."

"Tell me," O'Reardon said, "does your mom also plan on benefiting from your grandfather's good fortune?"

Falco, Michael, and Patti all shot a quick glance at O'Reardon.

"Well, does she?" he persisted.

Falco knew that this remark was another of O'Reardon's *rattle the cage* attempts.

Michael's initial reaction was to kick them out. He remembered the satchels in his attic and thought better of causing a stir.

"Lieutenant, did you drive all the way out here to enhance my family's grief? We are honest, hard-working people who have absolutely no association with my grandfather other than Christmas visits."

Falco thought it best to say nothing and let this play out. Patti had an anguished look on her face.

"No, we drove all the way out here to retrieve stolen money," O'Reardon said.

Patti spoke for the first time, "Now why in the world do you think *we* would have it?"

O'Reardon leaned back into the couch, put his arm on the backrest, and addressed her. "Why do *we* think that? Tell ya what, Mrs. Marchetti, first I'll tell you what we *know*, then what we *think*. We *know*, from witnesses, your father-in-law Salvatore Marchetti had two hundred fifty thousand dollars shielded from the holdup men, either by accident or by design. We *know* he left the bank with it, and it was kept somewhere in *his* house. We also *know* that he gave part of it to Marie Werner, about fifty thousand, supposedly for her grief.

"Now, here's what we *think*. We think your dad was an honest man who got in over his head in a desperate, well-meaning attempt to leave more than a meager pension behind. We *think* you folks are, as you said, hard-working, honest people, who nonetheless had this pile of dirty money suddenly in your laps. We also *think* you are looking for a way out of this, especially now that the dogs are on your trail."

Now Michael was looking at his wife's reaction, hoping she wouldn't give away any emotion. Falco sat, watching the old man at his best.

"That's a big jump from a Maspeth basement to my possession out *here*, don't you think, Lieutenant? Not for nothing, but if this money does in fact exist as you say, there *are* elements in my family that are much better equipped to handle it than me. Wouldn't your time be better served on a different island, namely Staten? It's shorter ride for you guys, too."

O'Reardon was impressed. "Ya know, we thought about that, until a little bird told me that your father wouldn't trust your grandfather with his library card let alone—"

"My father trusted everyone. Which is probably why he barely made assistant manager after thirty years in that shitty bank. Do you believe that he would jeopardize his son's life by dumping this on him?"

"Why not? The oldest son, a Wall Street guy with nerves of steel. It's the choice I would have made if I were him. '*Take care of your family with this,*' is what I would have told you."

"Are you finished, sir?" Mike asked tersely.

"Not quite."

O'Reardon tugged at his mustache which meant to Falco that he was deep in thought. Finally, he looked up. "How did you know the money was in your father's *basement?* No one mentioned that."

Patti softly groaned as her husband righted himself. "We hid *everything* down there! Christmas presents, Playboy magazines, cigarettes, you name it."

O'Reardon just nodded. "Listen to me, Mike, I'm satisfied that all the guys who were involved with that crime have been dealt their punishment in one way or another. I, or should I say *we,* don't want to pursue and arrest any more people if we don't have to. We've got enough to do. I just want the loot back so we can close the books and get on with our lives, and I can retire." He then feigned an amused look at the heavens. "So, here's the deal.... if you know someone who *might* have the money and doesn't want a bunch of grubby city cops pulling onto their nice suburban lawns, yanking out their underwear drawers and punching holes in their walls, they can do this: Take a drive to Delmonico's, treat yourself to a juicy steak dinner and a bottle of Cabernet, compliments of Mr. Morgan, then simply drop off the remaining money at the 104th Precinct. You can leave it with the desk sergeant and walk out. No questions asked, ball game over."

"You finished?" Michael asked.

"For today."

"Well, you guys have a safe trip back to Queens. It's a shame you drove all the way out here for nothing."

Patti sank into the sofa while her husband showed them out.

The detectives headed up the driveway.

"He's our guy," O'Reardon said matter-of-factly.

"*You* seem pretty sure."

"Trust me, he's got it."

"When did the DA give the okay on the *no questions asked* drop-off?" Falco asked.

"Who said he did?"

* * *

"Mom, there's a lady in the hall coming up," Angela announced as she arrived home from school.

"What? What lady?"

"I don't know, she asked me downstairs which apartment you lived in."

Laura Marchetti wasn't expecting company. She walked into the hallway just as Marie reached her landing. They found each other face to face.

Laura was less than cordial. "Marie Werner, what can I do for you?"

"We need to talk."

"You look as if you haven't slept in days. It seems to me your little adventure is taking its toll on you."

Marie wasn't surprised by the animosity. She was hoping she could convince Laura of her innocence in all this.

"May I come in? I think you might want to hear what I have to say."

Laura wrinkled her brow while looking over Marie's shoulder. "Come in."

She led her into the kitchen and directed Angela to take her milk and cookies elsewhere.

"Now, Mrs. Werner, what is it that you have to say to me?"

"Please, call me Marie. I don't know what information you have or where you got it from, but the fact is I do not have a cent of your husband's money. I've been accosted—"

"MY husband's money. Is that what it is? Like he alone did this . . . this robbery? You're saying you weren't involved in planning this thing with him?"

"May I remind you, Laura, that my husband was murdered inside that bank. I was a *victim* of this crime. Damn, I'm getting tired of saying that!"

"Young lady, if you look in here again, you're headed out, cold or no cold."

Angie snapped her head back into her magazine.

Laura lowered her voice. "Listen, Marie, I saw you outside with my husband the night he died. I saw you give him something and he came back and put it in my cellar. Then he returned to your car. You looked everything *but* a victim out there. You even *phoned* him to arrange the meeting. Remember? *I'm* the one who answered."

Laura was losing her cool. "Okay, you want to really know what happened?"

"Please, do tell," was her sarcastic reply.

"My husband Chubby told me what happened during the armored car delivery the night before the holdup. Chubby found it funny that the guys were standing there, what seemed an eternity, holding all this money while Sal fumbled with the combination. He said it reached the peak when the third guy, the driver, entered and started yelling from the entrance of the bank for his guys to hurry. Anyway, to make a long story short, the two of them, Sal and Chubby, carried the money into an adjacent office and locked it in a cabinet."

Laura, hearing this for the first time was frozen in her seat.

"Chubby told me that night that he didn't know how much was in the bags but they sure were heavy. The next day when the police informed me of the holdup and shooting, I was devastated. It never dawned on me that the money could have been left behind. The detective handling the case, who by the way is a good friend of mine—"

"How convenient," Laura interrupted.

Marie ignored the remark. "He told me he was pretty certain those Spanish guys only got around thirty thousand from the bank."

"That night when I called, I was drinking. My judgement was somewhat clouded but you're right, I *did* call Sal. I resented that he'd prospered on my husband's death and I told him so."

Laura straightened up. "So you blackmailed him!"

"No, I just wanted him to know that *I knew* what he was up to. He panicked and ran down to meet me insisting I take half for my 'pain and suffering,' as he called it. Yes, I took the money, if that's what you mean. I never spent a dime of it, never even opened the bag it was in. I'm guessing you already know that because the thugs your father sent got it. *All* of it, which they brought to you, I'm sure."

"You know, Marie, money does a funny thing to people. Especially people who never had it. It changes them. You go through life believing in God, honoring the Commandments, teaching your children the same, and *poof* it all goes out the window."

"It's called greed," Marie offered.

"No, you're wrong. It's greed if it's for my gain, me. This is for my children, who have done without the things all their friends have. I'm talking about basic stuff, not luxuries. It breaks my heart seeing them wearing worn shoes on the first day of school. To see them wearing their cousins' hand-me-downs at family gatherings *and* being reminded of it. Not always able to go to the movies with their friends. This can all turn around and I'm going to see that it does."

"Laura, I wish nothing but the best for you and your family. Your husband was a good man and I'm truly sorry for any grief I might have caused you. I do mean it."

Both women had tears running down their cheeks. "We both lost good men," Laura managed.

Marie grasped Laura's hands. "There is something I must know before I leave, and you don't have to answer if you don't want. Do you really *not* have the money?"

Laura slid her hands out of her grip. *"No, I do not."*

"Do you think *I* have it?" Marie asked.

"No, I don't think you do, not now anyhow."

About then Angela came into the room. "Ma, I got no homework, can I go by Nancy's after dinner?"

Marie smiled at the girl. "She sure has grown."

* * *

"Whitey, you awake?"

He stirred, opened one eye.

"Sandy wow! I was just dreaming about you, girl."

"Really! She sat down beside him on the bed and straightened his hair.

"'Bout what?" Sandy noticed Whitey seemed more coherent than the last visit. She also noticed the sheets hadn't been changed because the same stains were there.

"It was weird, babe. We were at the apartment. The sun was shining through those pink curtains your mother gave us and you were making me a sandwich for work."

"*You* were going to work! Where?"

"I have no idea, had a suit and tie on though. Looked good!"

Sandy hugged Whitey. "See, baby, we *can*. That's a message from St. Teresa. We're gonna be fine."

Whitey put his hand up. "Whoa girl! Let's give the saints the day off today, okay. It was just a dream."

"Believe what you want, someday you'll see I'm right."

"How's my boy?"

"He's been sick, throwing up . . . fever. He's better today. Mom's got him. Aren't you gonna ask me?"

"Okay, what happened? Did you find him?"

Sandy reached into her purse and pulled out three photos.

"Look familiar?" she asked.

"Wow, that's him. Why are they so dark?"

"What am I supposed to do, take a secret picture with flashbulbs?"

"What happened, what did you tell him?"

"Just what you said, that my old man's facing hard time and *you better come up with twenty thousand.*"

"What'd *he* say?"

"What I told you he would say. '*You crazy, lady? You got the wrong guy.*'"

Whitey grimaced. He figured Manny would do anything to avoid this rap.

"We got his picture. I wonder if we could find out where he works. He's obviously got a decent job, Whitey said.

"I'm thinking the waitress at the diner probably knows. I'll show her the pictures."

"Okay, people, times up," the young guard called in from outside the door without leaving his seat.

"C'mon," Sandy pleaded, "I just got here."

"The lieutenant said fifteen minutes, and fifteen minutes it is. Bye."

Sandy scooped up the photos and kissed Whitey on the lips. "I'll see what I can find out. Don't worry, just get better."

"Wait, give me one." Whitey took the clearest photo from her and slid it under his pillow.

* * *

Morgan's Bank, despite the bad publicity in recent weeks, still had a robust business and although Sal's position had yet to be filled, Manny and the girls managed to keep the boat afloat.

"I'm interviewing a guy tomorrow from Hamburg Savings in Ridgewood for Sal's position, so be on your best behavior."

"What's he look like?" Paula asked.

"Like he's gonna ignore you and get his work done."

"He knows what happened and he still wants to work here?" Rose wondered aloud.

"Why don't you switch jobs with him, Manny? You live near Ridgewood," Paula asked.

"I'd love to. One problem though. His salary won't even pay for my dry cleaning."

"Manny, your wife would throw you out of the house if you came home with a pay cut," Dana teased.

"You think that's why she married me? If I told you ladies the real reason she's with me you'll all leave your husbands."

A flurry of cat calls and "keep dreaming" came from the girls.

The group, ever since the shooting, seemed to have grown closer.

On the way home Manny passed that Hamburg Bank and wondered what working there was like. His wife greeted him at their apartment.

"Feeling better today honey?" Claudia inquired.

"I told you this morning I feel fine; there's nothing wrong with me."

"Manuel, you can't fool me, there *is* something going on. You've not been yourself for days now and it's got me worried."

"It's just work that's going on. The bills aren't helping either."

"That's never bothered you before. You sure it isn't something else?"

Manny dropped onto the leather loveseat. "You know, maybe it's better I told you."

Claudia put the frying pan down and sat alongside him.

"Remember the bank thing I cooked up last . . ."

"*I don't want to talk about it.* I told you I don't want it mentioned ever again. It never happened, forget it. Manny, remember our agreement, go on with our lives and learn from our mistakes."

"Are you finished? . . . I've been contacted by one of the girlfriends of the holdup men. The guy I planned it with. He's also the one in the hospital."

Claudia put her hand up to her mouth. "*What did she want?*"

"Twenty thousand dollars, or they'll go to the police."

Tears rolled down her cheeks and over her fingers.

"I don't think it's that bad," Manny said. "They don't seem to know who I am or where I work."

"How then, did they find you?"

"The Empress. I eat lunch in that shitty diner practically every day. If I just stay away from there and lay low, they'll never find me.

"What if we just pay them?"

"Pay them! That would totally break us, and they'd never be satisfied, after a year they'd—"

"I can't be losing you, Manny," she said out of the blue.

"Don't worry, these people are street junkies grasping at straws. Had Whitey followed my exact instructions they could have waltzed out of there, and with *all* the money. It was their stupidity that got them in this mess. Shooting the fucking guard. What morons. I'll be damned if they think they're dragging me under with them."

"You know, you're right. These people are shit. Just let them know they're out of their league. You don't even have to worry about the guys, they're gone. It's just her really. Intimidate her, scare her. Beat the shit out of her . . . No, don't . . . I don't believe I said that."

"Listen, Claudia, relax, you're making a big deal out of nothing. Like I said, they're not going to find me. End of story."

CHAPTER 22

"Michael, you're late. The dinner's ice cold."

"I'm sorry Patti, I thought I told you I was stopping at my mom to drop off money."

"Well, you thought wrong. How much did you give her?"

"Two thousand and change."

"What did she say?"

"She was ecstatic to the point of tears."

"Who cries more than your mom? How much more of that are you going to tap into before we decide what we're going to do."

Mike sat down at the table, folded his hands and looked at his wife. "I already decided."

"*Ohh?* I'm listening."

"I'm twenty-four years old. The last thing I want to do is wind up behind bars for ten years, wishing I had walked away from it."

"Walked away from it? How do we do that?"

"That's the problem. It's not going to be easy. One option is to give it to my grandfather. Let him launder it till this blows over."

"Mike, you saw it. If these cops don't get it back, they are going to be relentless. You bought a hundred shares of IBM stock. You said you used cash so's not to leave a paper trail. Leaving a cash trail, bank heist cash no less, is riskier. Don't you think? If they subpoena those records we're screwed."

"Giving it back to the police is ludicrous. Did you really believe that *mick?* No questions asked, my ass. If I walk into his precinct with those bundles, they'll be putting cuffs on me before the bags hit the desk. One of their own was killed in there and trust me, they're out for blood."

Patti was becoming increasingly unglued over this money. She wanted it gone, for her own sanity.

"I think you're misreading it, Michael. They just want the money to close the case. Let's just get it to them. I thought about it and say we return it to the bank instead of the precinct. We dump it and get out of there before anyone knows what it is, where it came from. Boom, we're home free. The only thing that bothers me is your mom being out the cash."

"That doesn't bother me, the way the market is moving I still can make her comfortable investing the insurance settlement, not to mention the cash I already gave her. I like your bank drop idea."

"So then, what's the problem?" Patti asked.

"I just hate to give in to that arrogant bastard. Don't you?"

"Mike, *giving in* to that arrogant bastard is holding out your wrists while he puts handcuffs on them. That's what we're *avoiding* here."

Michael started pacing around his large living room. He then stopped and looked up to the hatch in the ceiling where the money was. He shook his head. Looking at Patti and then at the half-empty rooms he'd wanted to furnish, he said in a low tone, "Easy come, easy go . . . let's do it."

Patti sprang to her feet and glided over to Mike. Hugging him tightly she said, "I feel as if a ton of lead was lifted off our shoulders. Thank you."

"Well, it's actually a ton of *cash* being lifted off our shoulders." They laughed and sat down to their cold dinner.

* * *

"O'Reardon! Falco!"

"Here we go again," Falco whispered.

Rogers motioned from his office doorway for them to come in.

When they entered, the captain was facing his prized map, which encompassed much of the wall. It contained the entire 104th Precinct layout.

"Can either of you tell me what the little red stickers on this map represent?"

After a few seconds of silence Falco replied, "Robberies?"

Rogers finally turned around to them.

"That's the yellow ones. Homicides! Homicides in January and February *alone*. Homicides in the 104th alone. We, gentlemen, have a fucking war zone going on out there. TAC has been helping out in the streets but we're not getting help *investigating* these crimes. Last Friday alone we had four homicides. Know where this is going?"

"You want us to hurry up and close the Morgan case," O'Reardon answered.

"No. You guys are *off* the Morgan case. All you're doing is chasing money while felons are parading the streets."

"Captain, I know who's got the money and where it is, if we—"

"FORGET IT, BRIAN. Starting today you two are on the Bellafiore hit on Elliot Avenue."

Rogers thumbed through a pile of manila folders on his desk and pulled one out. "Here's the file. I expect a report back in three days."

O'Reardon turned and stormed out without saying anything, leaving Falco to retrieve the folder.

"You really blindsided us on this one, Captain," Falco said. "Can we at least get the okay to peek in on the Morgan case now and again?"

"I'll grant you some phone time on it, but no more trips out to the boondocks chasing butterflies. I want to see results on that mob rubout Falco!"

"Okay."

Falco left with a sense of accomplishment.

"At least we still have our foot in the door," he told O'Reardon when he caught up with him.

"Here's what we'll do. You start on the new case while I take a quick ride to Cumberland," O'Reardon said. "I wanna see what Aparicio has for us."

He found Whitey heavily medicated. Apparently, fluid had settled in his lungs and now he was fighting pneumonia.

"Aparicio!"

No answer.

"Aparicio!"

Without opening his eyes Whitey slurred, "That's gotta be my Irish friend from the one-o-four. You know I haven't heard my last name called that loud since Navy boot camp."

"Shoulda stayed in, you wouldn't be lying on this bedbug ridden hospital mattress right now."

"Yeah, I'd be in a VA hospital instead, having Viet Cong shrapnel plucked out of my ass."

"Except you were in the fuckin' Navy. Listen, time for you to hold up your end. What have you got for me?"

"Can I get another week? I swear I'll tell you all I know about who set it up."

O'Reardon's face contorted.

Whitey knew he was running out of time. There was still a shot at Sandy getting that money out of Manny. He needed him out on the streets.

"My girlfriend is still living in the same apartment. This guy knows where she lives. She's moving out of the neighborhood on the first of the month. If you can—"

"Don't screw with me!" She'll be living in fucking jail unless you come across with this guy's name."

Whitey believed him. "All right. I don't know his name, but I can tell you where he hangs out. I swear on my kid I'm not bullshitting you."

O'Reardon reached into his briefcase and pulled out a tape recorder. He laid it on the bed and switched it on. "All right, from the beginning."

Whitey started to nod off.

O'Reardon shook him. "Start from the beginning."

"I met him at a party. He was well-dressed Puerto Rican about thirty-five."

"What did he tell you at this party?"

"That the bank was an easy mark, women and a couple of old men. He said they would have a ton of money in their vault because of some payday or something."

"Was he supposed to do the holdup with you?"

"No, he said he was going to contact me for his cut."

"Which was?"

"Twenty-five percent."

"Did he contact you?"

"No. He musta got cold feet."

"You mean because of the guard being killed?"

"Probably. I never found out for sure."

O'Reardon could see Whitey's face grimacing from the pain he was in. He began to realize that his prisoner wasn't going to be around a whole lot longer.

"That's it? How am I supposed to arrest this guy with what you're telling me. How the hell are we supposed to even *find* him?" O'Reardon reached over and shut the recorder. "Listen, amigo, that's not enough. Now if I'm going to have the DA go easy on your old lady you have to do better." He turned the recorder back on. "What else do you want to tell me?"

"He usually has lunch in that diner on Flushing Avenue, the Empress."

"Give me a full description, how tall is he?"

"I'll do better than that. In the top drawer there's a small envelope."

O'Reardon reached in and opened it, revealing a small photo. He murmured something, then looked at Whitey for a good while. "You really don't know who this guy is?"

Whitey sensed the urgency in O'Reardon's voice.

"No, should I?"

"Where did you get this?"

"My old lady waited for him at the diner and took it."

O'Reardon held Manny's photo up to the light. "Fuck!"

He started dialing the phone in the room. "Davis, is Rogers around?"

Whitey was straining to hear this.

"Yeah Captain, I'm here at Cumberland Hospital with the Aparicio kid. Yeah, I know, Falco's over there now. Listen, he just fingered the bank manager as the set-up man . . . I'm not shitting you . . . Yeah, I know . . . He looks like he *might* be able to. Whether he's willing, is another question though. All right, I'll find out. Be back there in half an hour."

He went back to Whitey, "Tell me something. Why did your girl-friend take his picture? You two blackmailing him?"

Whitey looked stunned. "Did you just say he's the *manager of that bank?*"

"Yeah, you heard right. Again, are you two blackmailing him?"

"Noo, she just went there to give him an update on my condition."

"An update on your condition ….yeah sure."

* * *

Mike chose this morning to make the drop-off at Morgan. The plan was for him to continue on to work afterward as if nothing had happened. Patti had an unexpected feeling of sadness when the two satchels were dropped out of the attic and onto the hallway floor. Mike noticed the expression on his wife's face as he folded the steps back into the ceiling.

"Having second thoughts, are we?"

"Oh Michael, it would have been so nice."

"Don't put ideas into my head. We're returning it. Patti, we been through this. It's for the best."

"I know! It's just not as easy as I thought it would be. How are you planning to do this?"

He pondered for a while. "Ideally, I'd like to walk in and leave it unnoticed in a corner somewhere."

"They're pretty big," Patti said. "It will look pretty obvious that something is amiss when you enter the bank with those two bundles."

Mike thought some more. "A laundry cart! Do we have still have one?"

"Actually yes. I saved it," Patti replied, loving the idea.

She emerged from their garage with the cart and a large laundry bag.

Mike reached into one of the satchels and pulled out a wrapped stack of twenties. He tossed it to Patti. "This is instead of the fancy dinner."

She giggled nervously while he jammed the bulging laundry bag into the cart.

"Fits like a glove."

An hour later she stood with him in their driveway.

"Mike, promise me you'll be careful."

"Imagine having an accident now," he joked trying to diffuse the rising tension he saw in his wife.

"Don't worry, I'm just walking it in, filling out a huge deposit slip, and walking out."

"Hey! I'm serious, don't do anything dumb and call me as soon as you get to your office."

He wiped a tear from her cheek, kissed her on the mouth, and was on his way.

The ride in was uneventful. Stop and go traffic, WMCA Good Guys on the radio. He sang along with the Four Seasons as he edged along on the Parkway.

Arriving at Morgan Trust, Mike was relieved that there was a half-dozen people on the corner waiting for the bank to open. It was while unloading the cash from the back seat when it dawned on him that several women from the bank might remember him as Sal's kid. He couldn't be recognized doing this. He pulled his Yankee cap from the trunk. Pulling it down over his sunglasses he felt comfortably hidden. Mike walked briskly, pulling the cart behind him. Seeing himself reflected in the glass window, he realized how ridiculous he looked in a business suit and baseball cap, towing a laundry cart no less. He yanked off his tie and shoved it in his pocket. He looked at his watch. It was five to nine. Standing outside in the cold, he tried to blend in with the group of early birds staring at the front door. Mike started to get nervous. He hummed the Four Seasons tune he heard on the way in. *"Walk like a man, talk like a man, walk like a man my souhuhon."*

There was a click at the door and the platoon of customers marched in. He glanced around through his shades and was relieved that no one was looking his way. Stopping at the center counter, he faked writing out a deposit slip while peering above the dark glasses. He was searching for a parking space for his wagon. He spotted Dana and Rose behind the window. Their heads were down taking care of the first two customers. The new guy who sat at his dad's old desk was laughing on the phone with what seemed to be a personal call. Manny, as expected, was in his office toward the rear with the blinds drawn.

Mike decided that was the quietest and safest spot to leave it. He rolled it back there and without breaking stride, he released it a few feet from Manny's door.

Smoothly turning around while still clutching the deposit slip, he strolled out the door without a soul looking toward him. Feeling eerily burden free, he hopped into his car and hurried toward the Midtown Tunnel and his work week.

Forty-five minutes later he was on the phone with his wife.

"We're officially broke again."

"You okay?"

"Fine. All I did was walk in, roll it to a corner, and walk out. My guess is there's a commotion going on over there by now."

"And no one saw you?"

Mike was surprised by Patti's nervous tone.

"Babe, I didn't *hold up* the bank. What are you so worried about?"

"I'm just so relieved it's over with."

"Yeah, well, in a coupla months we'll have another mouth to feed so let me get some trading done just in case the child wants to eat."

"Michael?"

"What?"

"I love you."

"I'll give you every opportunity to prove it when I get home. Meantime, I gotta go. Love you too."

The market was moving well. Mike needed it strong if he was going to fulfill his promise to his family. Thing is he had to do it legally now.

CHAPTER 23

The first taste of approaching spring was felt in the morning air as O'Reardon and Falco drove toward Morgan Trust. The latest development of the bank manager fingered as the mastermind had piqued the interest of Captain Rogers and bought the duo still more time on the case.

"Fucking traffic. Never fails, whenever we come down here it's the same shit," O'Reardon said.

"I still don't know why we're even going there. We can't do anything with this until we have more to go on than a photo given to us by a drug addict," Falco said.

"I know that. Like I said, I just want to get another look at him."

"You thinking that's not him in the picture?"

"Rich, this whole thing seems so fucking bizarre, I don't know what to think. It's eight-thirty. If we can get to the bank in ten minutes we should catch a glimpse of him entering work."

"Only one way we're gonna do that." Falco reached under his seat, pulled out the cherry and stuck it to the roof.

The sight of a black Dodge with a siren blaring tends to open holes in traffic. O'Reardon flipped the siren off two blocks away from the bank and they quietly pulled up to a fire hydrant across from the entrance.

There were no customers waiting to gain entrance. Marie and Rose walked up together and were let in by the stern-looking guard. They watched a yellow Mustang back into a parking space across the street from them. Stepping out, fixing his hair and adjusting his shades in the car window reflection was Manny..

His manner annoyed O'Reardon. "Rich, how do we get this fuck?"

"Don't know if we can. If we get a taped statement from Aparicio in a hospital bed, this guy's lawyer will chew it up and spit it out."

O'Reardon just nodded as he watched the manager strut across the street. Falco noticed his partner was uncharacteristically tense.

"You okay?"

He didn't answer.

"Wanna go talk to him, see how he's doing?" Falco asked.

There was a lengthy pause before O'Reardon replied, "No. I'll only get aggravated."

They sat parked there, silently staring at the entrance for ten minutes.

"Are we staking this place for another holdup?" Falco quipped.

Without speaking O'Reardon put the Dodge into gear and started down Flushing Avenue. About a block and a half down he suddenly pulled over to the curb.

Falco looked at him. "What?"

"Did you see who we just passed?" O'Reardon replied looking in his rear-view mirror.

Falco turned in his seat to scan the traffic behind them.

"No, walking. That was our junkie pal's old lady."

O'Reardon spun a U-turn and slowly came upon Sandy. He double-parked and watched her. Falco strained his neck.

"Where do you suppose she's headed? No, can't be. No way!"

"Sure as shit is," O'Reardon answered. Sandy made a beeline straight into the bank.

"What could she possibly want in there?" Falco murmured.

"Aparicio must have got word to her that he works there. Rich, you're less obvious, take this newspaper and stand on the corner. See if you can notice anything."

"Manny's office?" Sandy asked the guard who was curiously eyeing the detective crossing the street. He turned toward her and motioned to the manager's office.

"Back there, on the left. The one with the open door." He then turned his attention back to the street.

Manny was on the phone when Sandy walked in. She did not expect the huge maple desk and spacious office.

"Let me call you back, babe." He abruptly hung up the phone with a look of a deer in car headlights.

She stared back. "Looks to me like you're the fucking *jefe* here."

"Yes, I'm the branch manager."

"Been expecting me?"

Sandy had read his name on the door when she reached for the doorknob. She closed the door and walked toward him.

"Actually no. I figured you came to your senses and decided to go about your life in a safer manner."

"Whoa, that has a threatening tone to it. Let me ask you this, Manuel Figueroa, branch manager, did you come to *your* senses and decide to keep your ass out of prison?"

"How did you find me here?"

"It wasn't easy, you sure keep a low profile in these streets, but your face is popular!" She held up his photo. "There's a good chance you'll become a whole lot *better* known, in the near future."

He snatched it out of her hand.

"You can have it, we got others".

"What is it you want?"

"Thirty thousand dollars."

"What! What happened to the twenty thousand you asked for in the diner?"

"That was before we found out you *work* at this bank. *Manage* it no less. It's a whole new ballgame now. Robbery/Homicide will cream all over this. Inside job with bank guard murdered. He was a retired cop! You cost them one of their own."

Sandy noticed Manny seemed less combative at this meeting. She wondered why.

"I'd like it in hundred-dollar bills."

"Please . . . sit down." He slid the chair alongside his desk a bit closer to him.

Sandy, wanting to appear in control, slid the chair back to its original position, sat, leaned her elbow on the desk, and said, "Today's Tuesday, I'll be back on Friday for it."

"No."

"Well faggot," she abruptly stood up, "then you better be ready for—"

"No, not Friday. Come tomorrow. I'll have the *twenty* thousand, your original amount, ready for you."

Sandy was caught off guard, hesitated, then said, "Alright, but no bullshit." She locked eyes with him then got up and headed toward the door. He couldn't help noticing how perfect those stretch pants looked on her.

She turned around. "I'll be here at eleven tomorrow."

"Not here! The diner, at twelve."

Sandy hesitated again, then relented. "How romantic, the place we met. Noon then."

"I'll be looking forward to it," he said sarcastically.

As soon as the door closed behind her he pounded his fist onto his desk toppling the pen cup. Then he reached for the phone.

"Claudia, it's me. We can't wait any longer, she came here, *to my bank*! We *have* to make a decision."

"Not on the phone, Manny, we'll talk tonight."

Falco turned his back when Sandy emerged from the bank. Then walked down to the car, hopped in and shrugged. "She went into his office and was back out in five minutes."

O'Reardon shook his head. "Aparicio says he needs time so she could *get away* from this guy and she fucking walks into his office."

They watched Sandy walk back down Flushing Ave. "Don't you want to follow her?" Falco asked.

"What for? She was probably there looking for a new lay. Her old man's *johnson* will be shriveled up by the time he gets out of jail."

O'Reardon drove past her and headed back to the precinct.

"Still think the kid's got the money out on the Island?" Falco asked.

"Totally! As a matter of fact, we're going back out there tomorrow night with a search warrant."

Falco groaned.

<u>February 27</u>

It was five o'clock and already dark when Manny walked into his Himrod Street apartment. Awaiting him at the kitchen table was his wife.

"We eating tonight?" he remarked surveying the bare table.

"We'll get *chinx.*"

"Chinx! You know I don't like—"

"*She came to the bank?*" Claudia asked, with her palms upturned.

Before his wife was able to regain her composure and ask why, he spit it right out. "She wants thirty thousand."

"What? Stupid bitch." She sprang to her feet. "We didn't even have the last demand she made, now she wants more? Just fucking tell her—"

"I agreed to give her the original amount."

"What?"

"Tomorrow, twenty thousand dollars."

"Manny, that's all the money we have in the world. In a few months we'll have a newborn and not a dime in the bank. There has got to be some way for us to get out of this shit without handing over all our money."

"Sit down Claudia."

She did as he said, and looked up at him with a realization that there was more news coming.

"I have . . . well, uhhh . . . I should say *we* have," and he grabbed her hand, "in the trunk of the car right now, *two hundred and twenty-seven big ones . . . in cash.*"

"*Aii Dio Mio Manuel! Estas loco, hombre.*"

"No baby, I'm not crazy. It was returned to the bank by someone, *don't ask me who.* All I know is, it was sitting in a shopping cart right outside my office, yesterday."

Claudia sat looking at the wall while he spoke.

"Whoever had it probably got cold feet and wanted it gone."

"Well, yeah Manny, there comes a time when a person realizes it's just not worth it, no matter how much there is. The police were obviously hot on their ass, so they dumped their problem in *your* lap."

"Problem? Our only *problem* is the *lack* of money. This cartload is the *answer* to our problems! Babe, listen, I been holding this money for two days. During that time, I watched for any signal that indicated it was returned to my bank. I really don't think that person will be announcing it, and worst-case scenario, if he or she does, all they can say they did was leave a shopping cart unattended in a busy bank."

Claudia looked at him sideways. "Do you think these cops are just going to say 'Poof, it vanished, let's all go home?'"

"I don't care what they say or do! Fact is A, there's a *lot* of money out there in my car, B, they will always believe Sal's family has the money. And C, I don't plan on being around these parts very long to even become *part* of the investigation. I'll give that bitch her twenty thousand tomorrow and warn her never to show her—"

"You make it sound so easy, Manny. Just like you made the job itself sound easy when you *first* told me about it. If you think I'm having a baby with the father doing hard time a hundred miles away, you better—"

"LISTEN, if you're not with me, fuck it, I'll go alone. I'll be damned if I'm going to be another Sal Marchetti donating my life to that little bank and just have a wristwatch to show for it when I'm old. Babe, with this money we can live like royalty in Puerto Rico."

She was starting to see his point of view, but still felt a need to talk him out of it.

"As soon as you leave New York they're going to be on you like flies on shit."

"I know, that's why we're not rushing out of here. We'll wait until everything blows over before we leave."

Claudia raised her head toward the ceiling as if seeking divine intervention. "I'm with you Manny, I'll always be with you, baby. *Dio* help us." Then she cried out, springing to her feet and throwing her arms around Manny, catching him by surprise. "That's almost a quarter million dollars!" Only her half-mooned stomach kept them apart.

"Wow, you sure switched gears! Okay, listen to me." Manny said, "The main thing is we must behave like the money doesn't exist. Better yet, we have to *think* like it doesn't exist. Just put it out of your mind. If one of us gets spotted with even new shoes, it'll draw attention. I'll continue at work like nothing happened and you continue to be a pregnant Puerto-Rican and blend in with the rest of the women around here."

She slapped his arm. "You mess up *pendejo* and you'll be blending in with the Puerto Rican men *who got us pregnant* . . . on Rikers Island."

The two laughed.

"Seriously, babe," Claudia said, "how do you suppose we can find out who brought that money there?"

"What's the difference?"

"The more we know the better. Maybe you should be putting feelers out there."

"Feelers? To who?"

Claudia shrugged. "Don't know, maybe start by calling Marchetti's wife. Ask her how she's doing or find a form she hasn't signed yet. Another way is to call those detectives and ask how the case is going. See if anyone says anything that might be helpful."

He again embraced her. "Listen to you, all this scheming." Then he stepped back and ran his hands over her belly.

"Wish us luck, *nino*."

CHAPTER 24

"Take McLaughlin and Bryce with you."

O'Reardon shot a disbelieving look at his precinct commander.

"Come on, Captain, you know I can't stand that fuck, and the other guy, Bryce, just got his gold shield. I don't even *know him.*"

"Brian, you guys are going out to Nassau County to search a country home with only a pregnant woman inside. It doesn't require a Marine invasion force."

"Exactly my point, me and Falco is all I need."

"You know precinct policy calls for four minimum and I can't send uniforms into Nassau. Just take 'em. Leave them outside in the car if you want, I don't give a shit, and make sure that warrant is valid!"

After more fruitless haggling with the captain, Falco briefed the two detectives on the operation. An hour later the foursome were on their way out east. The new guy, Bryce, did most of the talking from the backseat of their shanty Plymouth.

"I hear these folks are related to Johnny Papa."

The two detectives in the front seat ignored him. Finally, McLaughlin looked toward him. "Supposed to be his grandson. Wall Street type, to boot."

Falco looked over at O'Reardon with a raised brow to suggest, *how did these two get that information?* O'Reardon remained stoic. It became still inside the car as they sank into their seats and gazed out into the February darkness. It was barely five-thirty.

"What would it take for these hicks to light up a few roads out here?" O'Reardon asked, squinting to read the exit signs. "That say East Meadow?"

Falco motioned toward the small wooden sign.

The rear-seat detectives righted themselves as O'Reardon exited the parkway.

There was but a single car in front of the Marchetti house.

"Good, she's alone," O'Reardon said, as he pulled up behind her in the driveway.

He then looked into the rear-view mirror. "You two wait here."

"Goodnight," Mclaughlin slumped back into his seat. Bryce looked bewildered as the partners simultaneously exited the car.

The porch light went on as they walked up the steps and Patti Marchetti partway opened the door before Falco's hand reached the bell.

"Mike's not home."

O'Reardon reached into his pocket. "Don't need him, we have a search warrant for this premise."

He handed her the document as they brushed past her and entered the house. Falco gave her a sympathetic glance as he went by.

"What's this all about?" Her voice cracked as she scampered behind them.

"It's about a shitload of money your dearly departed father-in-law withdrew from his bank," O'Reardon answered while looking up the stairs. Used to searching city apartments, he realized a suburban house would be a chore.

"This place is bigger than I thought, might as well have Heckle and Jeckle come in to give us a hand."

Falco went out to the porch and waved them in. "Officer, I'm expecting a baby, and this is all too much for someone in my condition."

An annoyed O'Reardon looked at her three-months-along pouch. "I think you'll survive. Just have a seat inside and relax."

O'Reardon then barked out the assignments. Mclaughlin and Bryce jogged up the stairs toward the bedrooms, Falco and O'Reardon stayed downstairs. What started as a meticulous search soon escalated into an upheaval of everything and anything they thought might shield the money.

O'Reardon was the most out of control. "You can save us a lot of time and yourself a lot of mess if you just tell me where you have it," he barked.

Patti was in the kitchen staring out toward the driveway in hope that Mike would pull up. She said nothing to O'Reardon. The foursome went from room to room yanking out drawers and overturning mattresses. They also scoured the attic and basement and found nothing. It was late and the guys were tired and hungry. Falco said to O'Reardon, away from everyone's earshot, "I knew we were barking up the wrong tree. It's got to *still* be in the city."

McLaughlin wasn't worried about anyone's earshot when he remarked to O'Reardon, "You'd think after thirty years on the job you'd plan searches that come away with more than women's underwear."

O'Reardon was in no mood. "Now you got something to get off on tonight, Mac." Falco was looking at the trembling woman and thinking of an appropriate apology. Patti really began to lose it when she noticed O'Reardon reaching for her purse that sat untouched on the counter. O'Reardon liked to look at bankbooks during searches. Won't be the first time someone was dumb enough to deposit crime booty into their own savings account.

"You think it will fit in her purse, Lieutenant?" McLaughlin said in his usual taunting manner.

O'Reardon held his hand inside while looking out her window.

"You're right, *McBushnell*, what are the odds of finding a still-wrapped bundle of cash in a pocketbook that's sitting in front of us?" He lifted the stack of twenty-dollar bills that Mike had tossed to her that morning. It still had the bank's band around it. It was marked one thousand dollars.

O'Reardon milked it, "Tell me something, Rich, I don't have my reading glasses handy, does this little band say *Wells Fargo Bank?*"

Patti was struggling to keep her wits, but at one point she called out Mike's name as a knee jerk reaction when O'Reardon held up the money. Feeling defiant against everyone, an angry O'Reardon stormed toward the trembling woman waving the two-inch bundle under her nose.

"Would you mind explaining to me how this cash made its way into your pocketbook."

"It was given to us this morning," she mumbled.

"Given to you?"

"Yes, as a gift to Mike and me for the baby," she replied in a low voice. She tried to hide her desperation. O'Reardon frightened her to the point where she almost blamed the whole thing on her husband.

The bewildered detectives closed in on her, not for any strategic purpose, just to hear everything she was saying. Patti buried her head in her arms and cried aloud.

The sneering O'Reardon had his arms folded standing above her smacking the money against his side. While her crying was genuine it also bought her a few moments to think up a better excuse. Her brain wouldn't overcome her fear, so she just kept crying.

O'Reardon waited no longer. "Patricia Marchetti, you're under arrest for possession of money obtained during a capital crime."

"I told you the money was given to us as a present," she cried.

"By who?"

Just then Michael arrived at the front door.

"Please come in, join the party," O'Reardon said.

"What's going on?"

O'Reardon took a few steps toward him. "You tell me."

Mike recognized the stack of money in his hand. He also noticed the handcuffs that Falco was holding.

"If you're to referring to that money in your hand, *I* gave that to my wife to deposit in the bank. It's a bonus one of my clients gave me."

O'Reardon shoved the cash in his face. "First off, that's not what *she* said, secondly, you do see the marking on this, don't you."

"I do, Wells Fargo is a big company, with loads of customers."

"You know what, kid, I've had enough of your bullshit."

O'Reardon then snatched the cuffs from Falco and while glaring at Mike he walked over to Patti, grabbed her wrists, and handcuffed her. She gasped.

"Why are arresting her? The money was mine!"

Falco was once again watching his partner at work. O'Reardon led her by the arm toward the door.

Without turning around O'Reardon replied, "The money was in *her* possession, not yours."

Mike bolted to block the door when the young detective grabbed him.

"It's all right, Bryce, let him go," O'Reardon said.

Mike moved in front of O'Reardon and his wife. Holding up his hands he said simply, "Just hold on."

O'Reardon stopped. The three other detectives stood motionless. All eyes were fixed on Michael Marchetti. He was fumbling for words.

"We're holding, is there something you want to say?"

Mike finally replied. "I did as you said."

"Excuse me."

"I did as you said, returned the money, no questions asked. Remember?"

Patti held her cuffed hands to her mouth. She wasn't prepared for an admission of guilt. The cops weren't either.

"McLaughlin, go out to the car and call the desk. See what they got."

"Don't worry, babe, it'll be all right." Mike said to his reeling wife.

McLaughlin was out the door before Mike could give them the rest of the information.

"I didn't bring it to the station house. I dropped it off at Morgan Trust."

"*Why? . . . When?*"

"Why? Because I wanted to ensure my anonymity. When? Monday morning."

"You gave it to, what's his name? Figueroa?"

"Yes. I left it outside a door that had his name on it."

"You're saying you just left two satchels of cash, a quarter million dollars, outside the man's office?"

Mike nodded. "Actually, it was in a large laundry bag stuffed into the cart."

O'Reardon and Falco looked at each other with bewilderment.

"I barely made that much money in all my thirty years on this miserable job." O'Reardon sneered. "To think here it was left alone in a goddamn laundry basket."

"They got nothing, Lieutenant," McLaughlin announced as he re-entered. "Should I call the bank?"

A frustrated O'Reardon snapped at him. "It's nearly seven o'clock. Who you gonna call? The bank closed four hours ago." He looked at Falco, shaking his head. "Why the fuck didn't I retire last month?"

"I swear to you, I walked in there when they opened the place and left it right there. He would have had to step over it to get out of his office." Mike exaggerated; fact is, he'd left it in the hall near his office. He wondered about the odds of someone *else* walking away with it.

"I did exactly as you said, and your word was 'no questions asked,' so I would appreciate you uncuffing my wife."

Falco spoke, "First off, leaving the money unattended in a bank is not *exactly* bringing it to the desk sergeant at the 104th—"

O'Reardon interrupted him. "Who gave *you* the money?"

An annoyed Falco completed his thought, **"Secondly, nothing was returned!"**

Mike's attention was on O'Reardon and meekly replied, "My father did." He realized the extent of the damage he was going to cause. As soon as he implicated his father his eyes teared up. Patti closed hers. O'Reardon knew he had at his fingertips all the information he'd been grasping at for over a month. Falco had his notebook out and was not going to miss a syllable.

O'Reardon was so engrossed in this he remained standing in their doorway holding Patti's arm.

"Your father, Salvatore Marchetti, physically gave you that money?"

"No, he actually called me the night he passed away and told me how he got it and where it was hidden."

O'Reardon started to speak, "Okay, how—"

"Most important," Mike interrupted, "my father made it clear to me, he did not plan this. It fell into his lap. Like I told you, the man was a cream puff."

Falco peered over his notebook. "We already know about your father's safe-opening issue and storing the delivery in the office and all."

Once again Falco's sense of justice got his partner rankled. "May I remind everyone, it's *still a bank robbery*."

"I understand, lieutenant," Mike said, "but you must also understand, he was dying, and he knew it. My mom, brothers, and sister would have been in bad shape after his meager life insurance stipend was gone. I realize that doesn't make what he did—"

"You realize correctly," O'Reardon said. "Listen, it's not my plan to spend the evening out here in potato land, so spare us the bleeding-heart sermon. When did you pick up the money?"

"I said, the night he died. I didn't know about his heart attack until I returned home with the money."

O'Reardon released his hold on Patti and allowed her to sit on a chair. The handcuffs remained on.

The other three detectives stood in the background and let the senior officer do the talking. Falco was still writing.

"Where was the money kept?"

"In his cellar."

"How much was there?"

"That's the weird part. My father said there was two hundred and fifty thousand there."

"And?"

"Well, we only counted two hundred".

"We?"

"Well, my wife and I, when I brought it out here."

"Did your mother know you picked it up?"

"No, of course not. I thought I told you she had no clue that my dad had any money from that robbery. Are you kidding, my mother? She would have never stood for it."

"All right, spare us the bullshit. You said that about your father, as well. Also, we already *know* your mother *is* involved in this."

Mike leaned his head back. He looked at Patti and shook his head in confusion. He then locked eyes with O'Reardon. "If this is some police tactic to break me down, you're wasting your time. I *know* my mother had **no** idea what was going on."

O'Reardon was losing what little patience he had. "Remember we spoke about your father's girlfriend, Marie Werner?"

"Yes, and I remember telling you they had a brief affair twenty years ago and you're referring to that whore as his girlfriend is *way* off and merely another way of pissing me off."

O'Reardon suddenly grabbed Michael by the collar of his suit jacket. **"I haven't begun to annoy you yet, you thief!** In case you're interested, your father gave that *whore from twenty years ago* fifty thousand dollars of what was supposed to be your family's money."

Falco couldn't believe O'Reardon was blurting out all this information. He knew Mike had set him off by referring to Marie in that manner, but physically grabbing the kid was uncalled for.

O'Reardon continued his tirade. "Also, in case you're interested, your sainted mother had your family goons beat the shit out of that *whore* and steal the money from her. I should say *re-steal.* Money your father provided to help get her through the murder of *her* husband."

"What you're saying is ridiculous. I know it's not true."

"Yeah, well, again, you also said that about your father."

About then Falco caught O'Reardon's eye and motioned for him to come into the living room with him.

"You're not leaving him behind, are you?" Falco asked.

"Fuck no, I'm leaving *her* behind; she has little to do with this. *He's* coming to Queens."

"Think he's on the level with the bank drop?" asked Falco.

"If he *is*, it's the most bizarre case I've ever had, partner. *Think about it,* this guy Figueroa plans the heist, gets cold feet, drops out, and weeks later the money gets delivered to his door . . . by someone not even in on it."

Falco lit O'Reardon's cigarette, then his own, and said, "In a fuckin' laundry cart no less! Can't make this shit up." They went back into the kitchen and O'Reardon confronted Mike.

"Okay, here's the deal, Wall Street man. I have your wife cold for possession of bank robbery loot. We can have her in night court for a bail hearing in two hours in front of cranky Judge Burnbaum."

There was a low chorus of *ooos* coming from the two backup detectives. O'Reardon looked back at them. "I take it you two know him."

"Kid, I suggest you get a good lawyer and a great bail bondsman," McLaughlin said.

Patti continued crying into her handcuffs.

O'Reardon put his hands in his pockets and leaned against the door. "I'm going to tell you this one more time: all the people who committed this crime are either in jail or dead. It's the busy season in the city, roaches are coming out of the woodwork, and we don't feel the need to further clog the court calendars. That said, if you can come up with the bulk of the cash in five minutes our original deal is still on. If not, someone is riding with us back home."

"Lieutenant O'Reardon, if you held your .38 revolver to my head with the trigger cocked, I would not be able to give you any additional information. I no longer have the money. I brought it to the Morgan Trust Bank Monday morning at nine a.m. Left it in front of the bank manager's office neatly packaged in a laundry cart. If getting your hands on that money is so important, I would not waste any more time out here, I would be at the bank."

"Thanks for the advice and it is getting late so it's time to go." O'Reardon then went over to Patti and removed her handcuffs. He then turned to Mike and said, "*You're* under arrest for possession of stolen money."

Mike calmly held out his wrists and replied, "So I take it you're either going back on your word or you just don't believe I returned it." O'Reardon clicked the cuffs together sharply and motioned toward the front door. "I never go back on my word." The five of them had started out the door when Patti ran to embrace her husband. Falco, who was leading him toward the car, gave them a minute.

"Don't worry, honey, by morning this will all be straightened out. Call my office tomorrow and tell them . . . something."

Mike was relieved *he* was being arrested and not his wife.

CHAPTER 25

The kids were off to school and Laura Marchetti was having a peaceful cup of coffee when her bell rang. She buzzed it open and saw her daughter-in-law at the foot of the stairs. Instantly she knew something was wrong. Patti, at the landing, started to speak when Laura held her hand up to her lips and waved her up. At the top of the stairs, it became evident that Patti had been up all night.

"What happened?" she whispered.

"Michael was arrested last night."

"WHAT! Wait, come in."

"Your husband, got him involved with that damn money."

Laura, surprised by her belligerent tone, said, "What money?"

"Oh please, don't act as if you don't know nothing about this."

What Laura *wasn't* aware of, was Mike and Patti's knowledge of *any* family involvement.

"Let's calm down for a minute. Tell me why Mike was arrested."

"Four detectives arrived last night with a search warrant and found a thousand dollars and arrested him for it."

"Was it part of the money?" Laura asked.

After a brief hesitation Patti said, "Yes, it was."

"Where's the rest?"

"I don't believe it! You're worried more about the money than your son!"

"Patricia, I only asked that because I'm sure that will have a direct bearing on what charges he's facing. Furthermore, I'm not pleased with your tone."

Patti relented and grabbed her mother-in-law's hand. "I'm sorry, I haven't slept all night, and my brain is scrambled. Let me start at the beginning. Mr. Marchetti left Mike a—"

"Oh, is he not Dad anymore?" Laura asked.

"*Dad* left Mike a lot of money to give to you... discreetly. He wanted it to look like his life insurance investments paying off, or something. Mike reluctantly went along with it for the sake of you and the kids."

"I knew *nothing* about Mile's involvement," Laura said, "and would surely never have approved of it. I'll tell you what I *did* know and between the two of us maybe we can make sense of all this. Not a word was said to me, Patti. I suspected something only after seeing that Marie talking to Mike's dad on the corner here, then watched him go into our basement and bring her back a package. Out of curiosity I went down and saw those big bags of wrapped money down there. I was mortified. Then, right after Sal's funeral I went back down just to see how *much* was there, and it was gone."

"Guess what?" Patti said. "That was because Dad called Mike that same night and told him where the money was and to immediately come in and get it out of there. He didn't want you or the kids to know what he did. Mike was going to give you the money in bits and pieces so as not to attract attention."

"So, *Mikey* had the money all along?"

"Yes, but that's when things started to go haywire. First off, we were never comfortable with that money in our house. The detectives kept coming out asking questions. I'm not sure if they *knew* we had it, or what. The one old guy seemed like he knew something."

Laura was frozen with anticipation with every word she was hearing.

Patti continued, "We were at our wits' end after their visit. When they offered us total immunity we decided to return the money. Well, all except for the damn one thousand they found in my pocketbook. DUMB!"

"So, you returned it, good. Then why did they arrest him?"

"Well, problem is . . . Mike didn't bring it to their precinct like they asked. Not trusting they wouldn't arrest him, he snuck it back into the bank instead. Mike called me this morning from jail and confirmed the police never received any money. Wait! What's worse, the *bank* is saying they never received any money! So now he is being charged with stealing all of it and his bail now is two hundred thousand dollars. I don't know if it's coincidental, but that's almost exactly to the amount we had."

Laura sighed and shook her head, asking Patti, "What do we do?"

"Let's keep talking," Patti replied. "Maybe we can put together a plan. That lieutenant told Mike and me that you contacted your father and were able, with the help of his *people,* recover fifty thousand dollars from Marie Werner that *Dad*, for whatever reason, gave her."

"Well, his *people,* as you call it, are just a couple of friends of his that owed him a favor."

"So, it's true! . . . Laura, why would you do that when all the while you distanced yourself from all this? I was certain you'd condemn it if you found out."

"I did, at first, but when I noticed the money was missing, I was convinced Marie had snatched the rest from down there. Knowing how I detest her, the thought of her doing that made me go against *everything* I stand for. I sought revenge."

"What did you do?"

"I went to the only one I know with any experience in this sort of thing: my father. I made him promise no one would get hurt, and he had it taken care of. Well partially anyway. They got *fifty* thousand back and insisted I accept it."

Patti tapped her forehead. "Not that it matters, but we wondered where that portion was! Dad originally told Mike there was more than what we found."

Laura thought for a moment….. "Why would he tell Mike *that* amount if he intended to give Marie fifty thousand? Ha! I'll bet she called him that night demanding money. She must have known something. *Of course*, she could have easily found out from her husband about the locker thing. I'll tell you this Patti, I noticed Dad had a very troubled look when he was talking to her on the phone."

Patti thought for a while before speaking. "Well, it all means nothing now. Important thing is we must find a way to get Mikey out of there."

"Still, I feel better knowing he didn't plan this thing with her . . . But enough of that. You're right, we must get Michael home! The smartest thing to do it is find out who has this damn money and get it returned to them."

"I'm listening," said Patti, a bit taken aback, but liking this side of her husband's old-fashioned mom. Patti reasoned that you don't grow up the daughter of a mob boss without some of it rubbing off.

Laura got up, found a pen and paper, and then sat alongside her daughter-in-law. She started listing all the people who had anything to do with the mess, from start to finish. They shared their knowledge of each of person, whether dead, alive, or in jail. They recorded notes about the cops, the robbers, the employees of the bank, the Werners, the Staten Island crew, the newspaper guys, insurance adjusters, and even their family. Laura wanted two things to evolve from this: first, an overall picture of the events that led to this breakdown of their parallel plans; and secondly, that they both could agree on the likeliest candidate to sic the wolves on.

"Gotta be Manny Figueroa," Laura said matter-of-factly.

"Could it be more obvious?" added Patti.

Laura picked up the phone and called Staten Island.

"Mom hi, it's Laura. Dad home?..... Still?..... No, don't wake him, just tell him I'm coming out today for a visit..... No, nothing wrong......About noon, I just need his advice on something ..... No, they'll be in school . . Okay, see in a bit."

"What are you doing?" Patti asked.

"Going with *you* to Staten Island to see my father and tell him about Mikey."

"Why do you need *me* with you?"

"Uh, you're his wife!"

"But he's *your* father and Mike's grandfather! I know your family over there refers to me as the Long Island hick, which is not far from the truth. Now you want me to go in and have a sit-down with a mob boss?"

Laura didn't find that amusing. "You know, you should really stop watching those movies. It's not like that. We're just going to tell him what happened and get his advice."

"When you said *sic the wolves*, I though you meant the police."

"If I meant them," Laura replied, "I would have said *vultures*. Enough wasting time, there's an 11:30 ferry we have to catch."

* * *

Sandy felt unsteady as she approached the diner. She didn't see Manny's car outside even though she was late. She had a folded Woolworth shopping bag under her arm as she walked up the four steps leading into the greasy spoon diner. After taking a seat in the first booth she gazed unattentively at the one-page menu leaning against the sugar bowl. She noticed there were four other patrons present: two guys at the counter sharing the racing form, and an elderly black couple, sipping hot soup.

She mistakenly sat with her back to the door but stayed there anyhow. Not five minutes later she saw the shiny suit moving along-side her. Manny knocked on the table and slid in the booth alongside her. She was taken by surprise, expecting him to sit opposite her. More importantly, Sandy saw that he was empty handed.

"Missing something?"

"No, I have what I need, just not in here."

"Why not in here?"

"Because when I'm giving away my fucking life savings, I prefer to do it at *my* speed. You here alone?"

Sandy mockingly looked under the table.

"Is anyone waiting *outside*, smart-ass?"

"I came alone. You have the money in your car?"

He poked her in the shoulder with force, "I don't want to ever see or hear from you again after today. *Comprender?*"

Sandy shot an indignant look at him. He looked around and then grabbed her by the hair and pulled her face close to his. "*Understand?*"

Her Latina blood was boiling, and she normally would have let out loud curses, but didn't want to draw attention to anything that was going to prevent her from pulling this off.

"You won't see me again, *now let go of my hair,*" she calmly replied.

Manny released her and sprang to his feet. "Come on."

She followed him past the approaching waitress carrying her order pad. His car was parked in front. She watched him unlock the car and start to get in. He stopped midway and looked at her.

"Well. "

"*Well, what?*"

Her stomach churned She didn't know what to do. She braced herself when he reached over and pushed opened the door. She dropped onto the bucket seat. Manny started the car and slowly entered Flushing Avenue traffic. A few blocks down he reached behind her seat. Sandy took a deep breath as her hand instinctively grasped the door handle.

"Relax. I'm not going to harm a hair on that body of yours." He then dropped a taped paper bag onto her lap. "There's twenty thousand in there, in fifties."

Manny removed the Wells Fargo bands and replaced them with rubber bands. After doing some quick math and sensing the unmistakable feel of greenbacks in her palms she let slip a small smile.

"It's all there, he said.

"I'm sure, you're not that dumb. "

"Corners fine."

"Are you sure you're okay on this block carrying all that?"

Needing, again, to portray an image of strength, Sandy said, "*This block* . . . is part of our turf. I never feel threatened when I'm down here." She unrolled her bag and dropped the package into it.

The truth was, she hated this area. It was a no man's land of dingy factories which, after closing time, surrendered the cobble-stoned streets to car cannibals and bruised-up hookers.

He rolled the car to a stop and Sandy, clutching her bag, eased out without saying a word. They both hoped they would never see each other again.

CHAPTER 26

The morning had a refreshing spring feel to it. The city streets flourish when a February day hits fifty degrees. The detectives shed their overcoats before they left the precinct.

"Captain says we haven't got enough for an arrest warrant, so why are we going to see this guy? Even better, what are you going to ask him? Falco asked.

"How ya doin', amigo?" O'Reardon replied.

"No, really."

"I'm not sure, I don't want to tell him about Whitey Aparicio's statement too soon. If he finds out we know about his part in the holdup he'll disappear for sure. Let's play it by ear."

The workers in the bank noticed the two detectives as soon as they entered. O'Reardon led his sergeant toward Manny's office.

"Good morning, Officers. What can I do for you today?"

"We're here, Figueroa, for your bank's report of returned money."

"Sorry to inform you, Lieutenant, there was no returned money here . . . that *I* know of."

O'Reardon feigned surprise. "You mean *nothing* was returned to this bank on Monday? No bags, laundry cart, maybe a quarter million in cash. Anything sound familiar here?"

"Not here," he said, shaking his head. "*I* certainly would have seen it if it were left here."

"I didn't say it was *left* here. I believe I said it was *returned* here."

Manny tried to remain cool. "Then tell me, sir, who was this person that *returned* it?!"

"Your girlfriend having a baby?" O'Reardon said, looking at the five-by-seven on his desk.

"Yes, we are expecting a child, and she's my *wife*," he replied glaring at O'Reardon.

The detectives both knew he was married. It was just another mean-spirited O'Reardon remark designed to rankle him and throw him off posture.

It worked.

"So, you gonna tell me which one of our employees is taking in laundry on company time?" Manny said sarcastically.

"How about you tell *me*?"

"*I* have no idea."

"Oh, I think you do. I think the guy that told us he gave it to *you* is telling the truth."

Manny remained smooth, which was no easy task considering the plunder was locked in his car trunk no more than a hundred feet from where they stood.

O'Reardon's style had always been to force their hand. Make them react. It had worked with Mike, it had worked with Whitey, and with the junkie in the park. Proven method, put the hammer down on them and soak up whatever squirts out.

"You're not planning on leaving the city any time soon, I hope!" Falco asked.

"I already had my vacation this year. Just got back as a matter of fact."

O'Reardon shrugged. "We're not talking about *vacations* here. You have no family member in trouble in Puerto Rico that you urgently must attend to, or a couple more kids stashed away over there that suddenly need their *Poppy*?"

That put him over the edge.

"Nope, no family trouble, and my kid isn't born yet so I think I'm a pretty safe bet to remain around here. I'm curious, Lieutenant, has it become department policy for drunken Irishmen to be the authority that monitors the lifestyles of other cultures?"

Falco looked at O'Reardon.

O'Reardon stared at Manny.

"The authority that oversees the lifestyles of other, what was it, cultures? Pretty impressive sentence! They should put shiny suits on all the dumb spicks in this neighborhood, works wonders."

Falco saw that O'Reardon was softening in his old age. Was a time when he would have hammered his head against the wall for that.

Manny took the insult in stride.

"I know you have that money," O'Reardon said, "and I'm going to take great pleasure in seeing you locked up."

"I have no idea what you're talking about. Just admit to yourself that you guys *fucked up* this case and go on to the next one."

O'Reardon moved close to him. Manny remained in his seat and looked straight ahead. "Listen, Poncho, it might interest you to know that we have your friend Wilfredo Aparicio on tape saying you were the mastermind of the holdup."

"WHAT? You're making shit up now."

"Am I?"

"Who is Wilfredo Aparicio, I never heard of him."

"You know him as Whitey," Falco said. "The guy who was stabbed in jail. He's sure as hell heard of *you*. Actually, lately, you've seen more of his *old lady* than he has,"

"Ya know, you guys are full of shit. First you say someone returned the money to me, now you're saying I *stole* it! Do you know how stupid you sound?"

O'Reardon turned to Falco, "Think we sound stupid, Rich?" He was scratching his head for effect.

"You know, maybe we *do* sound a little stupid," Falco replied, "but not nearly as stupid as arranging a holdup of a bank you're the manager of."

"That's total bull—"

O'Reardon interrupted, "Not nearly as stupid as allowing yourself to get photographed by the woman who was blackmailing you."

Manny recoiled.

O'Reardon pulled out the photo Sandy took and held it up.

"That supposed to be me?" Manny said, reaching for it.

O'Reardon held it away. "Spickskin suit and all."

"Agree, it certainly doesn't look the Sears rag you're wearing! Listen, this is obviously a ploy and it's not working. You know as well as me, if there were any facts in all this you would have me in handcuffs by now."

"Oh, don't worry, you'll be having peanut butter sandwiches with your amigos on Atlantic Avenue before you know it," O'Reardon remarked.

"Well, until then, I have a lot of work to do and also a fine lunch planned at the Rathskeller in Ridgewood." Manny said, "You know, I see a lot of police brass getting their *complimentary* meals there. I guess they don't extend the same courtesy to you street humpers."

"I recommend their pastrami on rye," O'Reardon said. "I also recommend you chew it slowly and hold onto the memory."

The insult war ended, and they exited the bank without saying more.

Manny's heart was racing. *Do these guys really have shit on me?* he wondered. *How did this happen?*

Crossing the avenue, oblivious to the traffic and blowing horns, the duo hopped into their Plymouth.

Falco spoke first, "Well, so much for us not tipping our hand too soon."

"I don't know why I fucking did that. I should have left that photo inside my desk. What's our book's first lesson . . . Present your evidence *after* the arrest.... *Dumbass.*"

"Think he's sticking around?" Falco asked.

"Sorry man, I get so riled by these motherfuckers, my anger gets the best of me. Back in the day, you let out your frustrations on their fucking skulls. Nowadays, you have to bite your lip just to avoid fuckin' Internal Affairs. Glad I'm getting out of here. By the way, notice he said *I* didn't find anything, instead of *we.* There were four other employees in there."

"Yeah, good point. Think he's sticking around?" Falco repeated.

O'Reardon looked at him, then turned to the road. "I don't know. What I *do* know is no way the captain is going to assign a tail for him."

"Nope. But he may put a tail on *you*, though!"

O'Reardon just shrugged and smirked.

* * *

"Jesus Christ, I hope you don't have the baby *here!*" John Paparelli said.

Patti laughed. "It's a little soon yet," she said, rubbing her belly.

"Dad, I wish you wouldn't use the lord's name in vain," Laura scolded.

"It shows how seldom you get here, or you'd be used to it," Mama P. said.

That was the last of the lighthearted conversation.

"Come downstairs, you two," the old man said.

Walking down the stairs Laura started to speak, "Dad, we came today because—"

"Wait, I don't want your mother to hear," he said in a low voice. "I know about Mikey. Sit here."

The three of them settled in a triangle.

"How did you find out?" Patti asked.

The other two looked at her as if it was a dumb question. "Dad has friends." Laura said dismissively.

"I was told he was being held for possession of stolen money," he said. "One thousand dollars? What the hell is that all about?"

Patti was content letting her mother-in-law do the explaining.

"Dad, Michael had the money all the while. He's the one who removed it from the bin. I wasn't aware." Laura said. She paused waiting for a response. There was none.

"Sal called him and told him about it and to come and get the money out of the house. He must've known it was going to be his last day. God rest his soul."

Still nothing.

Patti, embarrassed by their criminal behavior blurted out, "But we returned it!"

"What did you return?" Mama cheerfully asked as she descended the stairs carrying a tray of pepperoni and cheese. She saw the look on the old man's face. "Never mind, I'm leaving."

"Thanks for the snack, Ma. I'm hungry."

He looked at Patti, then addressed his daughter. Laura wasn't surprised by his response.

"*You returned it?*"

"I didn't, Dad, Mikey did . . . and rightfully so," Laura said.

He leaned back with a bewildered look on his face. This time he stared ahead, at nothing.

"Why then, are they holding my grandson?"

Patti was feeling less intimidated by this powerful man sitting alongside her. The police had said if we returned it there would be no questions asked so Michael returned to the bank and left it outside the manager's office.

"So why is your husband in jail?"

"They claim they never received it. He was actually arrested because the police found some of the money we *stupidly* held back."

Another pause.

He thought about the woman he wrongly ordered beaten up.

"I don't believe it; I'm surrounded by morons all day and now my family . . . He stopped short and turned to his daughter. "Why would your husband drag his own son into this bullshit? Why didn't he come to me? With all the resources at our disposal here, why would he put this on a schoolboy's shoulders?"

"Dad, he was sick. He wanted Michael to get it to me disguised as investments." Laura avoided telling her father that he was the *last* person Sal would trust.

"**He got his son locked up**, was all he got!"

"I know it was reckless, but, Dad, he wanted his kids provided for. If it wasn't for the bank guard's wife finding out, all this would probably never have happened."

"Who do you think got the money?"

They both spoke at the same time; Laura was first. "We know exactly who has it, the manager of that bank. He was Sal's boss, a Puerto Rican guy named Manny, a real *schevatz*. Michael rolled a laundry cart with the money inside right in front of his office, *while he was in there!* Mike said he couldn't have left his office without falling over it."

"Did he leave a note with it?"

"No, he didn't want to incriminate himself."

The women chewed on the snacks while the old man stroked his mustache.

"First thing is, we gotta get the kid out. I was told the bail is two hundred thousand. We have a bondsman who will take ten grand to put up the money. I'll have to vouch for Mikey though."

Patti was anxious. "How soon can we go over there?"

"First things first." He got up and walked over to the far wall, then pushed in a section of wallpaper in and slid it over. Behind the wall-papered board was his safe. It wasn't even locked. He counted out ten thousand in hundreds, spun the dial, and slid everything back. It all simply disappeared.

Laura was concerned for her father. "Dad, I know this is not the best time for you to be doing this with all your cases and lawyer's fees this year . . ."

He waved his hand. "The main thing is to get Mikey home."

* * *

"Hey, honey, you're early." Claudia called from the bathroom.

"We got a change of plan," Manny said. "The shit's coming down."

She came out wrapped in a towel. "What happened?"

"The cops know I have the money. They don't have any proof yet or they would have arrested me."

Claudia hand covered her mouth. "What did they find out?"

"I'll tell you all that later; right now we gotta start getting things sorted. Pack a small bag, we'll buy everything new. Be ready to go by tomorrow night."

Manny was talking above her moaning.

"Listen," He took hold of her. "We'll drive to Miami, sell the car there, and take a cruise from there to Ponce. You always wanted a cruise, right?"

"Manny you're not going to sugar-coat this. How the hell are we going to survive as fugitives?"

"Very comfortably, we don't need this place anymore. Most of your family is in Puerto Rico, no more cold winters. No more being called spick . . ."

"Who calls you that?"

"All the fucking time. Today. A high-ranking cop."

"Then let's leave tonight," Claudia said.

"No, tomorrow's better, I need one more day at the bank."

"Why? What if they come for you tomorrow?"

"They won't. If they didn't arrest me today what difference would twenty-four hours make? Besides, tomorrow's Thursday, you know what that means."

She squinted her eyes. "You gotta be kidding."

"Another hundred big ones coming for Friday's run."

"Manny, let's leave tonight, don't be greedy."

"Listen, grand larceny is grand larceny, whether it's two hundred or three hundred thousand. I'm going for it. We'll leave this place tomorrow morning. I don't want this money at my address. You can drop me off at work then go to a hotel for the day with two cash-filled suitcases."

"Where's this hotel and what am I supposed to do there?"

"It's the St. George, downtown Brooklyn and you're *supposed* to lock yourself in the room and keep that money out of sight. I'll leave the bank right after closing, about 3:15, and you'll pick me up out front. I'll have the third bag and we'll head due south with at least three hundred big ones. We'll hit that island like fucking royalty!"

"Yeah, well, calm down Poncho Villa. It's not going to be that easy. Don't you think there's going to be people watching us?"

"Claudia, I know how this city works. The cops can't keep up with all the crime here. There's no way they're putting a twenty-four-hour tail on me. They don't have the people. When they get around to charging me, we'll be on a sandy *playa* far away from New York City."

"With our newborn," she relented.

Chapter 27

"Hey Rich, got a *bit* of news this morning, actually *two bits*, that might interest you," O'Reardon said as Falco arrived at his desk, coffee in hand.

"What happened?"

"That junkie died last night."

"Whitey Aparicio?"

O'Reardon smirked. "Yup."

Falco was jolted and annoyed at his partner's callousness.

"Got a call from Cumberland twenty minutes ago—he just stopped breathing."

Falco straightened his slumped shoulders and regrouped. "You usually do when you bite it. What do we got today?" He sighed.

O'Reardon looked down at his notes. "First off, we gotta get down to Pier Seven in Red Hook and talk to the longshoreman who spotted the floater. Then we gotta interview the two hookers who saw the Graham Avenue shooting, one of which is locked up in the Village."

"I hate that fucking dungeon, when are they going to close it?" Falco said, referring to the Women's House of Detention on Greenwich Village's Sixth Avenue.

"How could you say that? I love going there."

"What about Figueroa?"

O'Reardon shrugged. "The captain's busting my balls to get these other cases rolling. Told me flat out to stay away from the bank."

Falco was flipping through the usual newspaper on O'Reardon's desk. "Easier said than done. And what was the other bit of news?"

"Oh yeah, the Marchetti kid made bail last night."

"No shit, where'd they get that kind of money?"

"With a grandfather named Paparelli you don't spend much time in the pen."

Falco was looking at the calendar on their bulletin board, finally saying, "How many days you got left?"

"And here I thought you were staring at Sophia Loren's cantaloupes. Counting today, seventeen."

"That's all? Speaking of big jugs, have you heard from Marie Werner?"

"I talk to her now and again. Looks like she's off the bottle again, which makes for a boring *now*. I'm thinking she calls mainly for gossip on the case. Can you believe, for a while there I was actually thinking of settling down with the woman?"

Falco noticed the empty stare on his partner's face. He broke the mood. "Okay so she's not her sexy flamboyant self, *sober*, and she becomes an obstinate bitch when she drinks too much. Reminds me of a book I finished last week where this woman hires a famous out-of-town gunfighter to protect her ranch from ruthless cattle barons. Two weeks later her hero arrives rolled up stoned-drunk with the stagecoach luggage. She sobers him up and his shaking hand couldn't shoot the side of a barn. The townsfolk are dismayed at their prospects until someone buys him of a bottle of rye whiskey and has a slug. He then starts to hit a few targets and after a couple more he is dead-on accurate and back to his old gunslinger self. The crowd starts cheering until a few more gulps and he begins to falter. Twenty minutes later he almost shoots his own leg off. They huddle in a frenzy and decide it's best to keep him *half* drunk."

"Yeah, what happens?"

"He winds up killing all the bad guys and they live happily ever after."

O'Reardon looked at him sideways. "What's that, a bedtime story you tell your kids?"

"It's actually being made into a movie, with Lee Marvin. It should be out soon."

"Keep Marie Werner half drunk, huh? Could work. All I would need is an IV drip to regulate the dose. Nah, she'd probably squeeze the bag and throw up on me."

Falco spit out his coffee. When he was done laughing, he looked at his deadpanned partner biting his lip and realized, probably for the first time, he was going to miss him.

"Ya know partner, if you insist on banging suspects, Laura Marchetti is more your type."

"You're right, Rich, she is. I told you she reminds me of my Jenny. It's just the kids thing, not up for all that at this stage."

* * *

"Hey Enzo, it's ham and eggs time, we got a ten o'clock sit-down with the boss over in Stapleton," Ragusa said.

"When now? I'm just leaving to get a haircut."

"Yeah, well forget it. I'll pick you up in ten minutes."

Richie Ragusa and Enzo the Monk were soon hustling along Victory Boulevard to meet with Johnny Papa for breakfast at the Empress Diner.

"How's Mikey doing?" Enzo asked the old man before he reached the booth.

"*Minca*, the kid spent one night in the joint and everyone's acting like he hasn't seen the sun in years. Don't worry 'bout him, he went to work today like nothing happened."

"Come on, sit down. **Waiter!**" He didn't wait for individual orders. "Bring us each ham and eggs. A couple pieces of sausage and some coffee."

Richie and Enzo were used to this, and they took it all in stride. They noticed he was more businesslike this morning.

"What's up, boss?" asked Enzo.

"I wish I could give you more time to get squared away, but this has *got* to be done this afternoon."

The guys looked at each other.

"Is this about that broad Marie what's her face?" Richie asked.

"Hey Ragu, how's about *you* closing it and letting me talk. This is not about her, but it is about the same money. We got this Puerto Rican bank manager over on Flushing Avenue who needs a visit this afternoon. Now listen to me, you can't fuck this up. You know that private investigator over on Cornell Street?"

"Yeah, Jimmy Starks, did he ever finish paying you?" Enzo asked.

"Not all of it, which is why he's standing outside the Hotel St. George as we speak working it off. I had a feeling that manager wasn't sticking around here too much longer so I hired Starks yesterday to stay glued to him."

"What's with the St. George? I thought this guy lived over in Bushwick," Ragusa said.

"That's the fucking weird part. I figured a couple days minimum before they make a move and two hours into it he calls me and says they're loading their car with suitcases."

The Monk started to speak, "Sounds like they're—"

"Will you fucking let me finish one thought! Rich, how do you put up with this washwoman all day?... So, he calls me and says they're loading up the car. I'm now calling people to grab this fuck. Ten minutes later he calls back and says their lights went out, but they didn't leave. Turns out, *they went to bed!* This morning she drives him to work, then checks in at the St. George. You tell me, what do you think is going on?"

"It's obvious, they're outta here tonight," Ragusa said.

"Why not last night? Why go in another day?" the old man asked.

The two of them hesitated and looked at each other for a response. Ragusa scratched the back of his neck while he looked off to the side, then snapped his fingers. "Another heist!"

The old man snaps his finger and points at him. "This one he does alone."

"So, she has the other money with her. Think it's in the car?" Enzo said.

"If I thought that, you think we'd be sitting here on Staten Island? No, Starks said she carried two suitcases into the hotel. An awful lotta clothing for one night's stay, ya think?"

Enzo got stoked. "Why don't we just go up there, knock on the fucking door and—"

Ragusa interrupted, "No, too noisy, we wait for her to come out and we lead her to the car, like gentlemen."

They turned toward Johnny Papa for his reaction. He was slowly spooning his eggs. He then abruptly looked up at them. "They're being greedy, so we're gonna be greedy. The money at the hotel isn't mine, it's rightfully my daughter Laura's. However," he then took a long sip of coffee while salting his home fries, "whatever he carries out of that bank at closing is ours."

"What if he comes out empty handed?" Monk asked.

The old man thought a second. "Then that'll be like the Seagram's truck leaving the docks you and that dope fiend from Red Hook grabbed in sixty-two."

"Was that the empty one?" laughed Ragusa.

"Everything's fucking funny to you," Enzo growled.

"Enzo, how do you *not know* the truck was *delivering* the booze for export, not loading it up!" the old man said while dribbling out his breakfast.

Enzo couldn't help but laugh with them. "You should have seen that fuckin' stoned piece of shit I brought try to drive an eighteen-wheeler down DeKalb Avenue. I'm yelling at him to stop; he drives all the way to Bed-Stuy bouncing off parked cars."

"Fuck you doing *in Bed-Stuy*?"

"We pull up at the Marcy Projects and he hands the keys to some moolie for three bags of dope."

The customers in the quiet diner were looking over at these three guys in mohair suits rolling around the booth.

"I haven't a clue what became of that truck."

Then the boss gathered himself, looked at Enzo and said, "Listen to me, this guy's taking as much as he can carry out of that bank this afternoon. *I just know it!*"

"Hey boss, what if he leaves before we get there?" Ragusa asked.

"Don't worry, I thought of that. If he skips without closing the place they'll be on his ass like a pimple. If he leaves at closing, he'll have all night to get away, and if he calls in sick on Friday it'll be three or four days before anyone knows what happened."

"So, what's the plan, boss?" Ragusa asked.

"I want you two outside the bank, unseen, by noon. If he leaves for lunch, tail him. If he's carrying anything, tail him closer. Remember he hasn't got his car so he's expecting his wife to pick him up."

"Anybody gonna be with her?" Enzo asked.

"Yup, she'll be escorted by our guys, right to his bank." The threesome leaned back while the waitress poured more coffee. Then forward.

"These two need to be convinced that the other one's life is in peril. Carry your pieces where he can see them."

Paparelli thrived on planning these jobs. He had a habit of instructing the guys like it was their first time out there.

"Listen close . . . the first words you speak when you come alongside him, 'Figueroa keep walking; we have your wife from the St. George.' Now he knows he's screwed and he's at your mercy."

"Think he'll be packing?" Ragusa asked.

"No, no way."

"Who's gonna be with the broad?"

The boss hesitated, knowing the bad blood. "Fat Vinny and Joey."

"JOEY FINGERS?" Enzo said.

"Lower your voice, moron, and his name is Joey Stubbs" Paparelli said.

"Boss, he's a fucking maniac. You forgot about the airport thing already? There's a reason he's not made, he's *pazzo!* I mean *out of his mind!*"

Ragusa apparently agreed with him. His eyes rolled as he rested his head on his hand.

"Listen you two, don't worry about Joey. That airport shit was a long time ago, he's not a kid anymore."

"*He cut off his own fingers for Christ's sake.*"

Richie Ragusa shot a look over at his friend as if to say, "Don't push your luck."

"Vinny is one of our best men and he'll be right alongside Stubbs. Who, Mr. Fucking-know-it-all, wasn't made because his *grandmother's* a kike, not because he's nuts. I like loose cannons, the crazier they are, the more money they make me."

Johnny Papa looked at the phone booth in the diner vestibule. It hadn't rung for an hour, meaning everything was going according to plan.

"You two better get going, you got a long drive to Brooklyn."

* * *

There were two more homicides at the precinct.

One was an infant dropped from a third-floor window. The squad was already light due to vacations, injuries and sickouts, so Captain Rogers held the men there on a short leash. The smoke-filled homicide suite was bustling with grumpy overworked detectives, angry relatives, and shady stoolies.

"Don't even waste your time, Brian, he won't agree to it."

"What if I tell him I'm willing to put off my retirement a week or so?" O'Reardon said.

Falco couldn't believe his ears; he turned his head from his desk and aimed a perplexed stare at him.

"Why would you even do that? This guy means that much to you, or you got a ransom worked out with the insurance company?"

O'Reardon found his humor a needed distraction from the chaotic room. "Actually, they promised to insure my boat for free."

Falco grinned. "Now *there's* a huge risk for them, especially since the tub never leaves the dock. Then again someone could trip over the tie line, fall into your boat and get impaled with a beer bottle. *Huge* lawsuit."

"First warm day this spring, wiseass, I invite you to drive down to Sheepshead Bay at 6 AM and watch the *Mister Meanor* steaming into the sunrise."

"Yeah, a lot of *steam* comes out of that little rust-bucket." Falco then got serious. "So then, why would you want to give up a week of that just to chase around a bank clerk?"

"First off, the channel is frozen. More important, I look at this case like a plump cherry on top of the unwanted fruit cake that represents my thirty-year career."

"Wow, thirty years! Do you ever wonder what you'd be doing these days if it wasn't for that accident and had retired after twenty, like you planned?"

O'Reardon thought awhile. "Well, my daughter Kelly would have been twenty-seven next month, so you know what I'd be doing? At six every morning I'd be steaming off in the distance with a boat named," he paused and pulled out at his teenage daughter's faded picture, "*Grandpa's Ferry.*"

He then swung his chair away toward the other side of the desk to grasp an unnecessary folder. Falco briefly placed his hand on his partner's shoulder as he passed behind him. "You wait here, I'll go talk to Rogers."

The captain was on the phone with a deputy inspector, explaining the area's spike in crime when Falco walked up to his door. Rogers waved him in and pointed to the seat alongside his desk. Hanging up the phone he said to Falco, "They think I have a goddamn army here!"

"I take it now is not a good time for this."

"What does O'Reardon want?"

"We *both* want to toss this guy Rodriquez' apartment. We think he's dumb enough to have the money stashed either there or in his car."

"There are four other cases on your—"

"Yeah, yeah, I know, but he's about to skip out with a quarter-million dollars that doesn't belong to him."

Captain Rogers was silent. A good sign, Falco thought. "It will only take an hour," he added.

Rogers looked amused. "An hour, huh? How come you guys put four hours on your overtime slip on the other house search?"

Falco thought fast. "That was a *house* search, this is a small apartment, *and* this one's not thirty miles away."

"Ahh shit, call Goldfarb and get the warrant. Do the search first thing this morning and then get right on the important cases."

"You got it, Cap."

O'Reardon was still lost in thought when Falco walked over to him. "C'mon partner, let's go see the judge."

O'Reardon grinned. "Well, goddamn."

A half hour later they were cruising up Bushwick Avenue on their way to Manny Figueroa's place.

"Make a left at that white church, Himrod Street."

They went east a few blocks until they found number 229. Falco didn't see the Mustang anywhere on the block. They entered and saw his name on the hallway bell labelled 3A. O'Reardon rang what he figured was the janitor's bell to gain entrance through the second door.

The janitor came out and knew these two were cops. "Who you guys here for?"

"We have a search warrant for Figueroa's apartment," Falco said holding up his badge.

He led them up two flights of stairs while feeling for the key on his massive ring.

Falco knocked, then pounded on the front door. **"Police! Open the door!"**

He then nodded to the super and the key was inserted. In they went with their right hands on their service revolvers. The furniture was there but their day to day was gone. Drawers and cabinet doors were left open, closets were mostly filled with clothes they'd left behind, and their cat was also left behind with a large open bag of food and bowls of water. A note on the counter said simply, *Cat's name is Willie.*

"Shit, I figured the *end* of the week," the lieutenant said.

"Why the end of the week?"

"This would give him a chance to add his *coup d'état* and clean them out one last time. Scumbag."

He picked up the wall phone and got a dial tone. "Rich, call the desk. Have someone check all flights to Puerto Rico. His wife's name is Claudia. Manuel and Claudia Figueroa."

While Falco was on the phone, O'Reardon rifled through their remaining effects, to no avail. Nothing was left behind they would need.

"They're working on it, Brian, there's a lot of flights to check."

"I'll bet he's fucking gone. We should have been out there . . . *shit!*"

"Maybe, it's a blessing in disguise," Falco reasoned. "Let's just head up to Glendale and see about that mob hit from Tuesday."

O'Reardon was in no mood for the Glendale thing. "That's a bullshit case. Nobody knows nothing. A guy gets a bullet between his eyes in a crowded restaurant, and no one sees a thing. Why even go?"

"It's your call, but there's nothing here to do."

They thanked the super, who was on his knees playing with the young feline, then Falco added, "looks like you have a new pet, name is Willie."

The duo then headed to their car and east toward Glendale.

CHAPTER 28

"You all right, Manny? You didn't eat lunch and look like you haven't slept in days," Rose Marino, the head teller said.

"Not really, I feel like shit. That's why I hardly left my office this morning."

"I'll bring you back soup from Mario's, it'll do you good."

"Nah, I'm just going to continue with these ledgers and get my mind off things."

It was nearly one o'clock and he had two hours to get the money out of the vault. His receipts showed one hundred ten thousand in mostly small bills back there. Getting it out the door was not going to be as easy as he'd thought. Manny had a shopping bag he stashed in his closet. He tried to remain as calm as possible and make it appear as just another day.

His last chore was a huge business loan for his friend Mundo's bodega expansion. He knew it was a bad loan and one the head office would certainly question but little did he care.

He cut Mundo a check for thirty-six thousand dollars. Manny chuckled when Mundo offered him a thousand out of it. He thought about having his amigo carry the briefcases out for him at closing but thought better of it. He hadn't heard from Claudia and worried if she's going to be out there with the car when he left.

At two p.m. Manny gave his assistant manager the rest of the day off then quietly shuffled the flattened paper bag into the vault. He scooped the bundled cash into the sack, nearly filling it. He peered out from the vault to make certain the tellers were occupied, then nonchalantly carried the money the ten steps into his office and placed it behind his desk. After fifteen minutes at his desk spending his fortune in his daydream, he walked to the front of the bank and peered out the window to make sure no one was lingering. He looked for his car. Not there—a good thing. It was too early, and he didn't want her sitting out there with all that money. *This is going to be one long hour.*

**

After an hour and a half of knocking on doors in Glendale, Falco suggested going to Kings County morgue to check the slain mobster's corpse. Arriving there, they were led to the vaults, where an annoyed orderly slid open the drawer.

Falco winced. *"Right through the eye."*

"Come on, let's go," O'Reardon suddenly said.

"What's the matter? *You've seen worse.*"

"No, just thought of something . . . Let's go to the bank."

"Morgan?"

"Yeah, it might not be too late."

As soon as they got into the car O'Reardon radioed the precinct. "Any word on those flights? Okay."

He looked at Falco. "Nothing."

"Think they're still around?" Falco asked.

"Only one way to find out."

* * *

Joey Stubs and Vinny Bracca were miserable from spending that same afternoon sitting in their car watching Jimmy Starks watching the St. George Hotel.

"It's two o'clock, time to join this guy," Vinny said.

"Come on, Vin. Why so soon? It's fuckin' cold out there."

"She'll probably be leaving soon. Don't forget, she's got the car."

The yellow Mustang was a half block up from the small doorway the private investigator was standing in. The duo entered the cold air and jogged over to the doorway. "I thought you guys would never get here. She ought to be coming out soon."

Joey looked at him. He seemed jittery with these two there. "Don't worry about us. Just worry about pointing out this broad, then disappearing."

Starks motioned up the block. "That's her car up there, the yellow Mustang."

It was twenty-five degrees on this February afternoon. The experienced private eye was bundled up pretty good, while the other two were less adequately adorned to counter the biting wind. For twenty minutes they bounced and slapped their sides before Starks exclaimed, "That's her, in the blue coat!"

Claudia was walking rapidly toward them lugging two suitcases and her unborn kid up Fulton Street. After she went by, Starks went in the opposite direction as instructed.

Vinny put his hand on his friend's shoulder before he started after her, "Joey, remember, no dramatics, stay calm, *capeesh*?"

"Yeah Vin, come on, before she gets in the fucking car."

They were upon her as she was loading the trunk. Joey grabbed her by the wrist and made a hand shaking motion. "I'm so glad to see you, Claudia. *Give me the keys.*"

His grip tightened and she did as he said.

"Which key opens these suitcases?" he growled.

She turned back while being pushed into the back seat. "None of them."

Joey Stubs slammed the trunk down and started toward her.

"Hey, what'd I tell you! Stay calm!" Vinny got in the driver's seat while Stubs sat alongside him staring back at Claudia and the back window. He lifted her wrists and cuffed them.

"*This necessary?*" she scoffed.

"Just shut up."

Her fear of these two became hate.

Before driving away Vinny turned and looked at her. "Listen, bitch, if you plan on ever seeing your old man, who's soon to be in the same situation you're in, except with uglier goons, I suggest you give me those keys."

"I don't *have* the keys, my husband does."

"Yeah? Well he fuckin' better!"

"Don't need 'em. Those suitcases will snap right open." Stubs said.

Fifteen minutes later they arrived at the bank. They made a U-turn at the corner and came back facing the entrance, a half block away.

"*Minga* where'd this traffic come from? What time is it?" Vinny asked.

"Ten to three, it's always like this down here."

Claudia stared angrily out the side window. Her tearing eyes hid her anger. She felt the baby kicking, as if to remind her there were more important things. They all sat there in the idling car for what seemed an eternity.

"Hey! Is that Ragusa over there?" Joey asked.

Vinny displayed an expression of disbelief at the stupidity of his partner saying his name. Vinny was shaking his head with his eyes closed when the door to the bank opened. It was 3:20. Manny caught a glimpse of his double-parked Mustang down the side street before turning to lock the huge, brass-plated doors.

He started toward his Mustang with the bag under his arm. The other duo sprang into action. Ragusa crossed the street and quickly walked behind him while Enzo followed slowly with the car. Approaching his car, Manny noticed two men inside there with Claudia. He stopped cold. He had a plan if the police were waiting for him, but this was different. He decided to continue to walk toward his wife.

She managed to roll down the window, **"Manny, behind you!"**

As he turned, a .32 snub nose was two feet from his face. Ragusa calmly said, "Drop the bag!" As he did, Enzo pulled up. "Get in the back."

Now he had two guns in his face. Manny, unaccustomed to street violence, was trembling while being shoved into the Caddy. Ragusa, still calm, walked up and dropped the sack on the floor in the back with the cuffed pregnant woman. He then hurried back to the Cadillac and jumped in. Vinny, Joey Stubs, Claudia, and all the loot were in front of them inside the Mustang.

"*Minga*, can this fuck move any slower?" Joey said.

Enzo was busy scanning the street for unwanted attention. Finally, the Caddy pulled alongside, and Ragusa leaned out the window. "Pull out in front of us and keep her quiet. You know where we're going, take Flushing Avenue to the Expressway."

The little caravan then traveled northwest. As they drove, Stubs could see Enzo and Richie Ragusa being very animated and jovial behind them. Claudia, as instructed, laid on her side in the back seat with handcuffs on. She alternated from crying to cursing at the two in front of her. She strained to see Manny in the Cadillac but realized he, too, was lying in the back seat. She had no clue where they were headed. She *did* know the direction was west after noticing the lowered visors.

"The cases still in the trunk?" Vinnie wanted assurance.

"Well, where else? In the fuckin' glove box?

* * *

"Hey! Isn't that his car?" O'Reardon bellowed.

"Where?"

"Facing us, the Mustang at the light! Now coming toward us!"

"No, that was two white guys," Falco answered as he spun in his seat when they passed him.

"Bullshit, how many yellow Mustangs are in this neighborhood? Turn around, quick!"

Falco swung a hurried U-turn at the corner, and they soon had them in sight two blocks ahead.

"I'm telling ya, Brian, there were two guys in the car and Figueroa wasn't one of 'em. We still got time to see if he's still in the bank."

"I don't think that car belonged to the guy driving it."

"Why you say that?"

"Bright yellow car, chrome hubcaps, dolls bouncing in the window, that's a Rican car, through and through!"

Falco shrugged, raised an eyebrow, and added a little gas. They were closing the gap.

"Keep a car between us, Rich. Stay behind this Caddy."

The trio of cars entered the Expressway and smack into stop-and-go traffic.

"Want to run his license and make sure it's his car? I'd hate to be going through all this for nothing," Falco said.

O'Reardon suddenly blurted, *"What the fuck!* Someone's head just popped up in that back seat!"

"Where?"

"There . . . **again!**"

"You mean this Caddy in front of us? . . . Oh, yeah! I *see* him!"

They edged up, closer still. The shackled Manny suddenly turned his head and looked directly at the detectives.

"That's fucking Figueroa! I think he *made* us," Falco said.

O'Reardon reached inside his jacket unsnapping his thirty-eight. "Something's going on here."

They continued rolling in the heavy traffic.

O'Reardon expected the Cadillac to maneuver through the traffic to evade them but it didn't happen.

Enzo turned in his seat and shoved Manny back into a lying position.

"See *that*, Brian?"

"Yeah, I did. Something's really fucked up here. Move back, Rich, we're too close."

Falco slowed down and a couple of cars quickly filled the gap.

He then reached for the mike to call for backup. His partner took it away. "No radio cars!"

O'Reardon instead had the desk sergeant connect him with Captain Rogers. After an eternity of no one answering he finally heard, "Detective McLaughlin."

"Where's Rogers?"

"Wait let me look under this desk and see—"

"Listen, fuckface, we need some black cars on the BQE westbound *like right now!* Who's with you?"

"An equally enthusiastic Davis."

"Both of you, drop the nothing you're doing and catch up with us. No sirens."

"Hey, Eliot Ness, when the fuck you gonna retire?"

"Listen, you dickhead, I know it's late afternoon which means it's a sure bet you're shitfaced, just get out of the fucking house and get over here. We're coming up on Metropolitan Avenue."

Sensing adventure, McLaughlin sprang up and his partner followed him out the door. They jumped in the car and Davis slapped the cherry onto the roof directly above his head. *"Where we going?"*

McLaughlin yelled over the siren, "They're on the BQE at Metropolitan Avenue. He said no noise, he forgets we're two miles away, in heavy traffic! How else we supposed to catch up?"

"You see us yet?" O'Reardon asked over the radio.

"Negative, still a ways back. Five more minutes. What's going on?"

"Looks like our asshole bank manager got in over his head. He seems to be taking an unwilling trip with an Italian travel agency. No doubt Paparelli's guys."

"We'll be up behind you shortly, Lieutenant. Got a plan?" Davis asked.

"First off, which one of you is driving?"

"MacLaughlin is. Don't worry he usually handles this shit pretty good, even though he almost got me killed on the way here."

"Yeah sure, I remember how you two handled the chase on Metropolitan Avenue."

"Fuck, I think we're being followed—black Plymouth two cars back!" Enzo yelled.

Ragusa spun around. "Bulls! Fuck they come from?"

"I don't know, but they're on *us* for sure."

O'Reardon spotted McLaughlin's car coming up behind him. "We have a yellow Mustang and a Black Cadillac up ahead of us," he radioed back. "Stay with us." Not thirty seconds later, the Cadillac screeched off the highway onto the Cypress Avenue exit. O'Reardon instinctively followed right behind.

"Nooo, he yelled as he looked in his rear-view mirror and saw his other guys right behind them.

He grabbed the radio, "Get back up there you fucking moron and go after the Mustang!"

"Yeah, how am I supposed to do that, they're long gone. You said *stay with us,* asshole!" McLaughlin snapped back.

O'Reardon hit his siren and the three cars pulled to a stop along the service road. Ragusa looked into his rear-view mirror and saw the four detectives standing outside their cars, apparently arguing. Enzo quickly uncuffed Manny in the back seat, confident he wasn't talking. They knew all the cash was in the other car, so they had broken no laws.

"Out of the car!" Falco yelled as they approached, guns drawn. **"Up against that rail!"**

"You guys all right?" Ragusa asked, taunting their discontent.

Davis and Mac held them at gunpoint while O'Reardon eagerly scanned the Caddy for bags of cash.

"Whose got the trunk keys?" Falco demanded.

Ragusa reached back and dangled them with a smirk.

A minute later, Falco slammed the trunk closed.

"Nothing," he snapped.

"It was in the other fuckin' car!" O'Reardon angrily whispered to Falco. He wanted to kill McLaughlin. The steaming detective rushed up to Manny and grabbed him by the back of the neck.

"Hey, spick! Where's your Mustang headed!"

The startled bank manager quickly replied, "I don't know what you're talking about, Lieutenant! I'm just headed out to a bar with my friends here."

"And I suppose you were taking a nap in the back seat there," Falco said.

"Hell yeah, these Caddies are comfortable as shit."

"And you two," McLaughlin called out, "what's with the empty holsters? Where did you toss you pieces?"

"Not at all, we're waiting on our carry permits, we're just getting used to wearing the leather," Enzo offered.

O'Reardon and Falco looked at each other in disbelief. "Put out an APB on that Mustang!" O'Reardon yelled.

"Already did," Davis answered.

"What about these three?" Mac asked.

Not being positive of Manny's latest embezzlement and having nothing else on them O'Reardon just shrugged. "Fuck 'em, let 'em go."

Not realizing their bright yellow Mustang was now a hot car, Stubs and Vinny headed toward the Williamsburg Bridge into Manhattan.

"Where the fuck they disappear to?" Vinny asked, looking up at the mirror.

"Who knows? Probably to lose their passenger."

"They better not hurt my husband!"

"No reason to, I'm sure they're just going let him out somewhere." Vinny replied.

A few minutes later Claudia moaned, "Can you take these off me, please?"

"Alright, but you better stay down!" Stubs said as he reached back and unlocked her cuffs. "And don't shit out that kid back there!"

"Where are you taking me?"

"Into the city," Stubs replied, "from there you can take your car home."

Claudia just sighed and slid back down in the seat.

"Where *you* going?" Ragusa asked Manny, as the wrinkled banker opened the Cadillac's back door.

"You can't leave me *here*!"

Ragusa pointed with his thumb. "Get the fuck outta here. There's a subway station down on Cypress Avenue."

They then also started west toward lower Manhattan while eyeing their miserable victim as he slumped toward the subway.

While stuck in the downtown mayhem of honking horns and crowded streets, Claudia slowly slipped her hand into the brown bag under the seat in front of her. Heart pounding, she wriggled out two ten-thousand-dollar packets. She slid them under Enzo's seat while feeling the car stop. They pulled up near the ferry terminal. Vinny shut the car and hopped out.

"Grab the bag in the back" he told Stubs as he opened the trunk and brought out the original suitcases. Vinny then helped Claudia from the back seat and handed her the keys.

"Know your way out of here?"

She ignored him, dropped behind the wheel, cranked the engine, and sped away. Joey Stubs and Vinny Bracca, three hundred grand in hand, melted into the Staten Island ferry terminal.

The two unmarked cars pulled up to their precinct and the four cops silently headed up to face Captain Rogers.

"You two can go," Rogers said motioning to McLaughlin and Davis.

"Have a great *weekend*, O'Reardon," MacLaughlin sneered as he exited.

"Fucking hack," Brian replied.

"What the hell happened out there?" Rogers asked.

O'Reardon shook his head. "All I know is that Manny Figueroa somehow wound up a passenger in the back of a car with two of Paparelli's henchmen. Get this, they were following *his* car being driven by probably *two more* of Papa's guys. We follow the one car off the expressway, and the *lead* car, no doubt with the all the fuckin' money, continued on."

The captain threw up his arms in disbelief and just shook his head instead of shouting.

"What makes you sure the loot was in the first car?"

"Didn't say I was *sure*; just makes sense."

"It's probably a waste of time but get a search warrant for the Marchetti apartment."

"Great! I'm guessing the cash should be on its way over to her in a day or two."

"Now that this shit is *hopefully* almost over, you still outta here at the end of the month?" Rogers asked.

"Before the end of the month actually, I have a few weeks of unused leave I'll be using."

CHAPTER 29

The phone rang at John Paparelli's house.

"Yeah?" he answered.

Joey Stubs was beaming. "*We got it, boss!* Just got off the ferry."

"We'll be right there, don't move!"

The old man summoned his driver and they headed to the terminal. Upon arrival they spotted the two of them sitting on the suitcases. Vinny was grinning while swinging the bag in his hand.

"Will ya look at this moron! Let's stay here a moment," the boss said, while checking the surroundings. "Okay, looks clear, drive up."

Vinny and Stubs tossed the four pieces into the huge trunk, casually got into the rear of the Lincoln, and off they went.

"Where's Enzo and Ragusa?"

"Dunno, boss! Last we saw they were behind us on the expressway," Vinny replied.

"You know that manager was carrying that brown bag out of his bank, so I'm guessing we got us some bonus booty here."

Paparelli's eyes widened. "We'll see soon enough. Anything *over* two hundred large is ours, or I should say . . . mine!"

The old man grinned.

* * *

A tired, disheveled Manny emerged from the subway onto Clark Street in the hopes of finding Claudia. As he approached the Hotel St. George, he spotted his Mustang parked nearby. He rushed into the huge lobby and found her seated there. Her eyes were red from crying.

She beamed. "Are you okay, Poppy?"

He sat beside her, and they held each other.

"I'm sorry, baby, *I'm so sorry*", he said. "They took everything."

"Not everything, Manny!" She discreetly flashed him her purse contents containing two packs of bills, each marked ten-thousand-dollars. "I snatched these from those greaseballs while in the back seat."

Manny shrieked a note of joy, stared up at the ceiling. "Let's go *right* to Idlewild airport! We'll sell the car to the first dealer we see on the way, grab a cab, then a flight to San Juan!"

The two were never seen again in New York.

* * *

Joey Stubs and Vinny were in the stately home's basement under Paparelli's watchful eye.

"Two hundred eighty-eight thousand, four-ninety-five, boss!" Stubs called out when done counting.

"Minga! That's more than I expected! All right, put two and a quarter aside for my daughter and, Joey, take it over to Maspeth tomorrow. Tell her *not* to keep it in the house. Tell her to stash it in a locker at Penn Station or something, *capeesh*?"

"Yeah boss, I'll take care of it. Want Vinny to come with me?"

"No, two of you will be too obvious. I'll call her and tell her to expect you for lunch."

* * *

"Captain, Falco is out sick, and our judge is in court most of today, so I guess we'll have to wait till tomorrow for the warrant."

"Just as well, maybe you can use today to clear up that mess on your desk before you're outta here."

O'Reardon hated nothing more than police paperwork but he settled behind his desk to see what he could get done. By 9:30 he'd had enough. First opportunity he slipped out and drove to Maspeth. He thought there was a good chance the loot was already headed there. He knew he had no legal grounds for a search today, but he just *wanted* to witness it getting there.

O'Reardon settled in his car a block up from the apartment with his bagel and coffee, while trying to find a radio station *not* playing the Beatles. By no means a patient man, he was getting antsy after ninety minutes when the shiny Caddy pulled up, of all places, directly across the street from him.

"Shit!" O'Reardon tried to lean back but his familiar black car was a dead giveaway. Joey Stubs, not known for being one of their brightest guys, spotted him and reacted by peeling off down the street. O'Reardon, knowing this now was his only shot, went after him. Stubs went screaming down the avenue toward the deserted old industrial *chop shop* neighborhood. O'Reardon, keeping his siren off, steadily gained on him. Luckily, there was no traffic in the area.

The speeding Cadillac tried to make a quick right turn onto an empty side street, but the big tires caught the curb. The Caddy flipped onto its side and slid, sparks flying, until it came, full force, into an abandoned car. O'Reardon pulled up twenty feet behind the battered car. The engine was now in flames. He jumped out, rushed up and peered into the upended car. He noticed the mangled driver spread out in the front seat and two suitcases in the smoke-filled back seat.

After quickly looking around the deserted street, he reached in through the busted-out rear window and grabbed the suitcases before the heat became unbearable. He was rushing toward his car when suddenly an explosion almost knocked him off his feet. He grabbed the Plymouth's rear door, threw the suitcases in, then reached into his front window for his police radio. O'Reardon paused, looking up and down the street. Amazingly, a junkyard bulldog behind a wire fence had the only eyes upon him.

Both the Cadillac, and the forgotten heap it slammed, were totally engulfed in ten-foot-high flames. He got into his car, backed it away from the heat and waited another moment. Then carefully looked around once more before putting the Plymouth into drive. As he made a wide pass all he could see of Joey Stubs was a black form.

He sped down the cobblestone street, eyes glancing up at the flames behind him. Oddly, at no point during the entire ride back did he hear fire trucks.

O'Reardon pulled alongside his personal car a block away from the precinct and tossed the still warm cases into the trunk of his T-bird. He peeked in one suitcase to assure himself of the bounty before snapping the trunk closed. Entering the 104th, O'Reardon strode past the desk sergeant and headed up to the detective division. He was glad the captain wasn't within view. Delving into his paperwork like never before, he spent the next two hours clearing loose ends.

* * *

"Whaddya mean he never got there!" Paparelli bellowed over the phone. "He left hours ago Laura. Are you sure? You been home all the while? . . . Stay put, I'll call ya back." He immediately dialed Fat Vinny. "Vincenzo, Joey disappeared. He never made it to the apartment."

"Wha? I told ya I shoulda gone with him!"

"Yeah, yeah. Listen, get over to Maspeth and look around for the Caddy, drive past the 83rd and 104th. Maybe he got busted and the car's outside. *Motherfucker!* That money better not be gone is all I'm saying!"

"Okay, boss, on my way."

"Call me the *minute* you find something out!"

* * *

Brian O'Reardon settled down in his apartment with the banded packets of tens, twenties, and fifties spread out over his couch. On his TV, The *Eyewitness News* reporter was breaking a story about a car fire in Queens. *"The charred remains are thus far unidentified,"* was how he concluded it.

After counting, he wondered what a quarter-million dollars would get him. More than he would ever need, he thought. *A house with a dock in the Carolinas would run thirty thousand, tops. Add to that a new boat another five maybe seven G's . . . Leaves a ton left over. Add my thirty-year city pension on top . . .* He smiled and swigged his beer.

* * *

"Hey boss, there was a crash off Metropolitan Avenue."

"Yeah, I know, they called me. They got the plate number. I don't fuckin' believe it!"

Then Vinny said, "Holy shit! I drove by to see it. I swear, all that's left is a charred heap, two actually . . . He musta hit another car."

"Vinny, I want you to handle this. Go down to the 104th and give his name if they don't already have it. You might have to go identify what's left of him. Say you're his brother if you have to. Call his girlfriend, too. I'm thinking all that money is now ashes. Jesus fuckin' Christ!"

"You don't think he mighta gotten robbed, boss? I mean what the hell is he doing over *there*? There's literally *nothing* down there!"

"You don't think that manager from the bank had anything to do with it, do ya Vin?"

"If he did, he's on his way to Puerta Rico by now," Vinny replied.

The boss grunted.

"You know what, I got enough fuckin' headaches. Just go take care of the shit I told ya."

* * *

"Ma, why ya crying *now*?" Angie asked, walking over to her mother who was slumped in the living room. "Was that grandpa on the phone?"

"It's nothing, honey, I was just expecting something that's no longer--" . . . Laura paused. "It's nothing sweetheart, don't you worry."

"Are you sure Mom, because I really don't need that coat we looked at."

"Oh no, young lady. We *are* getting that coat ....tomorrow! Go set the table and call your brother." Laura did her best to hide her anguish knowing now they were no longer able to get that house out by Mikey. She *did* have the fifty thousand yanked from Marie; however, with college and living expenses it was not going to facilitate a house purchase.

* * *

"Holy shit, Brian, was that one of—" He cut Falco short. "Yeah, one of Paparelli's cars . . . I'm pretty sure it was Joey Stubs in there! Good morning, by the way."

"As expected, in Laura Marchetti's neighborhood? Think he was ripped off?" Falco asked.

"Depends, if he was headed there or headed back. One thing is certain, he was sent over there to bring her the money."

"Are we still doing the search?" Falco asked.

"I don't know, might as well?" Brian replied, still going through the motions.

"Hey, might as well, it'll be your last!"

"All right then, let's go get the warrant signed and head over," O'Reardon said.

Sixty minutes later they pulled up outside the bakery. "At least the kids won't be home," Falco said as they entered the hallway. An annoyed Laura Marchetti answered the bell and motioned them up.

"We have a search warrant, Mrs. Marchetti, for stolen bank money," O'Reardon said in a low voice as they entered the apartment.

All Laura did was shake her head and motion them in. "Well, if you *must* . . . have at it then guys, just *please* don't destroy the place is all I ask!"

Falco surmised right then the rip-off, if there was one, had taken place *before* Stubs made it to the apartment. They quickly went through the search, knowing it was a large volume of cash and a rather small apartment. O'Reardon couldn't take his eyes off Laura as she sat in the kitchen dabbing her cheeks with a handkerchief. He felt her grief.

"We'll have to check your cellar as well," Falco said. Laura stood straight and pleaded. "Guys, my landlady is down there and will make life more unbearable if she sees policemen searching her cellar. I swear on my *children,* there is nothing there!"

"I'm sorry, Mrs. Marchetti, but—"

"It's okay, ma'am," Brian cut in. "I think our work here is done."

A surprised Falco looked at his partner and shrugged.

"I hope we didn't disturb you too much, Laura," O'Reardon said as they quietly exited down the hallway.

A somewhat bewildered and grateful Laura watched them go down the stairs and out onto the avenue unseen.

"I hope we didn't disturb you too much, Laura? Falco quipped, as they entered the car. *Softening this late in the game?*

"Yeah well, I really didn't feel like chasing my tail in a filthy cellar. I'm done with this fuckin' case. Besides, I've got a lot more shit to do if I'm going to get out of here by Friday."

"Yup Brian, it's a long time coming, pal! Seriously, what are your plans now?"

"Like I been sayin', looks like the Carolinas, probably North, around Raleigh but nearer to the coast. I can't afford anything decent up here."

"Bringing your boat with you?"

"Nah, think I'm selling old *Mister Meanor* and getting something nicer down there."

They entered the precinct and went straight into Captain Rogers' office. O'Reardon dropped the file on his desk. "Done. Nothing there, went through the whole joint."

"You sure?" Rogers asked.

"Hey, want us to go back?" Brian answered, grinning.

"Fuck NO! I'm putting this folder away for good! Are you through cleaning up?" the captain asked.

"Really want me outta here, huh? I'll be done by tomorrow, Friday the latest."

They all chuckled, realizing a lot of years together were coming to an end. As they walked out of the office, O'Reardon looked back at the captain. "Oh yeah, Falco told me he wants McLaughlin as his new partner."

Falco put his right hand on his thirty-eight. "How 'bout I just *retire* you right now . . ."

The next day went quietly. There were fewer loose ends remaining than he thought. The lieutenant shook a few hands and left at noon. Exiting, he turned around and gazed up at his old precinct for the last time. Feeling little emotion, he headed to his T-bird and drove home, listening to the same *damn* Beatles' songs. It was just another day.

* * *

That evening Laura was determined to keep things as normal as possible for her children. She realized life was more precarious now after hearing her father's account of the car fire.

"Ang, after school tomorrow we'll go downtown to Gimbels for your jacket."

"Okay, Mom, I already described it to everyone, so I hope it fits."

Laura smiled and turned to Paulie. "You stay here with your brother. If you're good, I'll bring you a surprise!"

Tuddy was in no mood to be saddled with his kid brother; however, sensing his mother's melancholic mood all day, thought it best to accommodate her.

CHAPTER 30

Three weeks later…

Life got back to normal at the Marchetti household until the postman, one afternoon, rang her bell carrying a large box. Laura signed for it in the hallway and carried it inside. Not seeing a return address, she plopped it on the kitchen table and started cutting through the tape. She wondered about the North Carolina postmark.

Laura fell back and gasped.

In front of her were neatly wrapped bills. She could see the same bundles of tens, twenties, and fifties that were once in her basement, except now held by rubber bands. Laura fumbled through it and then dumped the whole thing onto the table. She then leaned back into her chair, put her hands over her face, and started sobbing. After a while, when semi-composed, she stacked the piles and did the arithmetic on the box flap. Exactly one hundred fifty thousand dollars! She counted it two more times before neatly stacking it back into the box. She again made sure there was no letter or clue as to who sent it before squeezing the box into her closet, alongside the paper bag containing the first fifty thousand. Laura then dropped into Sal's worn-out armchair and prayed herself to sleep.

Five-hundred-twenty-miles due south at that same hour, with seventy thousand cold cash stashed in a Raleigh safe-deposit box, sat a cigar chomping ex-detective floating five hundred feet off the South Carolina coast in a brand new twenty-eight-foot Chris-Craft. On its stern was the freshly painted name, *Felonie*.

Finis

Epilogue

Laura Marchetti purchased her first home near her son Michael on Long Island, and soon after married her real estate agent. He gambled away much of her money. Her children loathed him. They divorced in 1970.

Mike and Patti Marchetti moved to Manhattan six months later with their two sons. He was acquitted of the stolen money charge due to the absence of testifying police but was subsequently investigated by the SEC two years later for his questionable securities trading. He was again exonerated. By 1980, before his fortieth birthday, Michael was a multi-millionaire and looked after his mom.

Richard Falco eventually became Chief of Detectives, Borough of Brooklyn, and retired in 1988. Mayor Ed Koch honored him at a City Hall ceremony.

Manny and Claudia Figueroa changed their names and opened a bodega near the U.S. Naval Firing Range in Vieques, Puerto Rico. In 1975 a stray shell from an offshore destroyer killed Manny and three of his employees. Claudia and her daughter were awarded $550,000 from the U.S. Government.

Marie Werner never re-married and lived comfortably from Chubby's pension. She reunited for a spell with Brian and made several trips to North Carolina, but they fought each time.

Hector Maldonado, convicted of one murder and two manslaughters, was electrocuted in Sing Sing Prison in 1969. His last words in Spanish were translated as *"fuck everyone!"*

Whitey Aparicio was buried with honors at the U.S. Veteran's Cemetery on Long Island. Junior Saez was interned on Hart Island near the Statue of Liberty, better known as Potter's field.

Gambino under-boss John Paparelli, a victim of District Attorney Robert Kennedy's investigations and mob turncoat Joe Valachi's testimonies, was convicted of racketeering. He spent eight years at Leavenworth Federal Prison before retiring to Miami.

Joey Stubs in '71, grieving after discovering his new boss ordered a hit on him for importing heroin, sat in the rear of the Staten Island ferry and shot himself through the mouth.

In 1967 Detective Lieutenant Brian O'Reardon finally ventured his boat farther into the Atlantic. Third time doing so, it took on water in a heavy sea. Neither he, nor the *Felonie* were ever found. A dozen or so beer bottles were seen bobbing in the waves two miles out.